Daisy Whispers

A RETURN TO COAL HAVEN NOVEL

MARIE JOHNSTON

LE PUBLISHING

 Created with Vellum

Alder Duke was my high school sweetheart turned husband, then he became a stranger who wanted his freedom. I gave it to him.

Fifteen years later, I'm a single mom who desperately needs a place to live. He's a powerful CEO who needs a wife in order to get the house he grew up in, thanks to a trust his grandma left behind.

He makes a deal with me: get married to him—again—and live with him for a year. Once the house is in his name, we can divorce—again—and he'll rent the place to me.

Just one year. No strings. No feelings. Simple.

But nothing about my ex-husband is simple. Gone is the man who wanted to stay out all night drinking with his buddies. This Alder cooks and cleans and unclogs sinks in gray sweatpants. He gets my stubborn daughter to like him. And with me? He looks at me like I'm the only woman in the world.

I can't fall for his sweet daisy whispers. I know how it ends. This time we planned it. My life was already derailed by him once, and I barely came out intact. He's had my heart forever, but he only gets one year.

Chapter One

Daisy

Tonight wasn't exactly a waste of a babysitter, but that was only because my mom was in town and she was watching my four-year-old daughter.

Sipping the pumpkin beer I'd been nursing all night, now lukewarm, I checked the time. Five more minutes and I would hit my socially acceptable amount of time spent at a pre-Thanksgiving Christmas party that was both fun and anxiety-inducing. The goal was to stay long enough that no one asked why I was leaving early.

My coworkers could be an adorable mix of clueless and nosy. They were chemists. They wanted definitive answers and would prod until they got one. While I was just as oblivious to some conversational nuances, I was extra sensitive to fielding too many questions. The urge to be fully transparent was too strong. *TMI, thy name is Daisy.*

I loved my coworkers. Really. We had a relaxed work

environment in the petroleum lab of the refinery outside of Coal Haven. My boss, Raj, had brought the newest additions to his coin collection to show off. Two other guys I worked with were getting animated over the latest manga live-action show. The series sounded interesting, but since Laila was so young, if it didn't have talking dogs and life lessons, we weren't watching it.

My friend and coworker Violet Duke had taken off earlier. Lucky duck. She was quite pregnant. After getting pictures of her holding her baby belly with one arm and her other arm tossed over a barrel in the party room at the back of the local brewery outside of town, she ate some of the catered pulled pork, reminisced about how she met the love of her life in this very brewery, then called it a night. Said love of her life had picked her up, his eyes glowing with adoration and affection.

Gah.

I wanted that.

I'd had it once. Yet tonight, I was at the Christmas party as a single woman. A single mom.

I needed to find a new place.

Another check of my watch. Close enough.

I stood and stuffed my arms into my winter coat. The fabric rustled as I zipped it and wrapped a cream-and-purple scarf Violet crocheted me for Christmas around my neck and tucked the tails inside.

"You taking off?" Raj asked as he pored over his coin box, his fascination stamped into his expression as if he didn't own the collection.

"Yep. See you all Monday."

A chorus of "have a good night" and "have a good weekend" rang out. I waved and walked out of the party room. I steeled myself to enter the main bar I'd have to walk through to get to the exit. There weren't a lot of people, but that initial discomfort of being noticed, of people looking my direction and having *thoughts* about me didn't fade.

No one is paying attention to me. I'm not the center of their world. My mantra didn't help, but it was so ingrained by now, I couldn't not recite it.

I strode through, my sights on the heavy wooden door that looked more like it should be in a castle and not a restored train foundry and repair shop. There was a table of guys close to the exit. I focused on the door until the din around me grew quieter.

A man pushed away, and I glanced up. My stomach dropped. Damn.

Jason. My ex. He had a ball cap sitting low on his head and slightly askew. I used to fix it. He thought it was adorable while my annoyance was off the charts. Couldn't he *feel* how off-centered it was? Why wouldn't he fix it if he did?

His crooked hat was no longer my problem. A lot of the emotions my relationship with Jason incited were very much my problem, but none of them were his fault, which he failed to understand.

I dipped my head and kept going.

"Daisy."

Shoot. I had almost made it to the exit. I stopped to face him. He tucked his hands into his jeans pockets. He wore his usual steel-toed work boots and the black T-shirt and flannel. Tonight's choice was red and black.

"Hi, Jason." The attention of his buddies, who were trying not to be obvious, prickled over my skin. Regardless that we were probably far enough away they couldn't hear us, I hated being the center of attention. Just one of the many things Jason couldn't understand. I gave him a tight smile. "Well, enjoy your night."

I was turning to go, but he stepped forward.

"Daisy, wait."

Crap. Did I sprint for the parking lot? Grit my teeth and smile through whatever he had to say, which was usually prodding me about what he'd done wrong? We were in public, and I refused to be a spectacle. "Yes?"

"Can we talk?"

My shoulders dropped. Not this again. I broke his heart. I had owned that, and we'd had some difficult conversations. At what point would that be over? When could he just let it be?

We'd had six years together. He was a good man. He loved our daughter, Laila. And as far as exes went, at least his attempts to talk after our split showed me he had cared. He hadn't vanished from my life like our years together had meant nothing.

One of the ends of my scarf came loose. I tugged on it and let the stitches of the yarn run under my fingers. "What more is there to say?"

The rest of the guys at his table surreptitiously watched us. I glanced at them just as discreetly. We all failed at looking like we were minding our own business.

Jason's hound-dog gaze intensified. "I know. I just... miss you. How's Laila?"

He'd seen her a couple of weeks ago, but he probably missed her after getting to be with her almost every day. "She's getting way too much candy from Mom."

His smile was faint. "I'm sure she's getting spoiled. Hey, uh, my mom called and was wondering if she could stay with them sometime over Christmas."

Longing tugged at my heart. His parents lived in

Minot, a little over two hours away. They'd take Laila and spoil her to the Nth degree, much like my mom. Only she'd have lots of little cousins to play with. Both of Jason's parents would dote on her. A big, loving gathering full of good food and lively conversation. Jason's family was one of those things I mulled over alone in bed at night. Were they one of the reasons I had stayed with him so long? The first being that we'd had a kid together. The second reason was doting parents who'd reminded me of another ex's parents.

I shook the thought off. "Sure. Let me know when."

Gratitude filled his eyes. "Great." His brows drew together. "How are you?"

"Fine."

He nodded, and I was tempted to take a step back, closer to the door.

"Listen, I've been thinking." He scratched the scruff on his cheek. "I sealed the sink back in place and replaced the entry carpet. Maybe you wanted to take a look."

I bit back a groan. He'd been such a sweet guy. He'd also been wasted on me. "Those minor repairs aren't why I left."

Despair rippled across his face. "Then why? I've tried working on myself. I've been lifting again."

He'd had a few drinks, and he was getting melancholy. Still, I'd have to reassure him. Again. "It wasn't your looks or your body, Jason. It's not just a cliché when I say it's not you, it's me."

"Daisy, I just miss you."

I didn't miss him. I missed the idea of him. The thought of having someone. I'd had that before, and I had the divorce papers to show for it. All I had realized was that it wasn't Jason, and staying with him wouldn't have been fair to either of us. "I'm sorry."

He lifted his hat and ruffled his short brown hair. "I talked to my boss about other shifts."

"It wasn't your job," I said with a sigh. *Here we go.*

"I could work less nights."

"It wasn't the nights."

He furrowed his brow. "Where did I go wrong?"

"You are fine. You just weren't fine for *me.*"

"We have a kid together," he said stubbornly, as if Laila had been sent to Earth just to prove that Jason and I were soulmates, and that I hadn't puked up an entire week's worth of birth control pills when I'd gotten salmonella from a catering-gone-wrong wedding reception.

"Laila is perfect. And you'll be the perfect guy for someone else." I took that much-needed step toward the exit. My back was to the door, but the waft of cold air from someone who'd opened it caressed my legs.

Jason ignored the newcomer. "Was it the bedroom?" he asked, not as under his breath as he probably thought. How many beers had he had?

"No." We'd been over this. Jason was insecure about his bedroom performance, and my main goal had been to weather this breakup without denting his self-esteem more.

"I've watched some movies."

A sigh gusted out of me. "Porn isn't the answer." *Please stop.* Whoever had just entered was getting an earful.

"No. YouTube videos. How-to ones."

I was ready to dart for the parking lot. My skin was

growing too tight, and people were watching. "Jason, that wasn't it."

He held his arms out at his sides. "Then what? Was it the orgasms? I can do better."

Frustration banged around in my head. "No."

"I know I struggled getting you off, but—"

"Jason, dammit. It wasn't the orgasms. Or the sex. Or anything about the bedroom. I told you, it's not you. I mean, I divorced a man who could get me off three times a night."

"That's true," an all too familiar, and supremely pleasing, deep voice said from behind me. "She dropped me like a burnt potato. Even though a few times, we got to four times a night. Didn't we, Daisy?"

Horror swamped me, squeezing my lungs together. Why couldn't I work with a bunch of physicists who could time travel me back ten minutes? I'd wait to leave. I'd give Jason a wave and charge out the door. I'd have been gone before the man behind me had arrived.

I squeezed my eyes shut. This was not happening. I didn't just belt out that personal of a detail and do it in front of *him*.

I spun slowly on the heel of my winter boot.

Yes. In fact, I had.

Because the person who had entered the brewery, who had caught the tail end of what should've been a private conversation with Jason, was a blast from the past, dressed in black slacks and a long wool coat that swirled around him like a cape. A man with neatly combed hair the color of strong coffee and touched with a few strands of gray at the temples. His flashing hazel eyes were painfully familiar. So was the humor in them. My heart wanted to wrench out of my chest and throw itself at the tips of his shiny black loafers.

Alder Duke. My ex-husband.

* * *

Alder

The gradual widening of Daisy's pale blue eyes inspired a slow grin to spread across my face. After years of avoiding her, of trying not to think about the woman who'd had the audacity to call me on my bullshit and leave, she was here, spouting details of what had once been an enthusiastic sex life.

Her pink lips parted and a squeak came out of her, like her vocal cords had failed.

I drank her in, along with the glimpse of deep emotion in her eyes. It'd be gone soon enough, and she'd return to the guarded, almost aloof, girl I had known and fallen in love with during our freshman year. "Hi, Daisy."

She snapped her mouth shut. An awkward beat of silence passed. The man behind her frowned, and his gaze jumped from her to me and back.

"Who is this guy?" he asked.

Daisy jolted like his words were pure voltage. "Oh, uh. Jason, this is Alder. My ex-husband."

"Nice to meet you," I said but stayed put. A handshake might escalate whatever had been going on here.

Jason took in my suit, the wool coat that I preferred on cold blustery nights like tonight, and probably recalling what I had said, he shrank right in front of me. "This is the ex-husband?"

She nodded, her gaze skating away and then right back. And away again.

Even after so long, I recognized the signs. A table full of burly guys in work clothing was gawking at us. A few other patrons were openly staring. Even the two bartenders were monitoring the situation.

Jason didn't seem like a fighter. He hunched like Daisy had beaten him down before I arrived and kicked him for good measure.

This was her fiancé? Yet his pleading tone with the talk of sex snaked through my memory. He'd sounded desperate. Hopeless, while also being hopeful.

A thrill washed cold through my veins. I recognized his special brand of heartache. He was now an ex too. Getting left by Daisy wasn't an easy event to endure. Dare I say, it'd been life-changing.

Did that mean Daisy was single?

She was shifting from foot to foot, her knuckles white as she gripped the ends of a scarf that matched her winter coat. Light purple had always looked good on her, but not as stunning as yellow. Just like her name.

I wiped those thoughts from my mind. Daisy was uncomfortable. She likely wanted to crawl into a corner and die. She'd relive this public exposure during future nights when she was trying to sleep.

"Were you just heading out?" I asked her.

She nodded and skirted around me. "Let me know about Christmas with Laila," she tossed back to Jason.

His expression stayed crestfallen. "Yeah," he said hoarsely. "Night, Daisy."

I gave him a tight smile and followed her out. I didn't

care if he or anyone else thought I was chasing her. The two things I did know were that I couldn't enjoy a beer wondering about the years Jason had gotten with her. Nor could I let Daisy go when she was distraught.

To the outsider, she'd look fine if a little embarrassed, but she was seething with feeling. I couldn't just let her drive off.

She walked fast for being a short woman. Her boots crunched on the ice of the parking lot as she scurried to an obnoxiously yellow pickup.

"Where's the Bug?" I called as I trotted and skated to keep up with her.

She stiffened and looked over her shoulder. "What?"

"Your VW Bug?"

She stopped. Her breath puffed out in a cloud of condensation. "I haven't had that car in years."

The vast distance of time landed hard between us. Fifteen years. Not quite a lifetime, but it might as well be. "Right."

She started walking again.

I didn't. "How are you?"

She stopped.

"What happened in there," I said, "it had to be uncomfortable and that's only what I caught."

She yanked her gloves out of her pockets. "It sure was awkward, yes."

"Can we go somewhere? And talk?" I closed the distance between us. The faint sound of engines on the highway that ran past the brewery was the only noise on a cold night. "Just to catch up? It's been a long time," I said softly.

When she finally met my gaze, my lungs froze. I'd

never seen that level of uncertainty in her eyes. Even when she'd laid down an ultimatum I'd ignored, then followed through with it, there'd only been steely resolve.

"I don't..." She sighed and looked around, those big blue eyes of hers searching for a reason. To accept or refuse? "Yeah. Why not?"

I repressed my grin. This wouldn't be a happy reunion. She'd been through the wringer before I arrived, and once I did I'd practically jump-scared her like a ghost in a haunted house. Her determination was weakened and perhaps that was why she agreed to catch up. Years of avoiding each other had worn on me. Was it the same for her? "Great. Is there somewhere that's open? Or your place?"

She shook her head, her chin-length blonde hair flying. "Not my place. No." I was about to be insulted when she weakly gestured to the brewery looming over us in its stony glory. "The house was Jason's, and the place I'm renting got sold. I'm moving again. Boxes every-where." She stuffed her fingers into her gray-and-yellow gloves. "There's a bar downtown, but I'd rather not get stared at all night."

"How about my pickup? It's still warm."

Her lips pursed as she thought about it. Small space. Me and her. We'd gotten up to more than talking in my vehicles before. Tonight, I just wanted to talk. To make sure she was okay. To soak in being in her orbit again. Would she want the same?

"All right," she said, resigned.

Yes. I hit the button to start my vehicle. A row over, the engine roared to life and the parking lights turned on.

She lifted her brows when she saw my ride. Yes, it had

cost nearly six figures, but unlike her, I didn't have kids. Or a spouse. I didn't even have a partner. Most of my money was invested, and the rest had gone into an expensive pickup.

I led her toward it and opened the passenger door. She climbed in, her coat crinkling from the cold, and I went around to the driver's side. By the time I got behind the wheel, her lemon-vanilla scent filled the cab. My eyelids nearly drifted shut while I took a long inhale. Crisp and sweet.

I adjusted the heating vents. "How've you been?"

She snorted and yanked off her gloves. "You witnessed it. Along with half of Coal Haven."

"That wasn't half of Coal Haven. Only about a third."

Her laugh was soft, but her expression remained sad. "What are you doing here, Alder?"

"I had a meeting today." I'd come for a beer and to figure out how I could move back to a community where Daisy lived a life independent of me. "A final interview at the refinery, more of a hammering out of the final expectations on both sides."

She nodded, then frowned. Her forehead developed the most adorable furrow. "You're leaving King Oil?"

"Yes. I met with them to nail out the specifics, but I got the CEO position at the refinery." It was as far out of Coal Haven as the brewery. A tiny city in its own right, its lights were a dull glow on the horizon.

Alarm flamed through her eyes. "You're my boss?"

Thanks to my sister Violet, I knew she worked in the lab at the refinery. "Not directly."

She rolled her gaze toward me. "You're everyone's boss, Duke."

The slip of familiarity was a balm to my eardrums. "Perhaps, but I'm not a micromanager." There were so many levels between us, it didn't matter if I was in charge of my ex-wife. Silence fell. Was she planning to job hunt first thing in the morning? "Will it be an issue?"

Her brows drew together, and her jaw tightened. "It's not like I hang out with the CEO. We don't have lunch together. He doesn't even know my name."

She didn't say no, it wouldn't be an issue. "To be fair, he wasn't married to you either. Will it be an issue, Daze?"

"We're both adults," she said with that familiar distance in her tone. "It's been a long time."

Yes, it had been. Sitting in the pickup cab with her, memories pushing at my mental doors, it felt like yesterday when we were parked in a field after she'd left a pasture party before it had even started. I'd seized my chance with her that night. So much had happened since then, since our divorce. Significant things. More for her than me. "I'm sorry about your brother."

Her eyes instantly misted over, and she looked down. "Yeah," she whispered.

"I, uh, would've come to the funeral, but I was in DC when I saw the obituary. I couldn't make it back in time."

"Mom got your card."

I had wanted to send it to Daisy, but there were no manuals for how to handle sympathy cards when you weren't sure the other party ever wanted to hear from you again. "Mind if I ask what happened?"

She sniffled quietly. "He kept getting sicker and sicker. Just unhealthy. You know how he lived."

"Nothing improved?"

She blinked at me suddenly, her gaze earnest. "No,

and that's what we all missed." Tears spilled down her cheeks, and she swiped at her face. My heart twisted for her. "He knew what he had to do to take care of himself, and he just couldn't."

I would've captured all her tears if I could, but she would shut down. Those moments between us were over. I grabbed a tissue from the console and handed it to her.

"Thanks," she mumbled. "I tried to help clean his place before he got kicked out and had to go to the shelter."

"He was homeless?" I had missed a lot.

"It was the healthiest he'd been. Structure. Regular meals." She let out a sad laugh. "He used to tell me how blah their food was all the time. It became a running joke whether I could smuggle seasonings to him." She dabbed at her eyes. "Getting that medical discharge out of the Marines was the worst thing that could've happened to him. He needed to be told what to do and for someone to have authority over him."

Her brother had been older than us, and I recalled those years after he had returned home right after training. He'd been so hyped to go, and then when he got back, he'd only gone through the motions of life. "Did he get fired again?"

"He didn't have to. He would just get scheduled fewer and fewer hours. You know how his hygiene was. That got worse too. I'd clean his place and..." A shudder racked her body. "I'd try to talk to Jason about it, and he'd gag and tell me he didn't want to hear it."

"I'm sorry. That bad?"

She nodded. "There weren't rodents, at least." Her mouth twisted wryly. "But I learned it was never rice in his kitchen."

"Not rice, then what would it be— Oh." My stomach clenched. That was bad. "Shit."

Her laugh was empty but needed. How had Jason dealt with that part of her? Daisy and her mom had a dark sense of humor, but it was how they coped. Others might think they were heartless or just plain clueless, but no. They felt things. Deeply. How they expressed them was different.

If Daisy was laughing about cleaning her brother's place, it must've been awful. Horrific, even.

"Yep. Fruit flies so bad the walls were brown." She swallowed hard. "Maggots and flies." She pinned me with that bright gaze again. "You know, I called a help center. I told them about Lee and asked for help. I said we weren't sure we could get conservatorship, and we especially couldn't afford to try. And there was how Lee ghosted people who butted into his life."

Lee had ditched everyone but Daisy. Still, that didn't mean he'd let her control him and his decisions. My fingers tingled to hold her hand, but she didn't always like to be touched when she was unloading her feelings. Add in that it was me, and this night could end just as it was starting, and I wasn't quitting before she was ready. We could have made superficial small talk, but Daisy dove all in. She only did that with people she felt close to. After all these years, I was honored she was telling me. I was also a sponge, soaking up every little detail about her that I had missed.

"The guy said 'he sounds depressed.'" This time her laugh dripped with bitterness. "Depressed? It took me an hour to clean just his *toilet*. Yeah, he was probably depressed, but there was also something else. Something major. His brain did not work like it was supposed to. We just couldn't find anyone to help us. The guy started talking appointments, and I wanted to cry. Make all the appointments you want—he won't go. But then if we did get conservatorship, then what was I supposed to do? 'Okay, Lee, go to the nursing home now.' Like I could force him." She dropped her chin. "It would've broken me and Mom, and dammit, that feels selfish to say."

I nodded, trying to imagine how hard it'd been. "That sucks for both of you."

I was rewarded with a small smile. "Sorry, I'm venting. We haven't talked in years and I just unload on you. But not many people understand the situation. Jason didn't. He was like Dad, thinking Lee was lazy or stubborn."

Daisy would've never worked with someone like her dad. I had acted like her dad when we were first married, and she'd walked. "Could you lean on him when Lee died?" I didn't want to be jealous of the guy, but I'd rather Daisy had a pillar of support in her corner. If Jason couldn't listen to her cleaning trauma, then who had been there for her? For her mom?

She chewed on her cheek. "He kept trying to hug me after Lee died. Every time I cried, he'd wrap me up."

"Oof."

"Yeah."

I would kill to hold her hand, but she wasn't someone who needed a lot of physical affection. She was like a cat. I had to let her come to me. I couldn't just grab her and force her to cuddle. She might hug me back, but she'd censor her emotions around me later. It was something I had learned when we were teens. Something I hadn't forgotten. There wasn't much I'd forget about Daisy.

"How are your parents?" I asked, relaxing into my

seat and breathing in her sweet scent. She wasn't running off. This was better than trying to kill a night by myself in Coal Haven.

"Mom finds something she likes online and orders ten. It's escalated more since Lee died. Jason got five tie tacks made from onyx last year."

I had once gotten five wallet clips from her mom. "Does Jason wear a lot of suits?"

"I've seen him in one once." We exchanged a smile, and her gaze dropped down to my coat, then my slacks. "I see it's become a norm for you."

And did she like what she saw? I'd been more like Jason when we'd been together. My similarities with him might be upsetting, so I wouldn't ask more. "Hazard of the trade."

"From the wells to the C-suite?"

"I put that on my business card," I joked.

She laughed. "Good for you." Her smile faded. "I knew you could do it."

After I was left single and working in the oil fields, it was either finish college or break my body by the time I was forty. "Helps to have a dad who's the King Oil CEO. A little nepotism goes a long way." Enough about me. My life had been a Daisy desert for too long. It couldn't happen again. "And your dad?" Her parents had gotten divorced before she was in high school. Pretty much after her brother barely graduated with his class.

She pushed her hair back from her face. A strand immediately fell out. Her ears flared out slightly, and I'd always thought they were cute as hell. She'd never covered them when we were together. Good to see she hadn't started. "I've met his newest girlfriend."

"He has a lot?"

"Yep." She popped the p, a small slip of emotion. The string of women had bothered her in high school, mostly because they had gotten her dad's attention over her. "She's nice enough. Stays out of my business. And hey, his third ex-wife made him get rid of all his family pictures."

"She did what?"

Daisy nodded. "They moved in together, and she claimed that there wasn't room. But when he was giving me the framed aerial picture of his parents' farm, she grabbed it and said 'Oh, you don't want to get rid of that, do you?' Yet they were off-loading all the photos of me, Lee, and Mom."

"Wow."

"Yeah. He was clueless." She shrugged. "Anyway, it's easier to be mad at her. Whatdya do? He sees Laila once a year. Sometimes remembers her birthday."

"Jesus."

She lifted a shoulder again. "Family was never his priority. We were his obligation. He loves us, but he doesn't want the responsibility. As long as I remember that, it hurts less. Now tell me about yours. How are Weston and Magnolia?"

Her self-awareness had always enamored me. I'd grown up in a chaotic house with four younger sisters and one brother. Daisy was calm. Mellow. She'd been my happy place. I hadn't found one since her.

"Mom and Dad are Mom and Dad," I said. "Acting like newlyweds and enjoying the grandkids."

"Are you enjoying being an uncle? Teaching them how to fish and hunt and snowmobile?"

I ran my thumb and forefinger over my bottom lip.

How much would she read into what I said next? "I haven't done any of that in years."

Nor did I see my niece and nephew very often.

Her wide eyes were on me, but she didn't respond.

The memory of our last married words together rose in my head. *I can't keep doing everything while you do nothing.* I hadn't done nothing. I'd played. "Busy with work. You know how it is."

She lifted a brow as if to say she absolutely did not when it came to me. Fair.

She stroked her gaze down my suit. "Things have changed."

"Thanks to you."

She puffed out a breath and looked at the passenger window. I didn't want our conversation to end. I missed her. The emptiness that had yawned inside me for so long wasn't so large when we were locked together into the cab of the pickup.

So I'd keep talking. "You already know Violet's having a baby and getting married, and I'm ecstatic it's not her douchenozzle of an ex."

"He was that bad? She hasn't said much about him."

"Willis was, in fact, that bad." I scratched the side of my face. "Lily is happily married with kids, and it's not with the douchecanoe Carter."

She laughed, the sound as delightful as I remembered. "Violet did tell me Lily's ex was, in fact, that bad."

"Worse, actually. He cheated on her and kicked her out when she was pregnant."

"What a bastard. But the new guys? Evander and... Eliot, is it?"

"Good guys." My sisters were happy. That was all I cared about. "Did Violet tell you how it all came about?"

Daisy frowned. "How they met their husbands?"

I nodded. "Grandma left a trust behind. We all get property, but there's a hell of a catch." I clenched my jaw. I hadn't talked about this to anyone. So why bring it up to my ex-wife? "We have to get married first."

Shock played over her delicate features. "That's why Violet and Lily are with—"

"No. Well, sort of. Eliot helped Lily out because she was already living in Grandma's house and would've had to move. The crux of the whole trust issue is that Dad and Aunt Linda have to sign off that the marriage is valid. Eliot and Lily fell in love for real. Violet met Evander before she knew he was renting her place, but she was ready to let the house go. They fell for each other anyway."

A faint smile graced her face. "How many houses did Grandma Annie have?"

A warm ball centered in my chest. She still called my grandmother Grandma Annie. "One for each of us."

"And what do you get?"

A dark cloud passed over my mood. "The house I grew up in."

Her expression turned impassive. "Oh. Are you...are you married?"

I barked out a bitter laugh. "No. God, no." Pinching the bridge of my nose, I locked up my annoyance with my grandma. If I was married, the whole house trust issue wouldn't be a problem. "She was renting it out. Just so happens it's open. Aunt Linda told me she'd just had it cleaned after the last renters moved. I can't live there because I'm single, so someone else will." And I'd have to find a place to live.

"I'm sure you'll get another tenant in soon."

"Probably." I hated the thought of yet another stranger living there. No one cared for the place like my family had. The house, the acreage it was on, had fallen into disrepair. Grandma hadn't updated it in the last decade, and Aunt Linda wouldn't put in extra work if it was just going to get sold off at the end of the trust term. That was, if I wasn't married. "I hate for Linda to rent it again. Nothing gets improved; it just keeps getting used."

"Oh, come on. I'm sure there are single moms who just broke off a long-term engagement who will take care of it."

That was specific. "You need a place?"

Having someone who had a history with it eased the conflict I had with renting it, which wasn't my decision. Aunt Linda could lease it to whoever she wanted. I didn't have a say. Until I was married.

She nodded but waved a hand. "I can't afford a space like that. With the land? I bet rent is half my paycheck."

"Being a chemist doesn't make bank?" I was half joking. Her work wouldn't pay nearly as much as mine.

She rolled her lips in and looked away. "I have other expenses. And Laila."

"Doesn't Jason help?" It wasn't my business, but I asked anyway.

Her features tightened. "He would worry and then he'd hope that meant we were getting back together."

He wasn't right for her. From what little I saw, he seemed like a heartbroken guy. His face had hung like someone had called his puppy ugly, but otherwise, he'd only been guilty of not letting go.

I could empathize. "Are there some good rentals in Coal Haven?"

She slid her gaze toward me. "Maybe an apartment."

Maybe? "A good one?"

She rolled a shoulder. "You'll have better luck than me. When I looked last time, both the houses and apartments in my price range were small or old. I'm just tired of moving, you know?"

I mulled over what she said. There was something she wasn't telling me about her living situation. Were her options really that dismal?

Regardless, she needed a place to live. I needed a place to live. I didn't want just any renter in the house that could be mine. And I needed a wife in order to claim said house.

To sum it up, she needed a place to live, and I needed a wife.

No.

It was a ridiculous idea. I shouldn't even think of it.

She'd never go for it.

But logically, I had to offer... Two birds with one *I do.*

"Shit." The curse slipped out, and she turned those big blue eyes on me.

My pulse sped up. I couldn't ask her. Too damn long ago, I had asked the same question. I had taken her horseback riding for the afternoon. We'd had sex in the shadow of a chokecherry bush, then I had proposed.

Simple. Just what she had wanted. Everything I had envisioned for my future.

But that was then. This would be more of a business deal. Unless it went from fake to real.

I pushed that hope in the far back of my mind. I would not use her disadvantage to my advantage. Besides, I had to ask first.

Or I could keep my mouth shut instead of ruining this night.

Except I hadn't said a thing before and it had been fifteen years before I talked to her again. I couldn't have that happen. If there was a way... I had to try. "I have an idea."

Chapter Two

Daisy

I zoomed around my apartment, tidying all of Laila's items. Both of her plush blankets were on the floor. I folded the one with a bunny embroidered in the corner. Mom had bought the blankie that was loaded with daisies. One of the many packages that randomly showed up.

Laila was still sleeping. She and Mom had been asleep when I returned last night. My sleep had been fitful, and I'd gotten up early. As soon as Mom woke, I took the opportunity to fill her in on Alder's scandalous offer.

"Can you believe it?" I stooped to grab a doll with floppy arms and legs. "Married. Again."

What if we married to get the house?

Married! What had he been thinking?

Oh, right. He'd laid it all out.

It makes perfect sense. You'll have a place to live for a year, and when that year is done, I'll get the house. I can even rent it to you after. It's five bedrooms, Daisy. Remember. Plenty of room for you and Laila.

He would have to live with me. Or I would have to live with him? We'd have to be *believable*. A divorced couple pretending they were in love. Then when the house was signed over to him after the year was up, we could divorce. Again. As if the first time hadn't ripped my heart out. A second time would resurrect all those emotions, fake marriage or not.

The audacity of that man.

"It was like he dropped a shovelful of shit on his real proposal." Which had been perfect. Complete with a small ring with a dainty square diamond and a wedding band with six diamonds that was now back in its little black box in my sock drawer. I only looked at it twice a year. The anniversary of the day he proposed and what would've been our real anniversary.

"It sounds like more of a business deal," she said.

Exactly.

I straightened and tossed the doll in an open box. I puffed a lock of hair out of my face and looked around for Mom. She was folding the daisy blanket.

"You do need a place to live," she said simply.

"You can't be serious."

She looked at the boxes lining the walls like it was obvious what she meant. I had to be out in two weeks. Even if I'd been able to renew my lease, the house was small. The second bedroom was little more than a glorified walk-in closet. The bathroom barely had extra floor space for a clothes hamper and a step stool for Laila to use with the toilet. The kitchen was as big as the living room, but that wasn't saying much.

"I'll find something," I said lightly, as if I believed

myself. There wasn't anything in my price range, and if there was, I couldn't justify moving a kid into those living conditions. Nothing like lead paint and asbestos around a four-year-old.

She gave me a plaintive look. "Anything new open?"

"That guy is trying to rent out the house that flooded on Violet."

Her lips flattened.

"He remodeled," I said weakly.

"Doesn't mean he's a better landlord."

No. It didn't. I sighed. "I can't marry Alder again."

Those words had streamed through my head all night. *I can't marry Alder. Again.*

"It'd be in name only," she said.

Did Mom seriously think this was a good idea? She was practical, but remarrying my ex-husband?

Tempting.

No. "But Linda and Weston would have to believe it to sign off on it or he won't get the house put in his name." Alder's dad might hate me. It'd be hard to tell with his aunt Linda. She seemed like she didn't like anyone, but she'd always been pleasant when I'd crossed paths with her around town. Kind but not interested in chitchat, which was her MO anyway.

"That doesn't mean you have to make out with him in front of them." I sputtered but she continued folding and refolding the blanket until it was a perfect square. "In fact, I think it'd be easier to believe. You two were tied at the hip for years."

Until we weren't. "I can't."

"Then don't."

I huffed out a hard breath. "That's not helping."

She pushed up her glasses and blinked her owlish blue

eyes at me. With her short, salt-and-pepper hair, she looked like a book-smart elf. "I think you want to go through with it. It'd solve a giant problem in your life. But you're afraid of what others will think, like Jason. You're afraid of becoming the topic of the grapevine. And maybe you're afraid of Alder himself."

"I'm not afraid of him." I couldn't summon any confidence. He was responsible for the biggest, longest case of heartbreak there was, but that had been my fault. Sort of. I'd divorced him, thinking he wasn't the man I had thought he was.

The Alder Duke in his suit and long wool coat who worked in the C-suite of an oil company was the Alder I had thought I married.

I slumped my shoulders. "He's even better looking than he was when we divorced."

"That's the way it goes."

Mom wasn't one for platitudes. I didn't need them. I'd never been a knockout, and I wasn't growing into one. There was no time for flat irons or curlers when I was getting Laila ready in the morning and off to daycare. I couldn't be bothered by dressing any way other than comfortable, and I forgot to put on makeup so often I just quit buying it. I was a "plain Jane" and okay with it.

But Alder? He probably woke up with his hair perfectly combed. He used to wear it longer when we were married, but now he kept it neatly trimmed. Only a couple strands of gray twinkled at his temples, but all they did was whisper promises. This man was going to be *fiinne* in a few years. And then keep getting better.

"Mom, I can't marry him."

We can sleep in separate bedrooms.

Would I get one night of rest while sleeping in the

same house as that man? When I knew exactly how he could make me feel? Just like his looks, he'd probably gotten better at sex too. Honestly, I didn't know how he could. He'd already been phenomenal.

I prodded my temples. A headache was coming on, and Laila would wake with a vengeance. Her routine was off, her sleep schedule messed up, and I'd pay for it all weekend.

"Then don't marry him," Mom said. "We'll figure it out."

We'd been trying to figure it out for three months. My rental had always been temporary. I needed to be out. In the middle of winter. Right before the holidays.

I didn't want to move. I loved my job, and it was one of the few lab positions that didn't require shift work. With Laila, that was critical. I also couldn't take her farther from her dad. She was still adjusting to not living under the same roof as him. Jason would always let us back in, but I couldn't do that to him. Nor could he take Laila full-time with his ever-changing schedule.

Reality was sinking in, one thought at a time. My living room was full of boxes I'd rescued from work. They needed to be filled, and I needed some place to haul them.

My options were few. Alder had presented the most comprehensive one. Yet I couldn't bring myself to call him, to tell him that yes, I would, in fact, dig out my wedding ring and tell him I'd love him through sickness and health when we'd failed once already. My stomach lurched envisioning the possibility.

No. There was no way I was getting married to my ex-husband.

* * *

Alder

I reclined on the couch in the house Evander rented, which would be Violet's after the two were married for a year. Until then, they were the picture of wedded bliss, and they weren't pretending.

Envy gnawed at my chest wall, and I rubbed my sternum.

I'd had what they had once. I'd fucked it up.

I could have it again, but I jacked that all up too. I kept trying to tell myself I hadn't overstepped. Daisy had told me her problems. I had presented a solution.

"You did what?" Violet's eyes were wide. Instead of resting her hands on her eight-months-pregnant stomach, she spread her fingers wide across it. The sweater I suspected was Evander's was pulled tight around her belly.

"All I did was offer." All I had done was watch her look at me like I'd sprouted horns and was tempting her to hell. She'd asked how I could even entertain the thought, and none of my logic was enough for my usually practical ex-wife. I'd spent the night regretting everything and nothing at the same time.

"Your offer was to *remarry* Daisy? The wife you've already divorced?"

"She and the kid need a place to live." I hadn't even met Laila. Did she have big blue eyes like Daisy, or fraught brown ones like her dad?

A crack in my heart that would never heal ached. Daisy had a kid, and she wasn't mine.

"There's gotta be something." Violet frowned and linked her fingers. She blew out a breath and inhaled like she'd been running. The baby must be putting a lot of pressure on her lungs.

Had Jason been around for Daisy when she was this far along? Had he rubbed her feet and made sure to take out the trash so she didn't have to? Had he picked his goddamn socks off the floor?

I tugged at the collar of my crewneck sweater. I had stayed with Violet and Evander last night. The empty house that was supposed to be mine had sat empty another day.

My phone buzzed. When I saw Linda's name, I scowled. "Shit."

Violet sat forward as much as she could. "Is that Daisy?"

"Unless it's to tell me I'm crazy and once again ask what I was thinking, I doubt she'll call." I worked my jaw back and forth. "It's Linda. She has a potential renter. She's showing them the house today."

"Damn."

"Yeah."

"If Daisy decides differently, you can just wait out the lease and marry then."

Stunned, I stared at her. "You want her to say yes?"

She pursed her lips like she was debating how much to say. "I'd hate for our family to lose the house."

There was more she wasn't admitting. Did she want me and Daisy to reunite? Regardless, I agreed with her about the house. We'd all grown up there. I'd been almost done with high school before Mom and Dad had moved.

The others might not be as attached, but we all had fond memories. Just like my parents' house was home, so was that place.

"Is there anyone else you can marry?" Her lips turned down like she smelled rotten eggs.

There was no one else I wanted to marry. Expectations would be set. I'd be ready to walk in a year when we fulfilled the requirements of the trust. Another woman might have ideas that included the real thing. Like babies.

No.

"It'd get complicated."

Daisy was nothing if not practical. She'd go into this knowing that there'd be an end date. She'd keep her distance. She'd play the part.

And the whole time, she wouldn't know that I was doing everything I could to win her back.

* * *

Daisy

"I want green cup!" Laila screamed. Her little fists were balled, and tears tracked down her face.

"That is the green one." I pushed my hair back, hoping the neighbors wouldn't call the cops—again— because Laila was in her "fierce four" era. She was opinionated, volatile, and tenacious.

"That one." She stomped and pointed to a yellow-green sippy cup sitting dirty on the counter.

Damn. "Okay, let me wash it."

"No!" She wailed some more.

So that was it. We'd reached the point where nothing would make her happy. She needed a nap, but she'd outgrown them. I needed her to nap, but that didn't count for anything.

"I'm washing the cup and then we'll go for a drive." I didn't frame it as a question. She'd fight it anyway.

Mom had left yesterday, and today, I didn't mind Laila's tantrum. The screaming took my mind off Alder's proposal.

Married. Again.

I shook my head as Laila dropped to her butt on the floor and sobbed.

I filled the cup with chocolate milk, her weekend treat, and went to the door that led to the garage. I grabbed her coat off the hook. "Come on. Let's go."

"No!" she shrieked.

"Okay. I'm going." I set the cup on the floor and shrugged into my coat. Next, I stepped into my winter boots and snagged my purse. We both liked afternoon drives. I could let my thoughts drift, and the hum of the engine and flashing scenery calmed her.

I retrieved her milk, opened the door, and stepped into the garage.

"Mommy." She raced to the door, flopped onto her bottom again, and tugged her boots on. Her pajama pants bunched over the tops, but I didn't fix them. One battle at a time.

I helped her with her coat, and she stomped out to the car with me.

Her fine, blonde hair stuck up in each direction thanks to her hood, but she got into her booster seat, and I buckled her in. She kicked her legs and guzzled her milk, probably to soothe her throat after hollering.

I backed out and drove through our dated neighborhood to the main highway going through town.

"Mommy, horses."

"Pretty horses," I replied. The excitement in her voice caused a pang of regret. She loved horses. I used to talk about how I couldn't wait to get my own place and have ponies. I hadn't shared those dreams with anyone—other than Alder—but Laila had picked her own fantasy about them anyway.

I hadn't ridden as a kid. I had just wanted a horse. To pet. To talk to. People didn't listen but a horse might. Their smell was soothing, and I loved the mellow way they munched grass. That was all.

Those dreams had been tabled after I divorced the ranch kid. Alder's dad had quit ranching altogether when they'd moved to Billings and the pastures the Dukes had used for their hobby ranch had been leased out.

Within minutes, the house Alder had grown up in came into view. I hadn't intended to drive here, but I drove by the house a lot on our excursions. The sight was calming, just like visiting it as a teen had been. The ditches were dusted with brown snow. We were supposed to get more next week and then a possible winter storm after that. Right when I was supposed to move.

The old place stood white against the tall pine trees Weston and Magnolia had planted shortly after they had moved in. Leafy green trees made up the middle row and lilac bushes that I drove out here to admire every June rimmed the third row on two sides of the house.

A layer of untouched snow blanketed the yard. When Alder and his siblings had been growing up here, there had been tracks all over. No mound of snow had gone untouched. The house had been alive and wild. So unlike mine.

Dad had been out a lot. He hung out with everyone but his family. Mom had quietly enjoyed my company, but I had been at Alder's every chance I had gotten.

Two cars were out front. I recognized Linda and Darren rounding a silver car. The pickup had a single guy, my stomach sank. They were showing the house. Another renter who had no idea of the history here and might not care if he did. The man wore blue coveralls and a flannel shirt. His hat had ear flaps, but he wasn't wearing a jacket. He probably worked at the mine or the refinery. Maybe the wind farm or the coal gasification plant.

Did he have kids who'd appreciate the wide-open yard? Would they watch the cattle graze on quiet summer days? Did he notice how little traffic there was? Except for my car, of course.

I kept peeking over as I passed.

Alder didn't have a wife. Linda would rent the house.

I gnawed on my lower lip. Before I knew it, I was crossing to the other side of town using back roads I still knew like my own reflection. I passed through Barron ranch land and ended up idling down a long driveway. A fancy black pickup with chrome detail, a locked bed cover, and brand-new tires was parked by the walk to the front door.

My hands trembled when I put my car in park.

"Where are we?" Laila asked.

"A friend's place." He'd told me he'd be here.

This was where Violet lived, but Alder came outside in a maroon, cable-knit sweater that wasn't one of the ten-dollar clearance sweaters I had once bought him. He wore jeans, and oh damn. Not only had his looks been refined, but his body had too with thick thighs and a powerful gait that spoke of all the hours he'd spent on horseback flying through the pastures.

If he put on a cowboy hat, I'd get pregnant again without touching him.

I didn't get out of the car.

"Who's that?" Laila gestured to the window with her yellow-green cup.

"An old friend," I said softly. I fumbled for the control to roll the window down, but he beat me to it, opening the passenger door.

When he got in, that new-leather-and-cedar smell wrapped around me like an old lover's embrace. My chest grew tight, and I struggled to take a breath.

"Hi," he said quietly, his gaze roaming over my face, his eyes full of curiosity and concern. After the way I'd stomped away from him when he'd proposed, he probably hadn't expected to see me drive up. He twisted in the seat. His eyes crinkled at the corners with his smile. "Hey there. You must be Laila."

Her eyes narrowed, and her lips puffed out in a suspicious pout.

"Your mom told me about you," Alder tried again. "Whatcha drinking?"

She hugged her cup to hide it from him.

"We like to go for drives," I explained, taking over. Laila didn't open up to strangers. "It mellows us out." I rolled my eyes toward the back seat to tell him that only one of us needed to mellow out.

The corner of his mouth quirked.

"We drove past your parents' old house." I stared out the windshield. I couldn't face him and have this talk.

Memories threatened to push out of the tidy container I'd tucked them in. Real proposals and old heartbreaks could stay locked up. "Linda was showing the place to someone."

"She said she had a potential renter."

A shudder traveled down my spine. I squeezed my eyes shut. Was I really doing this?

Picturing that stranger inspecting the house I remembered so well cut the air supply off from my lungs. I squeezed my eyes shut. He'd asked the same question twice in my life. To be fair, the second time, he'd said we should get married. But I was giving him the same response for a completely different reason. "My answer is yes."

I was met with silence, but when I snuck a peek at him, a wide smile stretched across his absurdly handsome face.

Chapter Three

Daisy

I feathered my fingers around my collar. I had just moved out on the guy. A six-year relationship and he'd been asking me to marry him the whole time. Now I had to tell him about my change of plans.

I had boxes lined up and ready to haul. Alder said the movers would be here at eleven.

Movers. I told him I couldn't afford movers, and he'd ordered them like he was buying a pack of gum. Not only that, he'd been able to schedule them on short notice, both at my place and his.

When we'd moved into our first apartment after we'd gotten married, we had paid his siblings in pizza and root beer floats. Basically pennies for a moving job back then.

Jason knocked, and I blew out a hard breath. My stomach was going to crawl out of my throat and launch itself across the room, but I yelled, "Come in!"

Laila skidded out of her bedroom. "Daddy!"

"Hey, hey, there's my girl." He crouched, and she flew into his arms. Seeing him so involved in her life even after we separated healed a hurt little girl inside of me. That girl wasn't so little anymore. A neglectful dad wasn't less hurtful as an adult. If anything, I could better see how little he wanted to participate in my life or in that of his only grandkid. I was his only living kid, but some days, I was just a name to clean up his affairs after he was gone.

"I'm almost done packing." Laila grinned.

I rubbed between my brows. "You know what, Laila. Why don't you go get the last of your things packed? I need to talk to Dad."

"Okay!" She buzzed away, singing a song that had been playing on the kids' station earlier.

Jason shoved his hands in his pockets and eyed the boxes. "So you found a place?"

"Yeah." That should be a good segue, but my mouth dried up. I'd managed some distance from the plans that had been set in motion, but speaking it all out loud? I pressed my hand to my stomach. "About all that... I wanted to talk to you first." Interest lit his eyes, maybe a little hope. "Remember Alder from Reservoir Barrel?"

The light died in his gaze. He cleared his throat. "Yeah. Your ex-husband."

I nodded. This was going to hurt him.

"You were talking to him in his pickup for a while." The betrayal in his voice shouldn't bother me, but the guilt inside me burned hotter. He must've seen us when he'd gone home for the night. Alder's pickup stood out even in a lot full of trucks.

"We were catching up. It was the first time since..." I blew out a long breath. "Look, there's no easy way to say this but you need to hear it."

"You're back with him?" His voice pitched up. Any higher, and it'd bring Laila running. I'd barely been able to conceal our plans from her. I'd wanted to tell Jason first lest she spill any details before I was ready.

"No." I was shaking my head, but stopped. "I mean, not like you think." He opened his mouth again, but I stuck a hand up. My own personal stop sign. He snapped his mouth shut. "He has a house." Only some of the tension eased from Jason's body. That might not last long. "I could live there, but I can't afford the rent. He can't live there or even get ownership of the house unless he's been married for a minimum of a year." I cringed and waited for his reaction.

Confusion swirled in his eyes, then a slow, dawning, disbelieving comprehension took its place. "You're getting married?"

"Yes," I squeaked. "But it's not a love union. I mean, we tried that and epically failed."

"You're marrying your ex-husband?"

I dipped my head. "Yes."

"But you wouldn't marry me?"

"This isn't about love."

"And not getting married was about love with me?" He exhaled roughly and looked away.

"Jason." I pinched the bridge of my nose. "I almost didn't do this because I don't want to hurt you more than I have. I'm really sorry. But this house is big. He won't charge me rent, and I can use that money to tackle my debt." That damn debt. The reason why my price range was so low.

The corners of Jason's jaw flexed when I mentioned debt. I had used it as an excuse to delay my acceptance of his many proposals.

"I told you I'd help with that," he said.

He had, but it'd been my lesson to learn, not his. And now, he couldn't promise his help wouldn't come with strings. He wouldn't mean to, but he was a loyal man, and moving on wasn't in his bones.

The marriage to Alder might help. The thought made me feel marginally better. Jason deserved happiness and paying my debt wasn't it. "When the year is up, we'll divorce, and I can rent the house from Alder or find somewhere else."

"You'll divorce?" he asked flatly.

"Yes." I held up a finger and peeked in on Laila. She had gotten distracted looking through a board book. I returned to where I'd been standing. "I haven't talked to Laila yet. I thought you should be the first to know."

His rigid stance softened, but the beaten-dog look remained. "Your ex-husband is going to be her stepdad."

My heart thumped. Stepdad sounded way too serious. Felt just as momentous as digging out the wedding ring that had wrecked me to take off. But stepdad? Technically, yes, but I couldn't get Laila to understand that many specifics. "We'll be more like roommates. We won't use that terminology. I don't want to confuse her more than all this will."

"At least you won't have to change your last name." His bitterness was undeniable.

Daisy Duke wasn't an ideal name to have. I was nothing like *The Dukes of Hazzard*'s Daisy Duke. No booty shorts for me and I couldn't tan worth a shit. But I hadn't possessed the will to change it after the divorce. I had lost enough.

"It's only for a year. I don't know if word will get out, but we have to be as real as possible while sleeping in separate rooms. His aunt and dad have to sign off after a year, and he won't get the house if they think we're lying about being a couple. His grandma was apparently quite a romantic." I sucked in a big breath. I was taking a gamble on this. Jason wasn't a vindictive person, but telling him was a risk. Yet my conscience couldn't live with lying to him. I'd have to use a few white lies for Laila just so she didn't announce at daycare or in the grocery store that I was just pretending to be married.

"Who else will know?"

"Mom knows. Maybe Dad, if he calls. You. Possibly Alder's siblings." I wasn't telling him that each Duke sibling had a trust. Alder's was taking up too much mental power as it was.

"Jesus, Daisy." He yanked his ball cap off and pushed a hand through his short hair. "Thanks for telling me, I guess."

"You're welcome."

He huffed out a quick breath. "That guy from Reservoir Barrel didn't look like a slacker who stayed out all night and couldn't be bothered to wash dishes or pick up his socks."

No kidding. "That guy" was nothing like the ex-husband I'd told Jason about. Alder could've claimed a wife by now if he'd wanted to, and she'd wonder what I'd been thinking ditching him. "Alder appears to socialize less these days," I agreed. "I don't know about the dishes or the socks. Like I said, we'll be in different rooms."

He gave me a steady look. "Unless his aunt or his parents visit."

A knot formed in my chest. I hadn't thought that far ahead. My sanity had hung on separate rooms. I couldn't do this if I thought I'd be sleeping inches from him again.

Not enough time had passed for me to forget what being pressed against Alder's hard body felt like. "I doubt they'd stay over."

His expression challenged me in a quiet way that was unusual for him. Jason pestered. He poked. He nagged. He didn't give me space to gather my thoughts.

But he was a decent guy. He'd find a good partner who would like to hunt and fish, and even if she didn't, she could fake it.

The faking had worn on me. In and out of bed.

I wanted all that for him. Not for me. "We'll have to deal with that *if* the time comes."

He didn't meet my gaze. "I'll have Laila back on Tuesday." I didn't tell him Monday would be the day I was remarrying Alder. "I'm sure she'll want to call you tonight."

"Call any time," I assured him, in case he feared I'd test Alder on his ability to give me four orgasms in a night.

Those days were over.

My body tingled. But what if they weren't?

Jason scratched the back of his neck. "I know I'm just a dumb pump operator." I hated when he did that. I'd never denigrated his intelligence, but I got tired of telling him to stop doing it. "But if you're going to pay off as much of your debt as you can before you get divorced, won't some of that be his when you two divorce?"

Shit. I would have to talk to Alder about a prenup.

* * *

Alder

. . .

I frowned at the document Daisy presented to me in the entry of the courthouse. There was a metal detector waiting for us to walk through and a bored deputy watching our exchange. "A prenup?"

She nervously fluttered the sheets in her hands. "I'm sure a standard form will work."

"I'm not worried about you taking my money." Daisy was the type to split the bill down to the penny without being asked. Plus, I had a hard time summoning one fuck to give if she got my wealth. I wasn't using it.

"I am." She shoved the papers toward me.

Frowning, I skimmed through them. It appeared to be a standard, boilerplate contract. "Shouldn't we have lawyers go through this?"

"If you want. Then the year countdown would have to wait." Her gaze strayed toward the deputy still quietly watching us, her hands hooked in her thick vest.

I was not waiting one more day for this woman. Yes, I wanted the house, but Daisy was almost mine again. A second chance was minutes from my grasp. I glanced at the table we were supposed to put our belongings on. A stray pen rested by some empty forms. I took the contract to the table and scrawled my name on it. "There."

Relief passed through her gaze, and she nodded. "Thank you, but we probably need a notary." She patted her square tote bag. "I have another copy."

Whatever the reason for the prenup, it wasn't wealth and she wasn't copping to it. I had no clue how binding this was, but I wouldn't pursue it. "Whatever you need, Daisy. We can also do a postnup and take our time. We have a year."

"We'll get this to work. Do you, um, have a ring?" Her gaze darted around.

"Yeah. I found my old one." I made it sound nonchalant, as if I'd happened upon it when I was packing.

I'd never forgotten where I had put that ring. A simple gold band, as pristine as when we'd bought it. I'd never been able to wear it to work in the oil fields for safety reasons, and I hadn't appreciated its symbolism enough when I did have it on.

"Okay. Good. Uh, I've got mine." She left it at that and put her tote in a bin to go on the conveyor belt.

Bolstered that she had likely kept hers in a special jewelry box too, I followed her through the metal detector. I was in the same sweater she'd seen me in last weekend, but I had worn slacks today instead. Seemed more fitting for a wedding. For my second wedding. During the first, I had worn black jeans, a crisp white shirt, a sport coat, and a cowboy hat. I'd even shined my boots. From there, my effort had dwindled.

That wouldn't be happening this time.

Just as we finished our short trek through the metal detector, my youngest sibling, Lily, walked in with Eliot. All of my siblings had been surprised but understanding. I hadn't missed the hopeful notes in their voices when I'd talked to them. My parents were a different story. They were thrilled. Ecstatic. I'd had to talk them down and keep them from rushing to Coal Haven to see Daisy again. They'd agreed to give us time to adjust. How long would remain to be seen.

Lily's smile widened when she spotted Daisy. "Hi!"

She didn't give Daisy a hug, and I appreciated that my sister remembered Daisy's discomfort with random hugs.

Daisy had been comfortable enough around me.

Once upon a time. I shook Eliot's hand. "Bring back memories?" I asked.

He grinned. "Good ones."

Lily practically swooned. I tried not to roll my eyes, but controlling my envy took too much effort. "Just remember that when I get to kiss the bride, that doesn't mean you two can let loose."

They laughed, but my gaze caught on a poleaxed Daisy. She hadn't realized we'd be kissing at least once as husband and wife.

My grin had to be wolfish. I wanted to make her comfortable with this arrangement, but I couldn't resist getting under her skin. Seemed only fair since she'd been under mine for fifteen years.

Her gaze skated away, and I held in my chuckle.

When we reached the office, a young woman clapped when she saw us. The nameplate on her desk said Ella. "Oh, I love starting the week with a wedding. Who are the bride and groom?"

"I am." I stepped forward. "And Daisy."

My ex-wife took longer to step toward the desk, and we were inundated with paperwork.

"Oh." Ella glanced from my ID to Daisy's. "Same last name?"

"I kept it from the first time we were married," Daisy mumbled.

Ella's brows lifted. "*Oh.*" She smiled brightly. "Well, it's efficient."

After we proved our identity and copies of everything were made, I signed in a few places, then Daisy did the same.

"Okay." Ella rose. "You both can come with me. The witnesses as well. You can hang your coats on the rack outside of Johanna's office."

I put a hand on the small of Daisy's back. Electricity tingled under my fingers. Did she feel it too? Her spine was ramrod straight. When she shrugged out of her winter coat, I took it from her and hung it up. Then I took my coat off, a blue L.L. Bean parka and not my wool coat. I'd been tempted to dress up more, but I was glad I hadn't. With her jeans, she wore a fluffy yellow sweater. Had she been afraid to put too much significance into today? Not enough?

Nothing would erase the memory of her in a fitted wedding dress, which had highlighted her slight curves, or the way her hair had been pulled back. Her big, blue eyes had held my future that day. They still did.

The corner of my mouth curved up. Yellow was her favorite color, and she'd pinned her hair back. The style was likely functional, but unless she said otherwise, I'd pretend she'd done it for me.

The justice of the peace introduced herself. "Good morning. I'm Johanna. I married your siblings. Both of them."

"There are three more after us," I joked.

"Good luck getting Jasper in here," Lily muttered.

Fair, but I had thought I'd never be saying vows again. I didn't like to repeat activities I had failed at, and I hadn't let someone down as often as I had Daisy.

"I'll have you two stand here." Johanna gestured to a spot in front of her desk, and she stood between us.

I took Daisy's hands in mine. Her brows pinched together. I ran a thumb lightly over her knuckles, and her grip stiffened. So damn familiar. Her skin. The vows. Daisy stared at my collarbone as she recited hers. When I said mine, she wouldn't hold my gaze. A line of pink crested her cheeks. Her fingers went limp, but I held on, supporting her in this moment. A silent promise I'd continue to do so this time.

All those years ago, she'd clung to me and had grinned while doing so, her eyes dancing. Today, apprehension filled her gaze.

She worried her lower lip as I finished. "'Til death do us part."

Her eyes drifted shut, and she sucked in a breath. From the corner of my eye, I could see Lily and Eliot standing quietly. My sister's expression was solemn. She could read the room. Part of the reason why I had asked her to be a witness wasn't just because Violet was the other closest sibling and too pregnant to make standing this long comfortable. No, Lily had been in high school when Daisy and I had divorced. By then, my family had lived in Billings for years, and Lily was likely to recall what things had been like between me and Daisy as teens. How inseparable we'd been. The way she'd laughed, her head back. How seamlessly she'd fit into our family, flower name and all. Lily hadn't been around to see how I'd let Daisy down in the most basic of ways.

"You may kiss the bride." Johanna beamed.

This kiss only needed to be a chaste touching of lips. A symbol, like our rings. But a starving man couldn't be plunked down in front of the best meal he'd ever had and be told only to sniff it.

I curved an arm around Daisy's waist, and her eyes went wide.

"What are you—" She looked around. Lily's eyes were saucers, and Eliot had judiciously dropped his gaze to the floor. Only the justice was watching us, indulgent smile on her face. We were supposed to be real.

Daisy's gaze collided with mine. I silently asked permission. Holding her like this was reward enough. If she needed me to give her only a peck, I would.

She gave me a little nod.

Fuck, yes. I lowered my mouth to hers. Her warm lips were everything I had dreamed of. Everything might've changed between us. I was no longer a rebellious slacker who thought life owed him. I worked out regularly and wore nice clothes. I'd be the CEO of one of the biggest employers in the state. Daisy had a daughter. She'd lived a whole life since our divorce.

But this kiss? Just as sweet as I remembered. She met me with the perfect amount of pressure. I didn't bear down on her, and I didn't nudge my tongue against her lips to sweep inside. We had an audience, and I had a fuck-ton of trust to build between us.

I added just a little more pressure, desperate for more, then I pulled back. I could control my desires now. I was no longer an entitled kid.

Her eyelids fluttered open and heat simmered in their blue depths. She'd responded to my touch. And now she was my wife. Again.

* * *

Daisy

I was in the bathroom of the courthouse, in front of the sink, staring at the ring on my finger. *My* ring. It'd seemed practical at the time. Why buy a new ring when I had this old thing lying around?

My vision grew blurry. A hot tear rolled down my cheek. I swiped at it and checked the mirror. My eyes would get bloodshot if I started crying. Everyone would know that I wasn't the unbothered queen of an arranged marriage with my ex-husband.

He was no longer an ex.

Alder Duke was my husband. Fifteen years later, I was Daisy Duke because I was married to him, not because I had been married to him. My life had gone full circle, and I had gone nowhere.

Another tear tracked down my cheek. I hastily wiped it off and sniffled.

The door opened, and I spun to wash my hands that weren't dirty. I hadn't used the toilet, I had just needed the quiet. The sensor on the faucet was touchy and the water wouldn't turn on. Damn.

Lily lingered by the door. The two stall doors were open if she needed to pee, but she ignored them. "How are you doing?"

The concern in her voice nearly made more tears well up. My mind was a mess. I should be happy, like any other bride on her wedding day. But confusion lingered because I had been that happy bride on my wedding day —when I was nineteen. I had a place to live in a gorgeous house that needed a little work. Renovations Alder said he'd do. Part of me was too scared to rely on him for anything. Life wasn't just about me. I had Laila to take care of.

I had in-laws I adored, but we were lying to most of them. How did I face West and Magnolia after I left their son once? What happened when I did it again?

"I don't know how I'm doing," I answered honestly.

Some days, I couldn't just toss out a "fine" and move on. I gave up on the water. "It's...weird."

She moved closer, leaning against the wall by the hand dryer. "I can't imagine. I was thinking that it must be nice to have a history with your temporary husband, but I guess when your history is, in fact, being married and divorced, then it's gotta be a trippy déjà vu."

"You're telling me." I mulled over her words. "You didn't have a history with Eliot?"

She smiled pure bliss. "I had met him twice. Three times if you count the day he overheard me tell Aunt Linda we were getting married. Otherwise, nope. No history. He was just a nice guy who thought I was a cute mess and needed a temporary husband."

Surprise crowded out some of my angst. "He married you when he didn't know you?"

She nodded and crossed her arms. "It was meant to be."

Good for them. She got the house *and* the love of her life. My astonishment dimmed. "Alder and I proved already that we aren't."

She shrugged. "You're married again. Never would've seen that coming." Her expression turned sheepish. "Can I say that I wished for it? I missed you, but then you two lived in different towns, never spoke, and I never would've imagined"—she gestured around us—"this."

"You were so young. I didn't think you remembered me a whole lot."

"You didn't brush me off like my sisters, and you talked about real things. It's not superficial. Not like all his other—" Distress filled her eyes, and she bit the inside of her cheeks.

"His other girlfriends?" Superficial or not, it had ended for all of us with Alder.

She pulled a face. "If you can call them that." She cut a hand through the air. "Fake marriage or not, I'm not talking about his dating history."

Yet here I was, hanging on every word, waiting to hear how they were so wrong for him. "I can discuss mine if that makes you feel better." I'd feel like shit, but my curiosity was strong.

She chuckled. "The only thing I'm interested in is meeting Laila. She sounds delightful."

"You've heard about her?"

Lily nodded. "Alder said she likes afternoon drives and treating him like he's invisible."

That got a smile out of me. "She's a ride or die for her dad."

"Good." Lily's grin was mischievous. "Alder can learn to work for a girl's affection."

I laughed despite the heaviness of the day. The good humor didn't last long, and I let out a sigh. "There's no way to fast-forward an entire year, is there?"

She laughed. "No, but I can tell you, the next year might be eye-opening in a way you never would've expected."

Her convenient marriage had worked out, and I was grateful for that little precocious sister who often had gotten lost in the shuffle of all her siblings. But we were all adults now. I needed routine and predictability. There was nothing routine about getting married on a Monday or predictable about moving in with the ex-husband I had only reconnected with a week ago.

But if there was one thing I could do, it was toss away

my old life and move on. One of these times, it'd actually be a good decision.

Chapter Four

Alder

The movers had arrived at Daisy's rental after our morning appointment at the courthouse.

Appointment. My wedding band was back on my finger. As the supervisor of the moving crew outlined the final contract I had to sign to say job well done, I fiddled with the ring, twisting it from side to side with my thumb. So damn familiar, yet so different.

I signed the papers and gave them a big tip even though they hadn't had much to move. The movers from Billings weren't showing up with my things until later this evening.

Daisy hadn't had much furniture, and her pile of boxes was minimal, but then she'd already moved once in the last few months when she'd left Jason.

The thought of Daisy leaving cracked open the crater in my chest, and fear welled out. Panic that she'd do it again. I had been easy for her to leave the first time, despite our history together. High school sweethearts. Inseparable. Then she'd been gone. I wasn't that man anymore. If nothing else came from this scenario, she'd know that.

She wandered into the kitchen where I stood by the stack of boxes, nervously tugging at the sleeves of her sweater. Her gaze dropped to my ring and slipped away.

Yeah. I was feeling the weirdness too. I was also still feeling the touch of her lips on mine. The same sweet flavor that was her, only richer. We were older. No longer young adults, we now had a history that didn't include the other.

My heart twisted. So many damn years lost because I'd been selfish and stubborn.

But I had her again. I'd learn about this version of Daisy, and maybe I wouldn't fuck everything up this time. "Where do you want me to start unpacking?"

"Oh, um..." She folded her arms and scanned the kitchen. Then she wandered into the living room. "It's like a different house."

"Yeah." Just like her and me, this house had a history that didn't include us. One of the previous renters had painted accent walls. A light cream covered three of the living room walls, and then a taupe where the couch would've been. In one bedroom, the same cream was on every wall except one light blue one. In the main bedroom, the one my parents used to share, there was a deep purple wall.

The bathrooms were wallpapered—poorly. None of the closets had been painted and opening the doors to them showed the age of the place. Some holes in the walls gaped open, likely from the most recent renters. Aunt Linda and Darren must not have gotten to it.

The carpets in the bedroom should be replaced, and the hardwood in the rest of the house needed TLC. The kitchen was in a different century. That hadn't changed much since I'd lived here, just the appliances.

"Laila's room should be done first." Daisy wandered down the hall. I started following her, but she turned. "I can work on that if you want to do the kitchen."

The message was clear. We weren't working in the same room together. No idle chitchat. No getting to know each other. No close proximity. This was a big house, and she meant to keep that distance.

"Okay." I had a year. Besides, she'd want to break for dinner. We'd only grabbed a quick bite at the cafe downtown with Lily and Eliot after our wedding. I had owed them at least a meal for being our witnesses.

As I unpacked boxes in the kitchen, I made a mental note of everything we'd need. The contact paper in the drawers and cupboards was either peeling or worn through. I ran the dishwasher with only cleaner because it stunk. The stove needed a better wipe-down and so did all the cabinets while I was at it.

An hour later, I had my sleeves rolled up and was elbow-deep in the corner cabinet, when I sensed a timid presence behind me. I'd always been able to tell when Daisy was in the room. Once upon a time, I'd taken it for granted. Never again.

I eased out of the cupboard, pulling an old packet of ranch dressing out with me.

Daisy kicked a pale brow up when she saw what I held. "That's probably the only food in the house." Her expression turned sheepish. "I came in here thinking I could make a quick snack."

I opened the fridge. All of her old condiments were now stored inside, but she had pared down her food to a point where she didn't have any. "We should grab some groceries."

Wariness entered her gaze. "I can go. Don't you have to wait for the movers part deux?"

"They're going to call when they're an hour out. Want me to drive?"

Her lips pursed. "I can get the groceries. You paid for the movers."

As if the cost dented my bank account. I made a lot more than her, had received more than a few bonuses, and with this new job, I'd earn even more. "I need a break." I didn't.

"Okay, then I can keep—"

"But I don't know what Laila likes."

She gave me a flat look. "We don't have to shop for groceries together."

I wanted to. "It's easier and faster. We could've been there by now."

She relented, spinning away. I smiled but dropped it before she could see. Logic for the win.

We got on our coats and loaded up in the pickup. I didn't open the door for her, or she might get more skittish and decide to stay home.

Home. This house was my home, and it was Daisy's. But it wasn't our home. Not yet.

*   *   *

Daisy

Awareness crawled over my skin. People weren't really watching me and Alder like I thought they were. Yet when I glanced at the registers, the two women working were muttering to each other and looking our way.

Alder held two packs of steaks. "You said Laila likes beef, Daisy?"

I took my attention off the employees who spotted the ring on my hand. I tucked it into my coat pocket. "Yeah. She likes beef just fine."

He tossed both into the cart. He discreetly looked toward the registers and hurt filtered through his expression. "Just a few more things and we can go. But if you want to wait in the pickup, I can ring it all up."

Guilt teased the corners of my brain. I was acting like I was embarrassed to be seen with him. I wasn't. I was self-conscious about what it meant, what people would think. Those who knew me also knew I had just ended things with Jason. Now here I was, wearing a wedding ring and being seen with a new man.

Word would spread soon enough through those who cared. I had remarried my ex. They'd fill in the blanks with what happened between me and Jason and then me and Alder. Some might even understand. And I'd have to just let them think what they wanted. A little messiness would help sell this relationship.

"No. I don't need to wait in the truck," I said. Besides, other people would take my attention off how achingly familiar it was to shop for groceries with Alder again. He still preferred sourdough bread, drank whole milk, got a small container of chocolate milk, and balanced his oranges in his hand to determine if they were heavy for their size. And now he was thinking of Laila as he shopped.

"Alder?" a woman said from behind me. "Daisy?"

Shock passed through Alder's gaze and he met mine. "Aunt Linda," he crooned. "How are you doing?"

I gave him a *seriously?* stare and turned. "Hi, Linda."

I'd passed Linda and her husband a few times in town. We'd shared tight smiles and had continued on our way. But I was part of the family again.

"Nice to see you again, Daisy." She glanced between us, the puff on the top of her stocking hat bouncing. She was swaddled in a thick coat with rubber-toed boots on her feet. They were similar to the pair I was wearing. "You got in the house okay?"

Alder grinned and closed the distance between us, wrapping his arm around my waist. "We did. We're between movers."

"The ceremony?" Her smile was faint. I had always liked Linda and her mellowness. "It went well?"

We hadn't invited anyone other than witnesses. Alder told his parents that this was so new, and being a second wedding, we didn't want to deal with any awkwardness. He'd also admitted we were moving quickly since the house was open. A little truth to add to the believability.

I hadn't been with him for the phone call, but I'd died inside the entire time I knew he'd been talking to them.

"It was great," Alder said, "but then we've had practice."

A nervous laugh burst out of me. "That's for sure."

"Like riding a bike, only this time I won't push her

off." He squeezed me to him. A solid wall of heat that our thick winter coats couldn't block.

"I'm happy for you two." The corners of Linda's eyes crinkled. "I think Mom's trusts are doing what she wanted and bringing all of you home." Her smile was remorseful. "I just wish she went about it differently."

My heart went out to her. She had to look after all the properties and the renters. A job she hadn't asked for. Then she had six nieces and nephews who were faced with getting married when they hadn't planned to. She was smart enough to know we'd rushed to get the house. Beyond that though, she looked at us as if she was happy to see us together again. As if she was relieved Alder and I had reconnected.

"Grandma had her own opinions," Alder said, "but she always loved Daisy. I know she's glad we're back together."

I blinked up at him. He'd spoken about her, about us, so easily. I could almost believe this was real between us. It'd be so easy if I weren't careful.

"Let me know if you need anything with the house." Linda gave us one last smile and walked away.

Alder didn't release me. Instead, I stayed tucked into his side through the meat aisle.

"Just a little longer," he said under his breath.

"I understand." I wouldn't admit to liking how solid he was next to me. Or that I couldn't bring myself to care who saw. We were selling this, and it was what we had to do. A little PDA was necessary.

* * *

Groceries were purchased and put away, and I had made myself a sandwich. So had Alder. He'd suggested some meals, but cooking with my husband was firmly in the danger zone. I'd start remembering how he used to come up behind me when I was at the counter chopping vegetables and washing dishes. He'd wrapped his arms around me, brushed my hair aside, and kissed the nape of my neck. Sometimes, he'd spin me around and lift me to the counter. And then we'd indulge our lust.

Yeah. Those memories. I did not need to be recalling them at all.

Laila's room was situated. Her bed and furniture were in place. She would not like the blue wall, just like I did not want a purple one. Alder's room upstairs had two navy-blue walls. I shuddered. Dark colors in the dead of winter. Ish.

I was in my room. Bedtime was approaching, and I was under the same roof as Alder.

Nerves fluttered through my belly. The first time we were married I'd been so excited for the wedding night. We had decided not to live together until we tied the knot. I had insisted we not go on our honeymoon right away but instead spend our first night in our new apartment. It'd been heaven.

Until school and work and the responsible, driven boy I had fallen for turned into a slug who couldn't respect me enough to preheat the oven when I called after I was done with school.

That slug dressed a hell of a lot nicer now. His wardrobe had to cost more than my annual salary. I'd seen the movers walk in with suits, still sharply pressed, on hangers.

That slug had also unpacked every kitchen box while

cleaning the damn cabinets and fridge, and he'd gotten his—expensive—furniture arranged in the living room. The place looked like we'd been living here for months instead of hours.

I pushed my hair off my face, some strands had escaped the small clips, and went to the living room.

Alder wandered into the room. He'd washed the dishes. All two plates and glasses.

This was not the man I had divorced.

He had his hands stuffed into his jeans as he scanned the room from corner to corner, his face expressionless. Several times today, I wished he was back in his suit. Then I couldn't tell how powerful his legs looked.

The walls were a different color but flashes of a young Alder streamed through my head. When I used to sit on the island and he'd get me water. How he'd hang out in this very doorway and just smile at me. The way he'd grin at me when I walked through the front door.

I knew all too well how that faded. How it had turned to eye rolls. To snarky comments and terse words about laying off him. To quit nagging. How he'd rather spend his evenings with the guys instead of me.

The weakly mended break in my heart threatened to crack open. "I'm, uh, heading to bed. Thanks again for giving us the main level."

His expression remained impassive. "I only need one room. There are two more upstairs. Does Laila need a playroom?"

There weren't enough toys for a playroom. I had taken half, and I had left the other half for Jason when I moved out. "Maybe after Christmas when Mom showers her with gifts that have a million parts."

The corner of his mouth lifted, but a flash of sadness sparked in his eyes. "You work tomorrow, right?"

"Yes, boss."

The corners of his eyes crinkled, and dammit, he had no business looking that good. "I'm not your boss yet."

He was going to be home for a little over a month before he started at the beginning of the new year. The old Alder would've stayed on the couch and gamed all day, then gone out at night with his buddies. "What do you plan to do?"

"I'll keep busy," he said as if he was promising me.

I shrugged like it didn't matter, and really, it didn't. We were roommates. I hoped he cleaned up after himself, but if he didn't, I wouldn't take it personally. Not like before.

"The house needs a lot of work," he said. "I'll grab some paint tomorrow."

An image of a teen Alder with his hat backward painting the barn with his dad and brother, Jasper, flashed into my head. The way he had laughed with Jasper and argued with his dad about getting the job done. My young heart hadn't been prepared. I might be older but it was a good thing I would be at work all day.

"It's your house. Or it will be."

His look intensified as he studied me. I was tempted to tell him I was picking Laila up most days after work, unless Jason was getting her, so I'd be home later than my shift—if he even knew what my hours were. I resisted. We weren't a couple, and he didn't need to know my business. Yet I had to bite the inside of my cheek to keep from chattering about my plans.

He finally dipped his head. "Good night, Daisy." Then he turned and disappeared into the kitchen.

The sense of loss that weighed on my chest made it hard to breathe. This was exactly what I thought I would have one day. Alder as my husband. A kid. This house. I had everything I had lost.

I could cry at the irony. "Good night, Alder," I whispered.

Chapter Five

Daisy

Laila kicked her feet against the seat. "Why can't I stay with Daddy?"

"He has to work. You'll be with him next weekend." I glanced in the rearview mirror. Her militant little gaze was pinned out the window. "I can't wait for you to see your new room."

She frowned like a disparaging governess.

Okay then.

I drove out of town to the house. Instead of driving by, I was turning down the drive. My chest tightened. Alder's pickup was backed up to the far garage door, which was closed. He'd saved the closest one to the house for me. The mudroom that connected the garage and the kitchen was one of the most worn rooms, but it was functional.

"Who's here?" Laila asked.

"Alder. Remember? He's living with us."

Her scowl wasn't heartening.

I parked in the garage and gathered my purse and lunch bag while surreptitiously trying to gauge Laila's reaction. The dubious expression on her face stayed as she scrambled out of the back seat.

I opened the door to the house and let her go inside ahead of me. The first thing that hit me was the savory smell. Yesterday, it had smelled like dust and cleaner. Today? Roasting meat. My stomach rumbled.

The next thing that hit me was the mudroom. A fresh coat of eggshell paint covered the walls, and the old wood on the bench and the board holding the coat hooks shone with fresh polish. The floor had been freshly scrubbed of all the footprints from the movers yesterday. Every time I thought of something that needed to be done, Alder had already done it. I couldn't identify the emotion swirling inside me, so I stuffed it away.

Alder appeared on the other side of the opening into the kitchen, a dish towel over his shoulder. He was in a loose, red, King Oil hoodie that still couldn't hide his wide shoulders. His jeans today were even more worn, hugging his thighs like a stripper on a pole. "Hey. How was your day?"

I blinked at him as if he were a sight I'd never seen before. I hadn't, actually. An Alder cooking in the kitchen wasn't in my bank of memories. He used to help his mom, and he'd been on a dishes rotation. But an entire meal? "Whatever you made yourself smells delicious."

"I tossed in a roast for all of us."

Laila flapped out of her coat and kicked her boots off. "Yuck."

Alarm passed through Alder's expression. Damn. He'd made sure to cook what I told him she liked.

"You love roast," I told her as I helped her hang up her coat.

She was a beefaholic to the point I worried that when she saw her first cow, she'd have an existential crisis. But no. She loved cows, and she loved her protein.

She kicked off her purple winter boots.

"Line those up on the rug, please."

She stomped her stockinged feet but did as I asked. "I don't want roast."

Her Rs still had a slight W sound. "Alder went to a lot of work to make a meal for us." I lifted my gaze to him. "Thank you."

His brow was furrowed as he witnessed Laila's subtle tantrum. "It's ready when you are." He stood aside for us.

I herded Laila to the large, solid-wood dining room table. My small folding table was in the garage. Same with the chairs. Three places were set with dishes that weren't the set I'd kept when we divorced. I still had most of the pieces, but he hadn't unpacked those. Instead, the plates and flatware were like the table. Sophisticated and quality, but lacking any flair, in a solid slate gray. A wealthy bachelor's belongings.

One plate was at the head of the table. The other two were on either side. One chair had Laila's pink plastic booster seat hooked to it. Ready for a happy family.

Dread crawled up my throat, robbing me of my appetite. With Jason's shift work and overtime, we had only eaten as a family less than a third of the month. I had looked forward to a nice meal then, but this was with Alder, and Laila was not impressed.

He was trying to be nice. Besides, this wasn't the Alder I had known.

I ushered Laila to her chair. "Here's your spot."

She didn't get into her seat. "I don't want it."

"Sit, please."

My tone prompted her to move. She crawled into her seat. When I turned, Alder was behind the island, watching me, an unreadable expression on his face.

I used to catch him watching me with a distant smile on his face. This wasn't the same. I folded my arms across my chest. "What's up?"

"You sounded like Mom."

I relaxed. "I learned a lot about parenting from watching her."

"From my mom?" He carried a dish with a small beef roast surrounded by cubed potatoes and carrots to the table.

"The warm and fuzzy stuff. My mom is perfunctory."

"What's that mean?" Laila asked, kicking her feet against the chair legs.

"It means there's a little of both moms raising you," I said. She talked like a grown woman because of my mom. But she was expressive and open with her feelings because of Magnolia Duke's influence on me.

Alder set the roast on the table and glanced between me and Laila.

"I don't want to be by him." Laila rolled her eyes toward Alder and adopted a mutinous glare.

Crap. "Laila—"

"I don't want—"

"It's all right." Alder picked up his plate and utensils. He smiled tightly. "There are more chairs."

Laila pointed to the other end of the table, the farthest from her, like a tiny dictator.

I bit the inside of my cheek before I giggled. Things had always been easy for Alder. People liked him. He bounced back from our divorce way better than me as the multitude of expensive suits attested to. Violet said he'd been head-hunted at the refinery because he'd left an impression on them when he'd worked there after high school. But he was not winning over a four-year-old girl.

He sat at the opposite end of us. I took some roast and cut it into small pieces for Laila. She poked at her potatoes and carrots.

"How was work?" Alder asked.

My knife was poised over my food. He was making small talk, but the idea crawled over my skin. Catching up about the day around an evening meal. It was what families did.

"Fine." I stuffed a carrot into my mouth.

Alder hesitated before he took a bite. We ate in silence. Laila finally ate some of her roast, and I coaxed her into eating a carrot. When I was done and Laila was finishing up, I rose to clear my plate. I carried it around the island and loaded it in the empty dishwasher.

"There's dessert," Alder said.

Laila snapped her head up and looked at me. If Alder thought he could buy her affection with sweets, he was correct.

"I'm sure there was plenty of dessert at your dad's," I told her. I never worried about Jason cheating. I worried about him eating the last piece of my birthday cake or chewing through Halloween candy by the end of the week.

The false innocence on her face made me hope that she'd be a terrible liar at least through her teenage years.

"We should skip tonight," I said. It wasn't about the sweets, although Laila got an upset stomach if she ate too many of Jason's mini candy bars. It was all of this. The set table. Dinner ready when we walked through the door. Dessert.

His gaze dropped like he knew exactly why I'd said no.

"Okay," she said mournfully and dropped her fork. She wiggled out of her booster still chewing her last bite of food.

"Ready for a bath?" I pointed to her place settings.

"I had one at Daddy's." When she grabbed her plate, it clattered to the floor. The dish busted into three large pieces and who knew how many shards. Juice from the roast, carrots, and potatoes scattered over the table and onto the floor.

She jumped back. "Sorry!"

I skimmed around the island. "Just stay where you are."

Alder was already on his feet. He plucked her out of the middle of the mess, spun, and set her on her feet by the table.

She ran around his chair toward me. "Mommy!" She rammed into my hip and wrapped her arms around me.

I rubbed her shoulders. "It's okay."

"Sorry!" Alder had his hands in the air. "Sorry, I should've asked. I was terrified she'd take a step and get glass in her foot."

I nodded, grateful for his quick reflexes. "Thank you. She's scared about it all."

He waved off the mess. "I'll get it. Don't worry. I'll clean everything up."

Since Laila was still clutching me, I'd take her out and calm her down. "Let's go take a bath. I think you'll like the new bathtub. There are no cracks in this one."

The crush of her arms eased. Laila liked her marathon baths. I gave Alder a small, grateful smile. The concern etched around his eyes only made him more handsome. So damn caring. So responsible.

This is the man I had thought I married the first time. Too bad he hadn't become that guy until the second time we'd married—when it was too late.

* * *

Alder

The broken shards were cleaned up, the table wiped off, and the dishwasher was going. I'd even gone outside to see if Daisy needed more stuff carried in, but there'd only been a backpack. Laila must have stuff at her dad's place. I left the cookies in the tray in the cupboard.

Daisy's dismay when I'd said there was dessert... Had I thought it'd show her what a good guy I was?

Maybe. I thought she'd be appreciative. She'd probably had a long day, and I had only wanted to help. Mom used to say cookies made everything better. Daisy used to agree with her.

But what did I know of Daisy these days? What did I know of her daughter?

I rubbed the sudden ache behind my sternum. Daisy

and I had talked about how many kids we'd have—two like her parents or six like mine? She'd agreed to start with two, but she had to be done with college first.

We'd gotten divorced before she'd graduated.

I checked my watch. The bath had been going for forty-five minutes. Had Laila turned into a prune by now?

I paced through the living area into the kitchen. My furniture had been purchased for a new-build house in Billings. The hard lines and shades of gray didn't fit the hominess of my childhood home. I had rarely crashed on the couch, but I could picture Daisy and Laila cuddling against the cushy armrest.

Several minutes later, the bathroom door opened, and I stepped out of the way. Laila wasn't comfortable around me, and I couldn't blame her. I was a strange man, and now I was living with her and her mother when her dad wasn't. The breakup had to be hard to comprehend for someone so young. Throw in a non-relationship and no wonder she'd wanted me at the far end of the table.

I pushed a hand through my hair.

"You painted the whole room?" Daisy's stunned voice carried down the hall.

I jumped to the doorway. Laila was swaddled from head to toe in a green towel that had a frog hood that went over her head. Only her little toes were sticking out.

They'd come into the house, and we'd eaten right away. Daisy must've herded her into the bathroom first without veering into the bedroom.

"Yeah. I just did the standard off-white for now. But if you decide what you want—"

"I'll do it." Daisy's gaze jerked around the room. She wasn't looking at me.

Shit.

"Laila and I will decide what she wants in her room, and I'll paint. If she wants me to."

Laila had the towel hugged around her, but she flipped the frog head back and gave me a plaintive stare.

Point taken. I gestured to the small unicorn backpack at the base of the bed. "I brought that back for you."

"Thank you." Daisy still wasn't looking at me. "Can you shut the door, please?"

"Sure." I was once again alone outside of the room she and Laila were in. I wandered toward the living room. All evening, I'd felt like I had stepped to the left when I should've been going right.

I could get started on the projects I'd planned for tomorrow, but I stood staring out the front windows. The yard light lit the driveway. Snow blanketed the ground and covered the bushes. In a month, it'd be Christmas.

I glanced around the living room. The walls were bare. Would Daisy decorate? She wasn't—hadn't been—a big decorator, but she'd always put a tree up.

Minutes ticked by before the door clicked open. It shut softly, and Daisy's stocking feet whispered across the hardwood.

I turned to take her in. She had her hands buried in the sleeves of her sweater, her fingertips gripping the end to keep it from pulling up. "About today..."

"I really thought I was helping. I had all the painting supplies out and—"

"Did you paint my room too?"

Her tone wasn't hopeful. Or appreciative. "You hate purple."

She finally met my gaze and sighed. "You can't keep doing this."

"I'm just trying—"

"We're roommates. You don't need to cook for us, and you don't need to remodel our rooms."

"It was just a quick paint job. I'm going to paint the whole house anyway."

She folded her arms across her chest. "I get that, but sitting for a meal? All of us?"

"Laila's not ready?"

A furrow formed in her brow. "Why should she be ready?"

The hint of challenge in her tone utterly deflated me. I thought she'd feel taken care of. I thought she'd feel less alone through all this. I thought she'd like seeing me be productive. Did she think I moved her and Laila in to have a ready-made family? That we'd start up where we left off?

Damn, it might look that way, but she was helping me. Maybe I wanted to prove I wasn't a lazy, selfish asshole anymore. While I might be hung up on why she'd left, she'd lived a whole life. Didn't mean I wanted to sit by while she had her hands full. "I'm not trying to overstep, Daze."

"Then what are you doing? Dinner and dessert?"

"You're doing me a favor. Your daughter is getting dragged along with it. I was trying to make the first night we're all under the same roof a pleasant one."

Regret flashed in her eyes, but her stance remained rigid. "I can't do this."

I waited for her to elaborate. The air between us thickened.

"This is too much like..." Her expression wavered, and utter sadness shone through her blue eyes.

"What we had," I finished quietly, wishing I could reach for her, pull her into my arms.

"I can't pretend we're a happy family. I haven't been single that long. Laila's getting used to not having her dad around. And you and I?" The crease in her brow deepened. "We divorced and went our separate ways. We haven't even been friends for almost fifteen years."

She had moved to Bismarck to finish her school and work, and I had moved to Williston so I didn't have to commute to the oil fields. Then I'd quit and went to school. Now I was in charge of a goddamn oil refinery and still as fucking alone as I had been after I signed the divorce papers.

I pinched the bridge of my nose. This arrangement wasn't supposed to stress her out, make her sad, or upset Laila. My mind spun for a solution. I was a CEO, dammit. I could figure this out.

Define the problem. "Okay, so, you don't want any semblance of family. We need to figure out what that means." Yes. That was it. Daisy liked cut-and-dried. "Mind sitting at the table? I'll find a pen and paper."

"Why?" she asked slowly.

"We're going to draft a roommate agreement."

She blinked several times. "A roommate agreement?"

I lifted my chin toward the kitchen and followed her in. I kept my gaze glued to between her shoulder blades. Roommates didn't ogle the other's ass.

I liked how hers had gotten fuller.

No staring!

I dug out a notepad and pen that I had unpacked last

night. Daisy sat at the spot she'd eaten in. To be safe, I took the end of the table Laila had banished me to.

"No family meals." I scribbled it down. "What about if I throw something in the oven or crockpot for all of us and you two just eat when it's convenient for you?"

She pursed her lips. One of the moves I'd seen her daughter do. "What about if the same time is convenient for all of us?"

"I can eat in the living room. Speaking of which, if you're watching something, should I stay away?" *Please say no.* I didn't watch TV, but I didn't want to be banished from any room they were in. I didn't want her to think I wanted an instant family, but I wanted...her. I wanted to get to know the new Daisy...and her daughter. When the year was over? I had to know whether there was anything I could've done or if splitting had been our destiny anyway.

She ran her teeth over her lower lip. "I mean, I like to watch my murder shows after Laila goes to bed."

"Murder shows?"

She let out a long breath. "If it's a documentary about a serial killer, I'm watching it. If people are talking about how or why they killed someone, I'm binging it. If a husband murdered his bride, I'm in."

That was new. "Why do you like those?"

"They keep my mind busy, and I can cross-stitch without missing a lot of plot."

"You cross-stitch?" The divide between us was growing, only I felt like I was on a small patch of ice floating away from the mainland. If I scrambled to get back to shore, I'd drown—or get taken out by a sea lion.

"It's not like I have homework anymore." She wrinkled her nose. "I guess if we're sitting on the same couch or love seat, it should be fine."

She couldn't sound confident. I noted it, but made an asterisk next to the sentence *Same room okay* to remind myself that she had reservations.

A bath and three bedrooms were upstairs. I could make one into a sitting room with my own TV, but I didn't offer that up as an option. I'd have no excuse to be around her.

"Do we do a 'first come, first served' rule with the TV?" she asked. "If you're gaming—"

"I don't game."

She recoiled. I hadn't snapped at her, but I'd been resolute.

"I was staying up late." Drinking and partying and gaming. "I was late for work one too many times." Napped on shift one too many times. "It was behave or get fired." Before she could question why I'd change for a job and not her, I had a question I needed to ask. "Thanksgiving is next week. Christmas is coming. Holidays?"

She slumped in her seat, her eyes dark with thought. "Jason and I talked about this year already. Laila's having Thanksgiving with me and Mom, and then he wants to take her to his parents' place in Minot. He's going to take a week off so he doesn't have to rush."

"Did he ever take that much time off when it was just you three?"

"No, he didn't—" She scowled. "No personal questions. Write that down, Duke."

Instead of being hurt, I bit back a smile. There was baggage around the holidays with Jason. Didn't she care to spend that much time with his family, or hadn't he made the holidays special? Daisy didn't wear her heart on her sleeve, but that didn't mean she wasn't having fun or looking forward to having fun. Sometimes, she'd even say it.

If Daisy said "I'm looking forward to Christmas," that meant she wanted it like a movie. Wake up to a mountain of presents, have a relaxed breakfast and lounge in pajamas, then meet with family and laugh and play card games all day. She'd gotten that experience with my family. With hers, the day was quiet, the presents subdued. The afternoons were trying to stay awake while idly chatting. I had tried to make it up the next day by arranging a gathering at my parents' place.

She hadn't answered about what she'd do for Christmas without Laila. I'd keep that in mind.

"If I invite Mom and Dad over, is that okay? Violet and Evander? Lily and Eliot? The others?"

Daisy's expression grew more troubled with each one. "You still entertain?"

"My parents and siblings," I reassured her. No single dudes who camped among empty beer cans and gaming controls.

She lifted a brow. "That all?"

"If I had C-suite parties at King Oil, it'd still be me and Dad."

"Dates?"

Not if I could help it. I tapped the pen on point three. "No personal questions."

Chagrined, she looked away. "What about dates now?"

"I'm married." That felt too good to say.

She snorted. "Like that's going to stop anyone."

"It'll stop me," I growled.

Curiosity entered her expression. "Has it always?" She shook her head and pressed her palms against her cheeks. "Oh god. Forget I asked. I didn't mean to dredge up the—"

"Of course it always stopped me." A punch of anger at myself hit me between the eyes. I'd make an exception for this. She'd lost a lot of trust in me after the way I'd behaved as a young adult with intoxicating freedom and enough money to be stupid. I'd been reckless, but not in that way. "I might've crashed at a friend's place, but I didn't land inside anyone. I didn't touch them, and I wouldn't let them touch me."

She shook her head like it didn't matter.

I leaned across the table. "*Never*, Daisy. I never strayed. And the first date I went on after the divorce made me sick to my stomach."

She blanched, her gaze glued to the tabletop. "It was hard, wasn't it?"

None of the dates had gotten better after the first. "I had no idea what to do, and I had felt like a cheater even though we'd been done for two years."

She snapped her head up. "Two years?"

"Yep." Part of me had thought she'd ask for me back. I'd had a game plan in mind. First, I'd play hard to get. Then I'd grudgingly say yes, and from there, it'd be back to normal. Only she had moved, and after she had graduated college, she had gotten a job even farther away from Coal Haven.

"My experience was about the same. Worst decision I ever made." Anger flashed across her face, but after she ran a hand over her face, it was gone, her features neutral. "So we have four points right now?"

"I'm not even writing 'no dating' down."

She crossed one leg under her. "Um, discretion. I know there's an upstairs bathroom, but if you could remain fully clothed while on this level? Laila shouldn't be seeing"—she fluttered her fingers toward me—"that." Pink dusted her cheeks.

I swallowed my grin. Her embarrassment ignited a long-dormant playful side of me. "No going shirtless?"

"Don't go around in just boxers."

"I still wear boxer briefs." Her blush darkened, and the struggle not to grin was getting harder. "What about just shorts, or is a shirt required one hundred percent of the time?"

"Yes."

"And when Laila's gone? Still no shirtless Saturdays?"

She sputtered, and laughter broke out of me.

Her flush spread to her neck. "Write it down."

"Bare feet?"

"Jesus, Alder."

I kept chuckling. "Just trying to be clear." I made the note but only about me. Daisy could walk around in a thong, and I wouldn't fucking complain.

"I'll pitch in for two-thirds of the groceries."

I shook my head. "Your little birdie isn't going to eat that much."

"Still."

I didn't write it down.

"Laila needs structure and that includes her food," Daisy said. "The dessert was a nice gesture, but it's a free-for-all at her dad's, and I've learned her moods don't free-for-all."

I nodded, jotting down *Food routine.*

"She goes to bed at seven. I know it's early, but I have to wake her at six to get us both dressed and fed and get her to daycare."

"I'll defer to you for anything Laila."

"Thank you." She picked at a loose string on the hem of her sweater. "She'll warm up to you. It's been a lot of change."

Touched she encouraged Laila not to hate me, I gave her a small smile. "I have to be honest, I didn't think it'd be so hard to win a four-year-old over. Lily's oldest lets me bribe her to be her favorite uncle."

Daisy smiled. "How does Jasper take it?"

"I strongly suspect he's also been told he's the favorite uncle. Now she has all of Eliot's brothers, and we're both screwed."

A bark of laughter left her, and I could only stare. Her eyes were radiant and her grin was wide. This easiness between us had been all but lost, yet here it was.

All I had to do was denigrate my uncle abilities. "The real reason I took the job was so I could be closer and bribe Lily's kids, and get a jumpstart on Violet and Evander's babies. Jasper has those little carvings that win them over. The refinery likes to claim they're a family-centered company, and I'm going to hold them to that."

She stifled a yawn. "I think I have to head to bed. I'm tired, but I also think Laila is going to find her way to my room in the middle of the night. She's scared about her new bedroom."

"If you need any help decorating it for her, let me know. I have a new cordless drill and I'm dangerous."

Her gaze softened. "Thank you, Alder." She got up

and pushed her chair in. She hesitated, her hands on the seatback. "That dessert still available?"

"Monster cookies from the grocery store." Which I knew full well she loved. The same family had owned the grocery store for fifty years. I'd make sure that cookie corner in the cupboard was always full.

Chapter Six

Daisy

The first three weeks of my second marriage had gone by without drama. Laila had finally slept in her own bed for the whole night last night. Alder had painted the whole main floor of the house. Two days ago, he'd had carpet swatches laid out on the table for us.

I hadn't been sure Laila would adjust to another upheaval of her room, so I would pore over the selection of the carpet to make sure she'd like it. Alder had said he could have it installed during Christmas when she was with her dad, or she could be home and watch the whole process. She'd opted for Christmas—and a new set of pajamas to help her adjust.

I pulled into the garage. Laila was thumping her boots against her seat, but she hadn't complained about the house for almost the whole week.

The bench from the mudroom was in the front of the garage, sitting on open newspapers.

"Is that darker?" Laila asked, her boots going quiet.

"Looks like he stained it."

Laila hadn't warmed up to Alder, but she'd fallen into a state of mostly ignoring his existence. He kept extending an olive branch, and at this point, I was ready to give him a bag of Skittles and tell him to bribe her.

Except there was no reason for him to. They cohabited just fine. Some nights, it was like he wasn't home, except for the thumps upstairs as he worked on tearing off the baseboards to stain after he painted the rooms. The noise was better than strangers moving around me in an apartment building, and his presence was comforting. The small house Laila and I had been in before could get lonely. This large place would seem cavernous without him.

When we entered, a familiar delicious smell wafted around us. I peeked my head out of the mudroom. Alder was in his designated spot at the table, his phone in one hand and a fork in the other.

He always had food ready, whether it was sandwiches or a casserole. I hadn't said anything because damn, he could cook, and because he'd respected the eating situation. He either took his meal before I got home, or he ate when Laila was getting ready for bed.

"Is that chicken and dumplings?" I asked.

He glanced over his shoulder. "Yep."

"Your mom's recipe?" Of course it was.

"She told me that you had to be the judge if I could ever make it again."

My stomach was twisting and turning, trying to get closer to Magnolia Duke's crockpot chicken and dumplings. She used to make it when she knew I'd be over, and she'd always have a dish to send home for my parents. My dad had usually eaten at the bar, but my mom loved the dish almost as much as me.

"Ew." Laila had been saying that about all his food. Yet I hadn't missed the gusto she ate with once she forgot her self-imposed stubbornness.

"Let's eat right away," I said to her as I helped her hang up her coat and put her boots on the mat.

Alder rose and cleared his place just as I entered the kitchen. He loaded his dishes in the dishwasher and went to the living room. Disappointment ricocheted inside of me. He was adhering to the roommate agreement, but did he have to be so compliant? The urge to have him at the table and have him ask me how my day went grew stronger each day.

Which was exactly why I had asked for guidelines.

I dished up a plate for me and Laila. I blew on her food and waved my hand over it until it was cool enough to eat.

I scooped the first bit of gravy and dumpling into my mouth and groaned. I was a decent cook, but I'd never gotten the recipe for this. Why would I have needed it? Magnolia had possessed a sixth sense for whenever I had a craving. I had briefly thought of reaching out to her and asking for it, but much of the enjoyment was that I hadn't had to make it.

I chewed through seconds and deliberated on thirds when Laila announced she was done.

"Hang on." I popped my head into the living room.

Alder was measuring the doorway, his broad shoulders flexing under his T-shirt. He'd taken off his flannel, and his biceps were on full display. The muscles bunched and stretched as he moved the measuring tape to get the height and width.

The tape snapped into its enclosure, and he grabbed the pencil from behind his ear and dug a sheet of paper out of his back pocket. His ass. I'd been trying—and failing—not to admire his legs as he wandered through the house like my very own handyman porn show, but I hadn't gotten a good look at his tight butt. Did he keep active in the gym? Were those ass muscles toned from pumping into his gorgeous dates all night?

He scribbled some numbers down and spun, tucking the pencil back behind his ear. "Daze?"

I yanked my gaze up. Oh no. I'd been staring at his butt. That was an unspoken guideline I hadn't thought of putting down. No lusting after the ex you're married to.

His questioning gaze was on me. It was the glint of amusement in his hazel eyes that kicked my brain back on.

"Leftovers?" I faintly gestured toward the kitchen. "Do you want all the leftovers, or can I take some for work?"

"Take as much as you need." His low drawl went straight for my belly, twining its way down.

"Thanks," I said with a squeak and ducked into the kitchen. Laila was kicking her feet and whipping her napkin around like it was a bird.

All through the meal cleanup, I gave myself a stern talking-to. No gawking at him. No thinking about his body and how strong he was. No remembering what he looked like naked. We were different now. He might be somehow bigger and more fit. I'd had a baby and not one article of my old wardrobe remained because I couldn't fit into it and I'd quit trying.

After the kitchen was tidied, I found Laila in her room, her tongue caught between her teeth and crayons scattered in front of her. My attention touched on the newly painted wall and dipped to the princess castle she was coloring, then yanked back to the crayon streaks on the fresh paint.

"Laila! Did you color on the wall?" Horror pushed out at my temples. Alder had rushed to paint this room for Laila, and she'd doodled all over it.

She pushed off the floor. Crocodile tears filled her eyes. "I didn't do it."

I pressed my fingertips against my forehead. "He painted the room just for you." She had never colored on the wall before. Why would she start now?

"I don't like him."

I crossed my arms. "Well, I do. He's helping us, and he's not trying to replace your dad."

Tears fell down her cheeks, and her shoulders shook.

I let out a breath and led her to the bed. I sat on the edge and lifted her to my lap.

She sobbed into my shoulder. "I didn't mean to."

She totally had. "I know."

"I miss Daddy."

"I know." Jason had hardly been around during her waking hours when we had lived together, but I couldn't dig into semantics. Her life had changed a lot in the last year. We were all allowed down days. Weak moments when we ogled our ex's ass. "Do you think calling him more often would make you feel better?"

I should've thought of this earlier. Before the graffiti.

She nodded, her hair tickling under my chin.

"Okay." I dug my phone out of my pocket and called Jason.

"Daisy?" he answered. "Everything okay?"

"Laila's missing you. Mind reading her some books before bed?"

"Yeah, no problem."

I left them, closing the door halfway. I stood for a few moments, listening to Laila's happy chatter with Jason. The art on the wall behind her, the squiggles, the stick figures, and the—I squinted—*flowers?*—glared stark behind her.

What would Alder think? I'd bitten his head off about painting in the first place. Now Laila, who he knew didn't like him, had defaced his work. She might be four, but she was smart. She'd done it on the walls to get back at Alder for being the guy in the house instead of Jason.

I pushed a lock of hair behind my ear. I'd have to talk to Alder and let him know that she was going to help me clean it off.

He was no longer in the living room, and I couldn't find him in the kitchen. I poked my head into the garage. Not there either. I stood at the base of the stairs. I hadn't been up there since we'd moved in. Another stipulation we should've included in our roommate agreement was that the upstairs was his den. Whatever he did there wasn't my business.

I could talk to him later.

Laila's voice still emanated from the bedroom. She would keep Jason on the line for a while. Maybe I could talk to Alder now.

I took the stairs, my mind filling in the blank walls with the portraits that used to hang in the stairwell.

School pictures. Family photos. Vacation images. I had been fascinated and maybe a little jealous. They'd always looked so happy.

My childhood photos had appeared happy too. And in those brief moments, we had been. Only I remembered how my dad and brother had been at each other's throats, so alike yet so different and unwilling to meet in the middle when it counted.

I crested the top. Technically, there were four rooms. Three were big enough to be comfortable bedrooms. Violet had taken the smaller office just to have a room of her own. That space was to my right and it was empty. The trim had been stripped out. Same with the bedroom on my left. The bathroom door hung open, but the bedroom door adjacent to it was closed. I had known what room he'd taken. The one above mine. His old room.

I tentatively approached. A crap-ton of memories resided in that bedroom. Lots of laughter and planning of our future. I faced the wood of the door. I was up here for *reasons*. I wasn't imposing. The house was like a business we were running together for the next year.

Blowing out a hard breath, I knocked.

The door swung open. Alder was holding a shirt in front of his chiseled bare chest, one arm already stuffed through a sleeve. He peeked around me, then relaxed and dropped his shirt. "Oh, good, it's just you. I was worried something was wrong and didn't want to make you wait, but I wanted to follow the rules."

He tossed the shirt on his bed.

No. I needed that on him now. I needed that broad chest with the sprinkling of dark hair that narrowed to a line traveling down his abs covered. My fingers twitched.

All I had to do was reach out and I could feel how hot his skin was. When had he gotten so brawny?

The walls! "Laila—uh..." My brain was sluggish. It kept reorienting on the rounded muscles capping his shoulders. Those biceps I'd seen earlier were completely visible.

He propped a hand on his hip while his other was on the doorknob. He was like a painting. *Here's what you didn't get.* "She all right?"

I shook my head and squeezed my eyes shut since I couldn't be appropriate. "She drew on the walls." There. I got it out. Was it hot up here? I wiped at my brow and opened my eyes. "I'll have her help me clean it, and I'll make sure she talks to Jason more often. She's missing him."

"She's really having a hard time."

He didn't ask, and I nodded. "I think so. I mean, it's probably not unusual for kids her age to draw on the walls, but she hasn't been inclined to before."

He grimaced. "But she's not a chicken and dumplings fan."

I giggled, grateful for the levity, but still concentrated to keep my eyes on his face. "I might have to ground her if that's the case."

"Exposure therapy. There are a lot of leftovers."

"No, there aren't. I saved enough for you for lunch tomorrow after I took what I wanted." It'd been a long fifteen years without chicken and dumplings.

The corners of his eyes crinkled with humor. "I'm glad it was a hit."

"Most of your food is. Laila won't tell you, but she cleans her plate most nights."

"You might have to let Mom know that she taught me a few things."

"Yeah. I will." The effort not to steal one last look at his chest was too much. "Just wanted to tell you in case I didn't catch you in the morning."

I was about to turn when he opened his door wider. "Hey, just a heads-up..."

Behind him, the king-sized bed took up most of the room. My full bed would work better in here while his bed should be in the main bedroom. The movers hadn't thought they'd actually get it in his room.

He scratched the back of his head, and damn, the *muscles*. "Mom and Dad asked if they could stay here."

Alarm posted in my veins, ready to spread through my blood until anxiety turned me into a shaking mess. Stay with us? "W-what?"

If his parents slept over, we'd have to pretend we were really married. That'd mean he'd have to sleep in my room. We'd have to touch. Maybe even kiss to sell this whole thing.

He held up his hands like he'd heard all the questions racing through my head. "I told them Laila was gone for Christmas."

A small, cool wave of relief helped slow my heart rate. "Okay, thanks. I mean it would've been nice to see them—"

"They'd like to come for the New Year."

"Dammit." We weren't getting out of their visit. Of course, they'd want to meet Laila.

He winced.

I pinched my eyes shut again. "I'm sorry. I knew this was part of the deal. I'm just not ready."

"I can tell them no."

"We'd never turn them away if we were really married." A pang of sorrow dinged off my heart. Not only wasn't this real, it wasn't our chance for a do-over. I adored his parents.

His mouth went tight. "No, we wouldn't. I'm sorry. Lily and Eliot have a full house. Violet's so pregnant and Evander's getting the rest of the house fixed up. Mom said the hotel was actually booked through the second week of January. Some ice fishing tournament."

Fucking fish. "No, of course. By the time they're here, we'll only have ten months or so to sell this so your dad will sign off."

"Clock's ticking."

"Tick-tock."

The crinkles of humor returned, and I smiled. The air between us grew charged.

"Mom!" Laila called from the base of the stairs. I jumped. "Daddy's done reading."

I yanked myself away from a shirtless Alder. "I'm coming." I stepped farther away. "Can you let me know the dates? So I can get ready?"

"Sure. Oh—the cabinet guy will be here tomorrow. Another heads-up."

"Yes, right." The cabinets? Already. "You're really moving fast. No rest for the wicked."

"I saw what being wicked cost me."

He'd worked hard and played hard, and it'd cost our marriage. Years had passed. For the last three weeks, he'd been toiling away at the house, taking only meal breaks. He worked like he was on the clock. "It's okay to relax sometimes."

His expression hardened. A distinct disagreement.

"I'll be home a little early tomorrow," I said. "Jason's

sister is coming through and wants to take Laila out to dinner."

"Mommy! Daddy wants to talk to you."

"Coming," I called toward the stairs. With one more peek at his abs, I scurried away. Why couldn't I have been this weak when I'd told him I wanted a divorce?

Chapter Seven

Alder

The doorbell rang. The cabinet guy was here.

When I answered the door, I blinked. "I know you."

He grinned, a shit-eating grin that almost reminded me of Jasper, except this guy had dirty-blond hair cropped close to his head, scruff lining his face, and despite the negative wind chill outside, he wore no coat, only a long-sleeved shirt.

Daisy would be home soon. Would she sneak glances at the way his muscles bulged in his sleeves like she had been doing to me? I'd caught her checking out my ass, then last night when I'd been shirtless, she'd had to peel her attention off my chest.

I did not mind.

The guy snapped his fingers. "Duke. Poppy and Clover your sisters?"

"Two of the four."

He stuck his hand out. "Jensen Hollis. I went to

school with them. Well, with Poppy. You get one, you get the other."

I gave his hand a firm shake, then stepped back and ushered him in. The house didn't have a nice front entry. The door opened right into the living room. When I had lived here, we'd kept the garage door open and ran through it at all times of the day.

He adjusted the brim of his ball cap that read "Hollis Cabinetry" and looked around. "This is one of those houses I've driven by a million times in my life but never saw the inside of."

"I bet you get to do a lot of that now in your line of work."

He flashed a grin. "Lots of old houses needing upgrades. I didn't realize this one was still in your family."

I led him to the kitchen. "My grandparents bought it when we moved and rented it out. They seemed to have a thing for collecting properties."

"I would, too, if I had the money. I just give them facelifts before people sell."

"Well, I have no plans to sell." I was finally where I was supposed to be. I just hoped it'd stay like this.

"You're back in town?"

"I got a position at the refinery. It took a while to get back to Coal Haven, but here I am." With Daisy and hoping like hell it would be for more than a year.

"Nice." From his shirt pocket, he tugged out a small notebook and a pen. He clicked it open. "Many of my customers worry about what's trendy and what's going to sell the house for the most money. You get to choose what you want. Counters and cabinets, correct?"

"That's the plan. Replace it all." What would Daisy want though? Did she think a butcher block section in the counter was necessary? Would she like granite or consider it too high maintenance? She hadn't commented on the stain I was using in the house. Did she like the darker finish, or would she prefer a shade closer to cedar? Hickory?

I had wanted to ask her, but I had lost the nerve. Nor had she offered any insight. To her, this house was mine, and it was too soon to hope it could be ours. I had her rules to follow. "My wife isn't home yet, but she won't mind if we get started."

My wife. That felt way too fucking good to say.

After Jensen reviewed exactly what we were replacing and inquired about any changes to the layout, he'd run out to his truck and brought in a bin. We were at the island, paging through a binder of the styles of cabinetry he offered, when cool air from the garage floated in.

Daisy glanced from me to Jensen as she entered the kitchen. "Hello."

"Hey." Jensen rearranged some of his wood color and types of samples. "You're just in time. I have a variety for you both to select from."

Her gaze swung back to me, eyes wider than before. She hadn't been prepared to pretend to be a real couple in front of Jensen, but at the moment, I was filled with gratitude we hadn't discussed it. I liked getting under that calm armor any way I could.

"I haven't made any decisions yet," I said to her. "I figured you'd be home soon...*babe.*"

Shock flared her face, but then she settled on a consternated expression. "No problem, *sugar lips.*" I made a choking sound. Her smile was saccharine as she crossed to me. "Thanks for stalling."

Since I was supposed to be a man in love with his

wife, I drank her in as she approached, uncaring if she noticed. She'd worn jeans like usual. She'd said once that they were durable, and while they weren't the cheapest clothing to destroy, at least they were versatile. Unlike the other labs she'd worked in as a med tech, chemists didn't wear scrubs.

She came around the island. I banded an arm around her waist and pressed a quick kiss to her lips, wishing I could do this when we were alone. "How was work?"

Her look shot daggers at me. "Good, but then I'm married to the boss."

Fuck yeah, she was.

"Oh, hey," Jensen said, either oblivious to our weird tension or uncaring of it. "You're the new CEO at the refinery?"

I kept my arm anchored around her. She was tucked into my side. Right where she fucking belonged. "Guilty."

"Gonna work out there for decades like Cameron Barron did?"

"That's the plan." Daisy went even more taut against me. She didn't like the idea that I'd be around Coal Haven forever? My heart would twist, but my body was too damn happy to have her pressed against me again. Too long had gone by since last time. I finally released her and tapped my index finger on one of the wood samples. "What do you think, Daze? I like the knotty alder myself."

"Are all Alders knotty or just these?" she asked in a voice full of innocence.

I pushed the three alder samples in front of her. "Run your hand over them and see," I said with a low purr, my back to Jensen.

She ignored me and studied the samples, but a blush painted her cheeks. "I like the knotty alder, but it looks like gunshots in the wood."

"I've heard that from others," Jensen agreed. "Some people like the look, others worry the holes will wear and get bigger, but I haven't seen that happen yet."

She ran a finger down one of the blocks with the darker stain. My blood would reroute and make this consultation embarrassing if I watched her stroke the wood.

"I like this grain and the color. With a lighter counter-top, I think it'll look sophisticated and not too dark." She snapped her hand back and looked at me. "But the final decision is yours."

It was, and I fucking hated the reminder. This house was supposed to be *ours*. "Let's do countertops next."

Her eyes glazed over with the countertop samples Jensen spread before her. He had samples of material and small cards with different marbled patterns.

"There's always laminate," he said. "Looks expensive but can take a beating."

"What do you think?" I could choose, but I'd rather have her insight. If I couldn't win her back at the end of the year, and if she didn't rent from me, then I could torture myself in this house that would have her touch everywhere.

She shrugged. "You know I'm more practical than anything. Whatever's durable and easy to clean and goes with the cabinets."

I tapped on laminate with the earth tones swirling through it in a cream color. "Let's do this."

"Got it." Jensen jotted down notes. "All I need to do is take some measurements, and I can put the order in."

Daisy disappeared from the kitchen while Jensen finished up.

Just as he was driving away, my phone buzzed. I had a message from Lily.

Lily: What are you doing for Christmas Eve?

Since our parents weren't making the trip from Billings until the New Year, that left me with a holiday to finish up projects around the house before I started my new job. Daisy hadn't mentioned her plans or whether she was going to visit her mom.

Alder: I'll be finishing some renovations.

Lily: Come over. All of you.

Alder: Laila will be with her dad.

Lily: Then make sure Daisy comes.

I'd give it a try. After years of quiet family holidays because my siblings and I had scattered away from Billings, I was getting spoiled by the larger get-togethers we'd had in the last couple of years. Now Violet was in town. Jasper wasn't far away. Poppy and Clover may or may not make the trip to Billings, but I doubt they'd come all the way to Coal Haven.

Alder: I'll let you know what she says.

I tucked my phone away. Christmas with Daisy was probably too much to hope for. She likely had plans with her mom. Most certainly she didn't plan to spend the day with me. Yet those damn hopes of mine wouldn't listen. She might want to spend the day with Lily and Eliot.

Daisy had retreated to her bedroom. It was just us in the house. Would she come out? I hadn't prepared a dinner. Had she eaten already?

"Daze?" I waited at the end of the hallway.

She popped her head out of her room. "Is he gone?"

"Yeah." I rubbed the back of my neck. "Want to grab a bite to eat?"

She cocked her head like she didn't hear me. "Like, out?"

I nodded.

"Why?"

I'd asked just because, but that one word caused all kinds of defensiveness to rise. "Because we're supposed to be married and married people go out to eat." She didn't respond. I let out a heavy sigh. All my offer was supposed to be was just that. A break from cooking and a break from eating in. "Don't friends go out to eat sometimes too?"

Her expression softened. She opened the door farther and stepped out. She was in fluffy pajama pants and a long T-shirt, the clothing she usually changed into once Laila was in bed. I loved her in every outfit I'd seen her in, but I'd missed this Daisy.

She flopped her arms out. "I'd have to change."

Ah. I recognized this resistance. I smirked. "The clothing or your mental status?"

"The clothing is easier to change." She tapped her forehead. "I'm in relaxation mode."

If I couldn't take her out, would she allow me to eat with her while staying in? "How 'bout I pick something up? What do you want? My treat."

"You don't have to do that. I can have toast or something."

Her something would be nothing if she didn't have toast. "I'm going to Rattler's anyway. Do you want a steak? Or some sort of chicken? Pasta?" She'd want a steak, medium, with sweet potatoes, cinnamon butter on the side, and steak fries. If she didn't, then I didn't know this woman anymore. A dull throb started behind my sternum waiting on her answer.

If she wouldn't let me pick up food for her, then this reconnection would be a longer uphill battle than I prepared for.

She folded her arms across her chest, the ends of her sleeves tucked tightly in her hands. She shifted her stance, indecision playing across her face. "I...guess I can take a steak. Medium. With a sweet potato, cinnamon butter on the side, and steak fries."

My grin spread wide with my relief. She had eaten the same damn thing at Rattler's since the day it had opened. "Anything to drink?" Lemonade.

"Um... No. Water is fine."

I couldn't win them all. "Should I get anything for Laila?"

"No. Her aunt Katie will be spoiling her."

I tipped my head toward the TV. "Get comfy. I'll be back soon."

*　*　*

Daisy's stockinged feet were kicked up on the coffee table. Once again, we were hanging out, watching TV, and eating food. This time, it wasn't gas station pizza and my siblings weren't running wild through the house.

I'd been able to sell my home in Billings without a second thought. This place meant a lot to me. The woman next to me meant even more.

I'd abided by her rules. I was being good. Only a few weeks had passed, but she was still avoiding me. That wouldn't do at all. I'd never win her back as a wife. I'd have to get her to open up, like I had the first time.

You like horses?

One question all those years ago had been the beginning of what should've been a lifetime together. My entitlement and immaturity had ruined it. However, my memory of Daisy was pristine. When she talked about something she was passionate about, she forgot about her walls and her self-consciousness.

What could I ask her about that she was invested in but wouldn't touch on issues we were avoiding?

Her job. But first, I had to ask about Christmas. There would be no good time, but she was relaxed, and Laila was still out with her aunt. "Lily got a hold of me. About Christmas Eve."

She cut through her steak. "That'll be nice."

"It's Christmas, and, uh, married couples are usually together. She invited all of us, but I told her Laila would be gone."

She paused mid-saw. "Oh."

I didn't want her to write the whole holiday with me off. "I can make up an excuse. Mom and Dad won't be here until after. Even if Aunt Linda decides to show, I don't want you to feel pressured."

"You can't help it, and that is my part of the bargain." She cut the rest of her meat and pushed it around with her fork. "We can't ask Lily or Violet or their spouses to lie if they're asked if we were both there."

"And you know they'll ask. Mom's trying to play it cool, but she's dying to see for herself that we're married again."

Stress tightened her brow. Was she wondering how

it'd be next year? Telling everyone we were divorcing? We'd be doing that if I couldn't fix what I had broken.

"It should be no problem. Just any other meal with friends." Her movements were more stilted while elation coursed through me. I was getting closer to my goal. Now it was time to take her mind off it, or she'd be worrying the whole night.

"Tell me about Dr. Adarsh." I hadn't met her boss yet, but I would soon enough.

She screwed her face up for a moment, then laughed. "You mean Raj? I don't know what he'd do if you called him Dr. Adarsh." She poked her cinnamon butter into her sweet potato. "He earned it though, but he's more about the chemistry than the status, and he's the best boss I've ever had."

"Yeah?" I relaxed into her tone. I wouldn't have to prompt her to keep talking.

"Most definitely. Take his PhD. I think he doesn't like being addressed formally because it takes away from the work we're doing. His ego doesn't need it. So, like, when it came to Violet, he didn't get all worked up over her maternity leave. He wanted her because he could tell she loves chemistry and wants to do a good job. Other bosses would have used it as a reason not to hire her, whether it's illegal or not."

I filed that information away. I was in charge, but I was a few levels removed from direct oversight over the lab. Yet I wanted to make sure we kept the good employees.

"I had this one boss," she said around a mouthful, then swallowed. "She had a PhD too. And I respect that, right? Those are a lot of work. But she was the lab direc-tor, and it wasn't a science-based PhD. Yet she whipped out the doctor label so often, it became an inside joke." Daisy glanced at me, her lips quirked. "Only with some of us."

This was the fire I loved in her. Daisy was mellow until she thought something was unfair. "You're a shit-stirrer."

"I believe her eval said I often failed to display a respectful attitude."

"She did not ding you about using her title?" I asked, incredulous, and furious on her behalf.

"Supposedly not." She stabbed at a steak fry. "You know, she got the director position over my supervisor? They both have the same master's degree in clinical lab science, and my supervisor had been doing the job for months before they hired her. Because"—she threw up air quotes—"she was so impressive with her PhD. Then I learned it's in history or something."

"No kidding. Was she a good director?"

"Alice—my old supervisor—was a good leader, and the lab ran well under her." Daisy put her plate down and faced me on the couch, curling her legs under her. "And don't get me wrong, *Doctor* Simmons is too, but she was never there. We'd be in the middle of an outbreak, and she'd be working from home. She did half the work of my old supervisor, yet if the hospital administrators arrived—there she was, addressing herself as *Doctor* Simmons. If she had put half that effort into clear communication about the issues we were dealing with, morale would've been a lot higher. But she's cute and smiles a lot. You know how that goes over?" She rolled her eyes. "Yet everyone thought I was petty when I commented on it."

Daisy saw through bullshit, and people hated her for it. I could see now I had resented her at the time. It was why I'd planted my hooves in the mud like a stubborn mule. I hadn't wanted to finish growing up. "It was disingenuous of her."

She flung an arm out. "Right? She was intentionally trying to mislead people. She knew full well people would think she was an MD or that her PhD was in microbiology, or at the very least, a science field, and they gave her more credit because of it."

"Which she then used to discredit others." Daisy would hate the lack of transparency. I still knew her so damn well.

Her hair flew as she vigorously nodded. "Exactly! It's manipulative. I don't know how many times I'd point out something, people would argue with me, but when she said it, and 'oh, doctor knows best.'" She slumped against the back of the couch looking vindicated that someone understood. "Thankfully, I got hired on at the refinery, or I probably would've gotten fired for some BS reason and no one would've questioned *Doctor* Simmons."

Daisy was right. She would've eventually lost her job. I used to think she should just stay quiet and protect her employment. Then I had started managing people. "For what it's worth, I relied on employees like you."

She snorted. "The ones who point out the weaknesses in the process and everyone hates them for it?"

"Yeah. The ones who respect my authority but talk to me like we're equals because we work for the same company and want it to succeed."

"You don't need your ego stroked?" She said it lightly, but the heaviness of her work history simmered in her eyes.

"Maybe at one time I did. But after the divorce, I had

to piece myself back together, and I guess after that, people's superficial words were easier to see through."

A stricken expression passed over her face. "Our divorce made you a better boss?"

It made me a better man. "It made me get my shit together to be a boss. The further up the ladder I rose, the more I noticed the...what did you call them? The 'I like your sweater' people?"

Her lips twitched. "I still call them that, but there aren't many in the lab. Raj hires people who are too nerdy to care about kissing ass."

I laughed. I wasn't nerdy, and I didn't care about kissing ass. "If someone is too gushing, I can't trust what they say. They're trying to appeal to me and not to the company's welfare."

"You just described my entire experience working for the doctor. Scientists tend to like a lot of validation, and that can be why they make horrible managers." She lifted a shoulder. "I guess that's people in general. We all want validation, but there are some people who will take it at the expense of others, and I could never stay quiet if I saw that, especially if they were in a leadership position. Because then not only were they trying to invalidate someone's work and intelligence, but they were using their authority to do it."

"I'm sorry it was so hard for you." Did she have someone who listened to her when she'd come home miserable and beaten down? "I'm glad the refinery is a good fit for you."

"Not gonna lie, I live in fear Raj is going to leave. Or that he'll hire someone exactly like who I've tried to get away from. I need this job."

I wasn't above using my position to make sure her

work environment didn't change. "Not many lab positions in rural North Dakota."

"You're telling me." She stuffed a fry in her mouth and chewed. "I cannot afford to move or get paid less."

Alarm bells rang inside me. Her worry over finding a place to live had been income-based. "I know it's not my business, but Jason helps, right? With child support?" She hadn't answered directly before.

"Yeah, but it's for Laila, and I make sure it stays for her."

I worked my jaw back and forth. There was something she wasn't saying. Tonight, I'd made progress, but our lives were still separate. "Other than housing, is there anything I can help with?"

Her gaze shuttered. "No, it's fine." She picked up her to-go container, shoved another fry into her mouth, and grabbed my empty to-go box off the coffee table.

Now she was avoiding the topic. Frustrated and a little hurt, I picked up my lemonade glass and followed her. She'd drunk half of what I had ordered.

In the kitchen, she was stuffing our containers in the trash, bent over with her ass toward me. Goddamn, that view was another one of my favorites. The clouds on her pajama pants sat on each cheek, inviting me to feel how soft they were.

She straightened, closing the trash drawer, and I yanked my attention to her face before she turned around. The distant look in her eyes washed out the desire. If she talked to me, I could help.

"Everything's not fine," I said.

She let out a long breath and swiped the back of her hand across her forehead. "It is. Either way, it's not your business."

"You're my business."

She propped her hands on her hips, that damn militant expression making her lower lip puff out. "No, Alder. I'm not."

We used to tell each other everything. When I'd behaved like an entitled dick during our marriage, she'd called me on it each and every time. Since we'd been together again, she'd even talked to me about Jason. But she wasn't telling me what was bothering her now.

I closed in on her at the counter. "You're my wife—"

"In name only."

"—and we live in the same house—"

"For a year."

"—so like it or not, you and your kid are my responsibility." I was towering over her. She had her chin lifted defiantly, anger flashing in the blue of her eyes. "I care about you."

She went rigid. "You don't need to."

"I never stopped."

"Alder." Her voice came out a whisper.

"It's true, Daisy." My gaze dropped to her puffy lips. She'd taste sweet right now from the lemonade and cinnamon butter. A little salty from the fries. She'd be even better than my surf and turf. Richer. Full bodied. Delectable. "I never stopped regretting how I failed you."

Her gaze dropped from mine. "You seem to have recovered well."

"I didn't do this for me."

A shiver went through her, but then she stiffened and deliberately lifted her attention to meet mine square on. "Did you do it for Sophia?" I jerked at the name. "Claudia? Hmm..." She tapped her chin. "Or was it Becca?"

Each name should've been a splash of ice-cold water,

but instead, a smug satisfaction filled me. "You kept track of me, Daze?"

"No." A flush painted her cheeks. "I didn't have to. Old friends and acquaintances loved sharing pictures of you with the woman-of-the-month on their social media."

I used to get tagged a lot by my dates until I finally quit social media altogether. But I hadn't shut down my accounts. How else would I spy on Daisy? To know she'd done the same? Satisfying. But I didn't like that she'd been hurt by the images she saw. "All those women were really attracted to my big...thick"—I dropped my head until my mouth was close to her ear—"wallet."

She sputtered. I let out a low chuckle, but I didn't move away.

She tipped her face toward mine, our lips inches apart. "You're just as incorrigible as you always were."

Much of the time, I was agreeable as fuck. Only one woman could call me on my shit. "Only around you, Daze."

I lowered my mouth to hers. The shock of energy when our mouths touched made her jolt and shot through me so strong I had to hold on to her or I'd rear back, and there was no way I'd ruin this moment. This kiss wasn't for show, and I'd waited too damn long for another chance.

She fisted a hand in my flannel shirt and a small whimper left her. I swallowed the sound and licked along her lips, seeking permission to take the kiss further. She opened with a small gasp like my tongue was the key and she'd been waiting an eternity for me to come along.

I'm right there with you, darling.

I curled a hand around the back of her head and sank into her while holding her still, mine for the taking. She wound both of her arms around my neck, and she rose to her tiptoes. I was bent over her and she was reaching up for me. An embrace that came as naturally to us as breathing. We were like two statues that had been pried apart but were finally fitting back together, just like we should've been all along.

She tasted sweet and salty and so damn familiar my chest ached. I'd missed this. I'd missed her. I pulled her impossibly closer to me, one hand stuffed into her hair and the other gripping her lush ass.

The doorbell rang.

She made a strangled noise and pushed away from me. Dazed, I blinked, the sudden loss hardening in my arteries like sharp icicles.

A little girl's voice drifted in from outside the front door. Laila had returned. The sound of her dad's voice responded. He must've met his sister and daughter after his shift.

Daisy scooted to the side, breaking my hold on her, and put her hand on her forehead. "Jesus." My mind was nearly back online when she spun and poked my chest with a finger. "Put one more rule down. No kissing between roommates."

Faint pounding resounded from the door, and she stormed out of the kitchen.

I continued to blink. Had I fucked up?

That kiss had been the final meal for a condemned man. Water on day nine in the desert. A lifeline when I'd been at the bottom of an empty canyon for years.

And she'd kissed me back like she felt the same.

No, Daisy. I would not be adding that rule.

* * *

Daisy

That kiss was... It was just... Uncalled for.

I couldn't summon the heat of anger. By the time I opened the door, I barely had my breathing under control, and my cheeks were still flaming hot.

"Mommy!" Laila rushed into my arms.

Grinning, I hugged her back. I'd missed her, but I wouldn't tell her that and dim her excitement about being with her dad. "Hey. Did you two have fun?"

"Yes! We made cookies." She went back to stand with Jason.

Jason winced. "They didn't turn out well. I had to put in an SOS with Mom and ask why they got so flat."

"The butter," Laila declared, scandalized.

"The butter," Jason agreed.

He'd never baked when we were together. Hadn't cooked more than hot dogs. He would've if I had kept on him, but my will had been lacking. I'd been down that road. But Jason was stepping up for his daughter. I might've picked a guy who didn't fit me, but I was grateful I'd picked someone who was a good parent.

"I'm sure they taste fine." I glanced behind me. Alder hadn't popped into the living room. He was either giving us space, or getting the erection I'd felt prodding against me under control.

What had I done by letting him kiss me? I hadn't been able to move away. I'd wanted it.

A real kiss from Alder Duke? With no witnesses so I

could just let go? No, I hadn't been able to walk away from that.

And unfortunately, all the kiss had done was show me that I'd done the right thing with Jason. I'd known, but the irrefutable proof was in the flush that was slow to leave my cheeks.

Jason handed Laila her backpack, then crouched to give her a hug. "Go on in. I'll see you next time and we'll get those cookies right."

"Love you, Daddy."

My heart melted. I'd given her the father figure I had missed growing up. A present man. She'd even have a doting stepfather if she let Alder in.

She crossed to my side and held my hand.

"Thanks, Jason."

His smile wasn't as sad as usual, but he scanned the room behind me, as if he was looking for Alder. Relief tinged his eyes. "See you girls later."

When he walked down the front steps, I let out a quiet sigh. The kiss might've reinforced the decision I'd made with Jason, but it'd created the question of whether I'd done the wrong thing getting married again.

Chapter Eight

Daisy

I waited in the living room with Laila. She was ready to go to her dad's and to see her grandparents for the next week. I would be heading to a Christmas Eve dinner at Lily and Eliot's. With Alder. Without my daughter.

I drew in a heavy breath. I'd miss her so much. One of many holidays I'd experience without her, but she'd be in good hands. She'd have a blast with Jason's family. And I'd be home. With Alder.

I had managed to avoid him for a week.

That kiss...

I'd gone to bed each night wishing he was on the other side of my small mattress. Wondering if his fingertips were still deliciously calloused and if he could still use the exact same pressure and tempo, the one he'd programmed into me as being perfect. The one no other man could replicate.

Not only that, Alder had been the only one who

could get me out of my head enough to enjoy sex, to be lost in it. But then I'd been young. So had he. The stress of those days was nothing compared to what I lived with as an adult with debt and a kid.

I was fantasizing about Alder. I had built up what we'd once had in my mind. Meanwhile, he'd probably had some excellent sexual experiences. Those women I'd seen him with had been gorgeous, sophisticated, and worldly. They had probably taught him stuff.

It'd been so hard to see those posts. Usually, the images had been taken by his dates, posted on their accounts. Some random person who'd known her or Alder would like or share the picture, and inevitably, Alder's dating life would cross my feed thanks to mutuals.

Had my life ever graced his screen? I didn't post much. My MO was to take a picture specifically to post and share with friends and family. I'd even have the draft post up with a caption. Sometimes I had written something witty or sweet. Then I'd think how insane it all sounded and delete it all.

Still, I had family and friends who'd sometimes post. So did the boyfriends I'd had over the years. Had Alder gotten jealous?

My big...fat...wallet.

Incorrigible.

The guys I'd been with between then and now had been attracted to my stability. I wasn't the crazy girlfriend, and sometimes on those early dates, I could tell I was the palate cleanser. They didn't *really* want a mellow girlfriend. The first date who had graduated to a boyfriend had been a mistake. I shouldn't have given him even a month, much less years. Then I wouldn't be where

I was now—remarried to my ex-husband so I could have a roof over my and my kid's head.

The guy after him had wanted a mom more than a wife. Then there'd been the one who'd had two other girlfriends. Jason had been a sweet relief after them. The sad fact was that I would've ended things long before last year but I'd gotten pregnant. He'd been so excited, and I had already gone through feeling like an emotionless witch in a big breakup.

In the end, the relationship hadn't been sustainable. Not for me.

Alder appeared in the opening from the kitchen. I willed myself not to look at him, but ever since that damn kiss, he'd moved like he was in the middle of a photo shoot. There was no simple stance with him. He'd drape his hands on the top of the doorframe and lean forward as if he were each month's feature in a calendar. Or he'd have a tool belt on and his flannel would be hanging over the back of a chair. Rugged Men 'R' Us. Other times were like now—his shoulder propped against the wall and his lean body on full display thanks to a tight T-shirt. Perfect for Mr. December.

"The carpet guy is good to go on the twenty-sixth," he said.

Laila aimed her pout at me. "I don't want new carpet."

"I know," I said, "but it'll be new *clean* carpet, and trust me, that's a treat." I couldn't wait. I didn't want to go into details and inspire a tiny germaphobe, but the bedroom carpets were gross. A million shampooings wouldn't change the grunge, and I died a little inside whenever I found Laila sprawled on the floor with her toys.

She glanced away, her little stubborn expression firmly in place. She hadn't warmed her cold shoulder toward Alder. Good thing she didn't know we'd kissed.

I caught the glint of Jason's truck out the window. He'd be turning down the driveway soon. I dug her gloves out of her winter coat and held one up. She stuffed her hand in.

"I think you should thank Alder for changing the carpet when it won't disrupt your use of the room."

She wrinkled her nose. The engine outside grew closer and a door shut. Footsteps crunched in the snow up to the door.

"Daddy's here," she said.

I kept my gaze on her. "Thank you, Alder, for being considerate about the carpet in my room."

She wiggled her hips and stomped her feet. "Thank you, Alder." Her tone was not full of gratitude.

"You're welcome," he said, going to the door. He met my gaze, asking permission to be the one to answer.

Tension knotted my stomach, but I nodded. The year was just beginning, and I'd rather not feel like I was hiding my husband. To stay transparent, I'd shared with Jason that Alder wasn't Laila's favorite person and that Alder was giving her room and time to adjust.

Laila sprinted across the room, and I juggled her suitcase and backpack.

Surprise lit Jason's face when he saw Alder. He nodded a greeting and bent to catch Laila. "There's my girl. Ready for the trip?"

"Yes! Can I go to the car?"

Jason glanced at us. He must have sensed Laila's disgruntlement. "Sure," he said, straightening. "Head on out."

She rushed around him. I handed her suitcase and backpack over.

Alder stuck his hand out. "Nice to see you again. At least we met once so you know me in more of a capacity than as the guy your daughter dislikes."

Jason chuckled, surprise in his gaze, like he didn't expect Alder to be charming in private as well as in public. It'd be easier on all of us if he weren't.

Jason shook Alder's hand. "Heard she's giving you a run for your money."

Alder rolled a heavy shoulder. "Can't blame her. Lots of changes, and I'm a good target." He let go of the door and stepped back. "Well, I'll let you two be."

My appreciation for him grew. Not only was he trying to do what was best to make this easier on Laila, but he was respectful of Jason and how all this made my ex feel.

Jason gave me a tight smile. "How's everything been going?"

Other than the smoldering kiss and that I wanted to scale Alder like my very own telephone pole so I could harvest all his power for myself? "Fine. Weird," I added quietly. "But we're making it work."

"No more crayon?"

"No, but it was an admirable fit she threw while cleaning it off. Thankfully, blasting Disney movie music helped."

"I'll keep that in mind in case there's any decorating at my parents'." He gave a resolute nod. "Well. Merry Christmas."

"Merry Christmas."

I closed the door and swallowed the swell of emotions. Regrets that I couldn't have loved Jason more.

Sadness. My first Christmas without Laila. She'd be bouncing between homes until she had a family of her own. Anticipation. I had told her we'd open gifts when she got home. Rushing through a Christmas celebration after work, between dinner and bath time, hadn't felt right.

I turned and found Alder in the same opening he'd been lingering in when Jason had arrived.

Empathy softened his gaze. "I can't imagine it's ever easy to do the exchange."

"No. Now I'm going to hang out with a happy family and watch them with their kids." I bit my lower lip. Damn. I shouldn't have said that. Some people leaned into others when they were hurting. Not me. I saw everything they had that I didn't, and I got angry. Resentful.

Jason had asked me once if it was possible to rewire my emotions.

I'd learned a lot about how I should feel, what I should express, but none of it changed how I actually felt. Parts of my brain were just hardwired differently.

Alder stuffed his hands in his pockets. "I can tell them you got sick. We're going to stay home and have chicken soup."

I cocked a brow. "You're going to tell Lily I have diarrhea and have to keep from infecting everyone?"

He laughed. "Isn't chicken soup for colds?"

"I don't know. I don't like chicken soup."

"You don't like the mushy stuff in the can and you hate making the good stuff yourself because it makes too much and the noodles are mushy the next day."

Texture was everything when it came to noodles. "Al dente or gag."

More laughter, deep and pleasing. "I'll make up any excuse you need. You don't have to go."

I pushed a lock of hair behind my ear. The offer was tempting. Alder wouldn't throw me under the bus either. "No, I can be a big girl and suck it up. Laila's going to get stupidly spoiled, and I won't have to get yanked into a ton of hugs." Jason's family was so *touchy*.

"No hugs. Promise." He wobbled his head from side to side. "Wait—I can't promise the kids won't hug you."

"Kids are less awkward."

He flashed a smile that could incinerate my clothes right off. Not because of his sexy smolder, but thanks to the easy humor and acceptance. "Leave in an hour?"

"Sure."

He pushed off the wall, his hands still tucked away. I clocked every moment like he was my special Christmas gift.

"What's your safe word?" he asked. "Snickerdoodle?"

I zoomed through space and time to when we were at a pasture party during one cool fall night. I hated breaking rules, but Alder had been invited. He'd been invited to everything, and he'd talked me into going, but he could tell I was growing quieter the closer we got. All I could imagine was police lights and sirens and trying to explain to my parents why I was drinking in some field with people who barely remembered me even though we'd gone to school together for a few years.

We can leave anytime you want, he'd said.

If I tell you I want to leave, they're gonna hate me even more.

No one hates you, Daze.

Because they forget about me.

He'd tugged me into him. *Snickerdoodle. Tell me*

*you're craving some of my mom's snickerdoodles and
we'll go.*

I don't like snickerdoodles.

Exactly.

I gave my head a little shake, scattering the memory
like droplets of fog. "Lily might actually have baked your
mom's snickerdoodles and then what? I have to eat disappointment."

"They're damn good cookies," he said, laughing.

"I'm sure they are once you get past the cinnamon
clogging the flavor of everything."

"You like cinnamon."

We'd bickered exactly like this plenty of times, but I
went along with it like putting on a favorite cozy sweater.
"In pumpkin pie and chai."

"Chai made with the powder and not real tea."

I shuddered. "If I wanted leaves in my cinnamon hot
chocolate, I'd drop it on the ground."

"Then you'll need to lean in real close and tell me
you're craving my..." His grin was wide as he backed out
of the room. "...chicken soup."

* * *

"I can't believe how good Jasper has gotten at carving," I
murmured.

Lily sat next to me with a mug of cocoa topped with
whipped cream. She was expecting her third, but it was
still early. Only her loose red sweater gave her away. Violet
and Evander would be here soon.

"His figures are amazing," she agreed. "He sticks with
horses, and Mom said once that she had an idea for a

book about a serial killer who leaves little horse figurines."

I coughed out a laugh, grateful I didn't have any cocoa, or I would've sprayed it over her couch. "She writes kids' books."

Lily smirked. "She's coming up with pen names for thrillers. M. D. Duke was her latest idea. No one will tie it to Magnolia, the children's book author."

"I'll make sure to buy a copy. I love thrillers, and a serial killer one sounds right up my alley."

We watched the kids play, and I didn't let my thoughts wander to Laila. She and Jason would still be on the road. As worried as I'd been about how uncomfortable this visit would be, it was nice to have some distraction. Lily was a lot like me as a mom. Supportive but not as doting.

"When Laila was first born..." I hadn't thought of actually speaking about my past without Alder, but his family had always been different. They'd been accepting. Welcoming. I could be myself around them. "I thought I had to be with her all the time. My brother and I were like free-range chickens growing up. No oversight." Part of me knew it was the times. The other part remembered the loneliness. How Mom could be in the room with us but so in her head that it was like we were by ourselves. "It wasn't until I recalled how Magnolia was with all of you that I backed off. A little."

"It's like anything else, I suppose," Lily mused. "Moderation. Not too much attention or they don't learn some valuable skills. Too little attention and then it's neglect."

Neglect. I rubbed my hands together. My parents had done their okayest, but they had each shown different sorts of neglect. Dad had been at the bar most nights of the week—not an alcoholic but a socialholic. Mom had been under the same roof, but Lee and I had been running wild outside by ourselves.

"How's it going?" Lily tipped her head toward the kitchen where Alder and Eliot were chatting about Eliot's small Arabian breeding program that he'd moved from Montana to the backyard. "You totally don't have to talk to me about it."

"You mean about my very *real* marriage with Alder?" I asked, smiling so she knew I was okay with the topic.

She winked. "The totally believable whirlwind wedding."

I winced. "Is our acting that bad?"

Her expression grew somber. "No, actually. I don't think you have to act. Alder regaled us with what happened and what he was going to do, and he didn't dive further into the story. Kind of like when you two split up. I think that's what sold it to Mom and Dad. He called and said he reconnected with you and it just felt right. You were marrying and that was that." She rubbed the side of her face as she thought. "Seeing you both walk through the door again, it was like the divorce didn't happen." She clicked her tongue like she was chiding herself. "Sorry."

"No, it's fine." Surprising, more like. "What do you mean?"

"It's like old times, but it's not." She blew out a long, slow breath. "You two were never touchy-feely so it's not like you have to suck face for us to believe it." She lowered her voice to keep her daughter from overhearing. "You're still comfortable around each other. You still know each other."

The way she said it sounded like I was very familiar with what he looked like with his clothes off in the last fifteen years. "He always understood me."

"Not always," she said softly.

Yes. The years we'd been married. "He did then too. He just didn't care. I can't blame him for wanting his freedom." It was one reason why I finally let him go. He had chafed at the almost daily reprimands and requests for him to change back to the boy who used to spoil me. I had been unhappy, and it'd made him unhappy.

"Well, he got his freedom." She shook her head. "We worried so much about him during those first few years." She glanced at the kitchen, then at her kids. A train set that circled the Christmas tree and the pile of presents underneath had them engrossed. "He took a nosedive. He'd work hard, then party hard—even harder than when you were married. I was still at home, so I caught a lot of worried conversations between Mom and Dad. People from here who knew them would pass on his antics. There was one with a tractor and a stock pond—anyway. He was wild in a destructive sort of way."

"Even worse? He's nothing like that now."

"A total one-eighty. He showed up one day, clean-shaven, with freshly laundered clothing that didn't have holes in it, and he was already enrolled in school. He took something like twenty-plus credits each semester and summer school to graduate early." When my brows lifted, she nodded. "And he finished his MBA in record time. After that, he got a basement-level office job at King Oil and worked his way up. It was like he was driven to prove it wasn't nepotism, or that if it was, he was still the best candidate."

"Now he's a CEO." Bile crawled up my throat. I

had seen a few of those party posts cross my social media feeds, then he'd disappeared. When he reappeared in a random post, it had been with beautiful Sophia.

"The change was drastic." She leaned away, peering around me like she was making sure the guys were still tucked into the kitchen. "But we still worried about him. He's all work."

He was using his time off before he started his new position, but he wasn't idle. The amount of repairs and renovating he'd done on the house in such a short time was impressive. "He seems to want to keep busy."

"He's driven to keep busy." Her tone made the distinction more than her words. "I hope this job gives him the validation he's seeking. I hope he learns to relax before his blood pressure bursts through his temples."

"He's not that uptight."

Her smile was soft. "Maybe not when he's with you."

Oh. No. That wasn't it. They weren't living with him. They didn't see the handyman side of Alder. Although he didn't sit very often, and he paced when there wasn't an immediate project. Anytime he was on his phone, it looked like he was answering emails and fielding work messages. Except for when he'd sat on the couch and listened to me unload all my previous employment trauma on him.

The doorbell saved me from having to respond.

Violet and Evander entered, and the next several minutes were a whirlwind of greetings and hugs between Violet and Lily's kids. I watched the warm commotion from the couch. Alder hung back, a wistful expression on his face. He caught my eye and adopted a smile that was almost regretful.

He crossed the living room to perch on the end of the couch next to me. "How ya doing?"

"Good." Surprised, I checked myself. I was enjoying myself. I might be discussing Alder's and my situation with Lily, but the young girl had grown into a woman I wanted to be friends with.

"Oh, good," Violet said to me as Evander helped her out of her coat. "I'm so glad you could make it."

"Me too." We'd talked at work, but I hadn't been sure about visiting my mom. Mom had reassured me that she didn't mind a quiet holiday and not to worry about me or her traveling. I refused to think that she was giving me one less escape route so I spent the holiday with Alder.

"Aunt Linda can't make it," Violet said and smoothed her Christmas maternity shirt over her belly. "She's not feeling well, and I think she believes..." She glanced at the kids. "You know? She doesn't feel the need to verify."

I would feel guilty for fooling Alder's aunt, but this sham marriage was solving a problem for her too. No renters to deal with and the house was getting much needed work. Thanks to Alder.

He stayed sitting next to me. Violet laughed and held her hands out to her nephew. She propped Kellan on her hip and Evander was behind her, a proprietary hand on her hip. It was easy to imagine this was me and Alder. Laila would be in the mix, playing with Cali, and maybe there'd even be another kid—

What the hell was I thinking?

I was not picturing this as my future.

Chicken soup.

Chicken soup.

But as I watched the family that I was once a part of greet each other, the words didn't leave my mouth.

Chapter Nine

Alder

I'd had worse Christmas days. I was in Laila's room ripping out carpet when I sensed Daisy at the door. Laila's bed was propped in the hallway, and her dresser was in the living room along with all her toys.

I sat back on my heels and arched my aching back. I hadn't minded the last few weeks of physical labor. It was like the old days, only I was getting paid a shitload more from my unused leave than I had made then, and as a single guy working in the oil fields, I'd been raking it in.

Daisy had her arms crossed over her chest, her thumbs through the holes at the end of her sleeves. She'd asked to help earlier, but I had shooed her out. It was her holiday vacation time. Instead, she'd called her mom and cross-stitched a butterfly.

I brushed my forearm across my brow. "What's up?"

"You don't have to work all through Christmas."

I shrugged. "It won't take long. I can wait until

tomorrow to move your stuff." The carpet layers would be here the day after tomorrow. "So you can sleep in your own bed on Christmas."

"It's fine. I've moved some stuff."

I frowned. She didn't need to be moving her furniture. "I can get it."

She cocked a brow. "So can I. I can probably even get the mattress and box spring by myself since they're only a full."

This was the perfect opening. She wouldn't like what I had to suggest, and a shot of adrenaline spiked in my veins at the thrill of using Daisy's practicality against her. Her bed was cheap and lumpy. I'd seen it when the movers hauled it in, nearly folded in half like a sandwich.

"Speaking of the mattress, with Mom and Dad coming next week, and since we're moving beds around, we should put the king in your room."

Her lips parted and her eyes flared. "No. It's..." She snapped her mouth shut. She couldn't refute the logic. My parents would wonder why the biggest, more luxurious bed was upstairs when I would be sharing a room with her. "I can't take your bed."

"I don't mind. I can swap them again after they're gone." I held in my smile. My logical argument was next.

A crease lined her brow. "That would be a lot of work for you."

Yes. She was buying it. The way she shuffled each morning like she'd slept on a wood plank with only a sheet for comfort would be over. That dollar-store mattress would be my problem. I'd buy a pad or something for it. Hell, sleeping on the floor might be better. "It's fine. I could actually have some room upstairs with a smaller bed."

She hugged her arms tighter. "I can't take your bed," she repeated.

"Take it. You'll be doing me a favor."

The furrow deepened. "I don't see how trading me for a shitty mattress is a favor."

"I almost broke my neck going to the bathroom in the middle of the night when I got stuck between the wall and the bed."

She narrowed her eyes, trying to sense my BS. I knew that look. I'd seen it a lot in the last year before she asked for a divorce. "Okay, but if we need to switch, I mean, Laila and I can move upstairs."

No fucking way. They got the biggest rooms and the best beds. "I doubt there'll be a need. I'm not as accustomed to the lap of luxury like you think."

Doubt darkened her eyes. "Your expensive suits say differently, Duke."

"Been checking out my wardrobe?"

She put her hand on her chest. "Did you witness the reverence with which the movers hauled them in?"

"I told the college kid I'd tip them as much as the whole move cost if they didn't wrinkle the suits. I hate dry cleaning."

She laughed. "Coal Haven doesn't have a dry cleaner."

I adjusted how I was sitting, putting my ass on the floor. I would not groan from stiff knees in front of her. "The motel has a special arrangement for when they get VIPs in, and they'll act as the go-between for a nice fee. It keeps their doors open."

"VIPs stay at the motel? The one with the fish-gutting station in the back?"

"VIPs like to fish too."

She chuckled. "It all works out for you, doesn't it?"

There was no heat behind her words but just a tinge of bitterness. She'd worked hard and had ended up worrying about a roof over her head. The quality of my life had skyrocketed after we split, but not right away. I'd had to wallow in rock bottom for a while.

"No, Daisy," I said quietly. "Not always or we wouldn't be pretending right now."

Emotions trickled over her face. Surprise, remorse, then discomfort. She shuttered the rest when we treaded close to an emotional topic she wanted to play keep-away with. "I think we glorified the idea of marriage."

"How do you mean?"

"Your parents are, like, a winning lotto number. I mean, look at the odds. Fifty-fifty, isn't it? They succeeded. My parents didn't. You and I failed. Just in that little pool, the odds aren't good."

I narrowed my eyes at her. "Is that why you didn't marry Jason?" Or the guy before him? And the boyfriend before that? For years, a hammer had been hanging over my head, just waiting to hear she'd fully moved on. Each update on her profile, each little tidbit of gossip I got, I had dreaded when I'd hear she'd gotten married and was no longer Daisy Duke. As long as she wasn't married, it felt like there was hope, yet I had kept my distance, not knowing when or if she'd ever want to hear from me.

I had added a goddamn hour to my workout each day after I'd heard she was pregnant. She was supposed to be having my kids and now some other man got to experience that with her. Fucking Jason. He had to be a decent dad too, so I couldn't hate him for that.

She skimmed her teeth over her lower lip for a few moments. "I was very aware that putting a ring on it was just the next expected step, and ultimately, I couldn't justify taking that step when I knew..." She took a step back. "When I knew that ending it all can be easier—and cheaper—than the wedding. Either of us could walk away at any moment, just as quickly as we walked down the aisle."

Acid flared like lava in my gut. "Jesus, Daisy. Did I make you that jaded?"

"A reality check is a reality check. Only this time, a kid would be involved."

And it'd be more complicated. "You wanted to be able to make a clean break—when he inevitably let you down?"

She gnawed on that poor lower lip. "Jason didn't let me down. He kept trying, and god, I wanted that to be enough." She hugged herself again. "We were just too different."

He kept trying. Jason had done more than me, and it hadn't been enough for him. If I had pulled myself together, stayed home more, done a few dishes, and quit treating Daisy like she was a live-in maid, then she'd have never had to keep trying with him.

"Anyway," she said in a tone that said she was done with that line of conversation, "I'm heating up some leftovers Eliot sent home with us. Want some?"

There'd been a ton of food yesterday, and we'd come home with ham and all the fixings and half a pie. "You're going to cook for me?"

"I can reheat like a boss."

I checked the time. It was that late. The afternoon was gone and now it was early evening. My stomach clenched and growled like it was afraid I'd pass on her offer. "Sure. I'll clean up and be right out."

* * *

I piled the remnants I had ripped up since the last load I'd carried to the back of my pickup in the corner. Next, I tossed my tools in the toolbox and ran a quick broom over the subfloor. After washing my hands, I found Daisy in the kitchen just as the microwave dinged.

She pulled out a large plate piled with food and stirred various parts around. Then she divided the contents onto two other plates, leaving some behind. She took a pot from the stove and poured gravy over my plate.

She might've remembered I liked a gravy-smothered holiday meal, but she'd also paid attention yesterday when I'd done it again.

She stuck a fork in the smothered potatoes and slid it toward me. "Bon appétit."

"Thank you. Are you taking the table or the couch?"

"The table. Why?" She carried her plate around the island to her chair.

"I can take the couch." I wanted to sit at the damn table and have a little holiday-fueled hope that I could get back the only girl I had ever wanted, but sitting my ass on the couch while she was at the table was still better than every Christmas I'd had without her.

She paused with her hand on the back of the chair. "You can join me. I promise I won't freak out."

"You won't get upset that you're eating at the table with me on Christmas Day?"

Our gazes met for a charged second. "It's better than being alone."

I knew what that was like. I took my food to my chair. "To be fair, we'd be under the same roof."

She smiled at me. Her gaze flickered from me to the chair opposite me, the one next to her. I'd been ousted from there by Laila.

Would she invite me over? I held my breath, but she tucked her chin down and grabbed her fork. My disappointment faded quickly. I was still a step closer to her.

"What was Fargo like?" I asked to make conversation as we ate, hungry to learn more about those years I'd missed.

She finished chewing. Took a drink. Let out a sigh. "I'm going to sound like a complainer again."

"Being critical isn't the same as a complainer."

Her mouth twisted. "I get told I'm bitching."

"I hope you junk-punched whoever said that."

She laughed. "We did break up not long after. And the whole time I was complaining, he was—" She snapped her mouth shut. "He was a lying jerk."

It was easy enough to guess what the asshole had done. "He cheated on you," I growled.

She snorted. "If only."

When she stuffed a forkful of ham into her mouth, I got the sign. She was done talking about that ex. "Fargo?"

"Oh." She dabbed her napkin at her mouth. "It was fun, in a way. You know, I was young and hungry and the lab was so busy, especially in the morning. It was go-go-go."

"But?"

The corner of her mouth lifted. "It's the competition. So, at the lab with the *doctor*, it was the competition between coworkers. We were colleagues, but it felt like a 'kill or be killed' environment sometimes. Who gets the recognition for an idea or a successful procedure? Who gets trained on the new, shiny technology? Because that means they're the smartest, and a lot of that was done by ass-kissing and backstabbing. Like, I'm sorry I don't play on your bar's volleyball league, but that new analyzer is for my department, for work that I do. So why am I not the first one learning to use it? But in a hospital setting, it was departments pitted against each other."

"But your colleagues?"

"They were amazing. A lot at the other lab were too. I'm still friends with many. Just, you know, not *Doctor* Simmons or the ones still attached to her backside."

I chuckled. I wanted to keep her talking. Did she realize we used to do this in school? She'd rant about unfair teachers, and I'd realize she was right. "How are departments against each other? Aren't they all working to help the patient?"

She nodded and that light lit her eyes. The fire inside of her. Fairness and justice. The ember was like a tiny jewel that needed to be locked up safe in this unfair world. "We're all under such tight deadlines, so it becomes the atmosphere. Pressure. It felt like nurses against the lab. Or the doctors against the lab. Or racing radiology to the patient so we're not blamed for delays, which doesn't matter. The lab is always blamed for delays. Some days, I'd almost get a panic attack when I had to call a critical value."

She hadn't been finished with school when we divorced. She had a whole career under her belt. One I was only just learning about. "Which is?"

"A test result that could be life or death. Not always that extreme, but we have to notify the doctor for each critical value or if there are any issues with the samples.

But the staff is busy, and some people just plain have egos and they'll put them before patient care."

"How?"

"Jake from ER." The fire raged in her eyes. Whoever Jake was, he'd been a dick to Daisy, and I didn't like him.

"Isn't he from State Farm?"

"No." She inhaled and slowly let out her breath. "Are you sure you want to hear this?"

"Absolutely. I've always been interested in your stories." Getting a glimpse into her brain had turned me on since our first study hall together.

She paused for a moment but then the flame licked to life in her blue irises. "So this wasn't in Fargo, but in Bismarck. I had this critically high blood sugar on an ER patient, but the sample was hemolyzed, meaning blood cells burst from improper collection techniques—sometimes it's a condition in the patient—anyway, the hemoglobin discolors the plasma and some tests are read by how it looks, right? Or extra things are released into the plasma from the cell destruction, so the result is incorrect. Ultimately, we can't get an accurate read. Glucose isn't one of them, so I called to tell the patient's nurse the sample needed to be recollected, but I told them that the blood sugar was critically high. Since a phlebotomist collected the sample, he basically brushed it off as the lab's fault. He yelled at me to do my job and then maybe he could do his about the high blood sugar."

"He didn't let you explain?" I had no idea what the issue was, but the indignation in her expression said it was important.

She shook her head. "He hung up when he should've told the doctor. They could do a finger-poke blood glucose and get that specific result in a fraction of the time, and the doctor could add on more labs in case we needed to collect another tube. I mean, the patient was in the ER for a reason, and that almost five hundred blood sugar reading might've had something to do with it. The patient's treatment was delayed because Jake wanted an ego boost. You can claim it's because nurses are busy or they're stressed, but I can talk to a nurse who just finished a code where they lost someone and she'll be as professional as ever. Can you imagine if you were a loved one of the patient? They probably thought Jake was a good nurse and they were lucky to have him. I'm sure since all the phlebs and techs that draw blood gush over what a hottie he is, he's boosted himself even higher in his own mind."

"Did you think he was hot?" I fucking hated Jake from the ER.

"I think he would've been more attractive if he took care of the patient properly." She pushed her stuffing around and the energy drained out of her. "It just got exhausting. I'd get yelled at because nurses thought I let the sample sit too long in the lab and it hemolyzed or clotted. That's literally not how hemolysis works. It's not how the additives in the tubes work. But then we'd have plenty of lab staff who acted like assholes and screwed up. I had a coworker who mixed up an order for red blood cells with platelets. They're different *colors*, Alder. It was alarming—and real fucking embarrassing to fix when it wasn't my appalling error."

Her breathing was speeding up, like she was reliving the stress. I was her safe space again, or she would've told me Fargo was fine and left it at that. "I hated showing up every day to do the best job I could do, a job I'd gone to school for, that I interned for, and got treated like I was jacking around when people's lives were on the line." Her mouth quirked. "I have my own pride too. Then I went to work for the *doctor* and there it felt personal. So yeah, I guess I did come home and bitch all the time. Now I'm saving the world by testing fuel." She gave me a furtive look. "I love my job, by the way. I probably shouldn't have said that around my boss."

"I'm not technically in charge of you yet." As if I ever could be. Daisy had a mind of her own, and it pissed people off. I wouldn't have made her feel like she was nothing but a complainer. "I'm a better boss because of your stories."

Her brows lifted. "I'm sure there's a lot more that went into your leadership."

Being single and living in an empty house without her. "You pull the curtain back. Poor leaders will resent you for it. Strong leaders evaluate the observations and criticisms as objectively as possible. That's what I strive to do, and I look for people who pull the curtain because there are a ton out there who are happy to sew it shut. Then they can't see the ship sinking. They can't look in the mirror and admit that they have some responsibility. I even used that analogy in my interview, and I think it helped me get the job." After I'd had a good hard look in the mirror at myself when I'd been on the brink of losing my job in the oil fields for being an idiot.

She blinked at me. "Oh."

"Either that or it's because I'm Weston Duke's son," I said with a tight smile. I couldn't deny that being his kid was a major secret to my success.

"Alder Duke is his own man." Her words were supportive, like she saw right through to that part of me that had to prove I deserved what I had. Daisy was the first one to show me that relying on superficial shit wasn't enough. I had to put the work in.

I'd grown up the oldest of six. Automatic authority. My siblings had looked up to me. My parents had trusted me. I'd gotten the girl. Life had been easy. Then I'd woken face down in cow manure after jumping a fence in the middle of the night with an angry bull on the other side. My buddies had been laughing their asses off, and police sirens wailed in the air.

If I had stayed in that moment, I'd have lost everything else. My job. The final shreds of respect of my siblings. My parents' patience with my wildness. There'd be nothing but more of the same, only I'd have a trespassing record at the minimum. "Now I am my own man, yes."

We shared a smile, and she pushed her chair back. "I'm having my pie right away. Do you want a slice?"

"It's my turn to get it."

"You've been making meals all week, Alder. I can get us slices of pie someone else made." She went to the fridge and dug out the pumpkin and whipped cream. Again, she didn't have to ask. She either remembered or paid attention yesterday.

Those were the parts of Daisy people couldn't handle. Growing up, I'd had the last name of a family in the community synonymous with money and power. Not to the level of Evander's family, the Barrons, but the Dukes hadn't been slouches. I'd been self-aware enough to know I had Dad's charisma, my mom's friendliness, and both of their looks.

Daisy had fascinated me since the first day of high school. Her first day in Coal Haven. She'd done her own thing, and when we'd had to work together in class, she'd treated me as competent, nothing more. During study hall, she'd helped me with algebra. The small country school she'd gone to had been light years ahead of the math I'd taken.

Then one day during our sophomore year, she'd brought me a chocolate chip oatmeal cookie from the coffee shop and a special jig for walleye fishing that one of her neighbors had made by hand.

Mom had always made oatmeal chocolate chip cookies, and I'd have some for a snack some days during study hall. When we'd chatted about our weekends, I'd tell her about fishing with Dad and that I lived for catching walleye. Two details of my life that were inconsequential while at the same time specific to Alder Duke. She'd paid attention to me. Without fanfare. Without wanting any recognition. She'd just handed the two items to me and said, "Is it graph day?"

I'd fallen for her then. Compared to her, everyone had seemed superficial. Too shallow. Nothing had changed after our divorce either. Dating had been as exhausting to me as her former jobs. I'd been left feeling used and sometimes betrayed. All because I'd been chasing that feeling Daisy had given me. Of being seen for nothing more than being me.

She brought me a slice of pumpkin pie and sat to eat hers. The silence was easy. We'd done a lot of talking and now we were enjoying a treat together. She'd always get quiet after a good rant and soak in the feeling of not holding it in.

When I was finished, I took my plate to the dishwasher. There was one more thing I wanted to do tonight, and that just might push everything too far, but I had to move the needle. I had to know if she was open to one day fixing what I had broken. "I've got something for you. Let me clean up and I'll grab it."

"Oh?"

"I just need a minute." I rushed through loading the dishwasher. I couldn't chicken out now.

Daisy usually cleaned up after herself while she was cooking, so the counters were already wiped. She stole the dishcloth to swipe over our spots at the table. Once I was done, I ran upstairs. I had hidden the package in my room. I studied the box for a minute. It wasn't too late to back out.

No. All that was inside was a little gift. At minimum, we were friends.

Downstairs, Daisy was tucked into the corner of the couch. The screen was dark and she scrolled through her phone. I closed in, the knot inside my stomach growing bulkier.

"Promise not to overthink it?" I held the package behind my back.

Her gaze grew wary. "Why?"

This would go fine. Just fine. I brandished the small, wrapped box.

Her eyes flew wide. "Alder!"

My heartbeat sounded between my ears. "Just open it."

Dismay darkened her blue eyes. "You bought me something?"

"No." Even I knew that would be going too far too soon.

Indecision tightened her mouth. "Okay."

Yes.

She lifted her hand, paused, then reached the rest of the way, her slim fingers closing around the box.

I sat on the opposite end of the couch, half turned toward her. I hadn't even been this nervous when I'd first asked her out.

She stared at the dancing candy canes. "I didn't get you anything."

"I know. I didn't expect you to."

Present buying stressed Daisy out. She always wanted to get the perfect thing. She used all her knowledge of the person to consider a gift, which was also what made it so hard for her to decide. This was my oatmeal chocolate chip cookie and fishing lure.

Tentatively, she peeled away the paper and leaned back, as if I'd wired it to blow confetti in her face. Under the green Christmas wrap full of dancing candy canes was a plain box. Her mouth set in a consternated line, she glanced at me before opening the box.

All my muscles went taut, waiting for her reaction.

Her pink lips parted and wonder filled her eyes. Then a slow smile spread across her face, and it was like the sun coming out. Out of the one piece of tissue paper, she withdrew a small wooden figure of a horse. Her reaction was exactly what I wanted.

"Did Jasper make this?" Wonder filled her voice, and she held it up to the weak light from the lamp.

"Yes. Out of alder wood." Before that tidbit could make her uncomfortable, I rushed on. "So don't lose it around the new cabinets after they're installed."

She laughed, the sound light and airy. A happy laugh. No discomfort or nervousness.

I might still toe the line too far. "I asked him to stain it the same color as Trixie."

She lowered the figurine to her lap and cradled it in her hands. "Trixie? That old girl?"

"She was old when you used to ride her."

"I think she was born old. Remember when she wouldn't cross that little creek that was three inches wide?"

"I had to get off and lead her across."

We exchanged grins, just like we would've done years ago. She bit her lip as she studied the little horse.

She held it up again. "I guess it has a name already. Trixie." She narrowed her eyes at the back hindquarter. "He added her scar."

"Dad couldn't believe she could still walk after that."

She ran a finger lightly over the ragged ridge Jasper had incorporated. "She got spooked, right? Flipped over a fence post?"

"Some teens partying in a field and they started a fire." It had been before I was born, but Dad had recounted the story often enough. A group of kids had thought the field was empty and started a small fire. It spread, and in the ruckus of the emergency response, the horses had bolted. Only Trixie had been severely hurt.

I should've carried that story closer to my heart. Those kids had been younger than me when I'd been an idiot in other people's pastures. Old enough to know better, too privileged to care.

"She was such a good horse," Daisy murmured, yanking me out of the past. "I adored her."

"She was fond of you."

"I didn't make her work hard." She grinned and closed her fingers around the figure. "Thank you. When did you see Jasper?"

I shrugged, fighting off a lump in my throat. "Eliot ran out there a few days ago for me."

"Right. Jasper manages Eliot's family ranch." She

continued to cradle her present. She hadn't gotten upset. How much did I read into that? We'd been friends once before. We were becoming friends again.

We'd been married once before. We were married again.

She'd been in love with me once before. Could she be in love with me once again?

I'd bow out before she got uncomfortable with how comfortable she was getting around me. I'd also leave her a little disconcerted. Maybe she'd entertain the idea of how cozy she wouldn't mind getting with me. "Mom said they'd be here on Thursday. Five days. They'll leave on the first."

She clasped the horse to her chest. "Yes, of course."

"I'll have the beds swapped by then. That way, maybe you won't make me sleep on the floor when we have to share a room."

"Oh..." Two pink blooms spread across her cheeks.

There it was. Just the right amount of uncomfortable. "Night, Daisy."

Now, she'd go to bed thinking about me. And I'd go to sleep content that after fifteen Christmases, today I didn't have to wish I was spending it with her.

Chapter Ten

Daisy

I let my car warm up as my breath puffed out. My vehicle was idling in the parking lot of the refinery. Today was one of my last days I'd come to a job where Alder wasn't over me.

A swath of heat crashed into me. Alder over me. In me. Under me. A full-body shiver racked me. Thankfully, it looked like I was cold and not lusting over my ex-husband turned husband.

I splayed the fingers of my left hand out in front of me. I wore a knit glove, but I could see the ring perfectly, like a hologram over the material. I could not afford to develop feelings for my husband. I was already the bad guy to Jason's family for breaking his heart. It wasn't like I could stay married. These things ended. Always.

Alder had been out of my league back then. He wasn't even in the same stratosphere now. Next week, he'd show up in the head office, in one of the shades-of-gray power suits he had, and he'd be my boss. He'd be in meetings with women who didn't wear lab coats and didn't have marks from her safety goggles lined into her face.

There was no way to look sexy in a lab coat.

Those women he'd dated after me had probably worn nice blouses with power suits. Hadn't one done some modeling before working in the PR department of an energy company? They'd probably had friends in school. Alder had seen by now how much better he could do than me. Once he had the house, he'd be free to do whatever he wanted. Whomever he wanted.

But he'd given me a carving of Trixie. Scar and all.

I blew out a breath. Warm air was starting to pump from the vents. I had to get home. Laila was still with her dad, so I had no reason to delay.

Weston and Magnolia would be there. I'd walk into that house again and be thrown back in time. To when I had been loopy in love and enamored with the vibrant house so full of energy.

My parents loved me. In their way. But growing up, our house had been cold and quiet. My parents hadn't been the touchy-feely type to the point where I wondered how my brother and I had even been conceived. Emotions hadn't been a bad thing, unless it was anger. Conflict. But on the flip side, they hadn't been encouraged or expressed.

The butterflies in my stomach went wild. There'd be *feelings* walking into that house today.

I closed my eyes. I could do this. More so, I *wanted* to do this. I liked Weston and Magnolia.

How awkward would this be?

Only one way to find out.

For the entire drive, I sucked in long breaths and blew them out slowly. Nothing like a little Lamaze to wrangle the mass of unruly butterflies. I parked in the garage, passing an unfamiliar large black pickup on the way.

I could barely keep my hands from shaking when I walked into the house. Magnolia was at the table, her salt-and-pepper hair pulled back in a puffy ponytail like she'd often worn it when I was younger. Her simple black sweater and loose black pants only highlighted the red Converse on her feet.

Her smile grew wide and she rose. "Daisy." She rushed toward me.

I hastily dropped my tote bag and hung my coat up before she reached me. I was enveloped in a floral-scented bear hug. Her strength hadn't diminished over the years.

I returned her embrace and soaked in her unrestrained delight. When Magnolia embraced me, I never questioned the action. She put her all into her hugs. It was one of the few times a hug didn't make me uncomfortable.

"I'm so happy to see you." She stood back and beamed at me. "I didn't even mind missing the second wedding because it meant you were part of the family again. I admit to being a little disappointed I can't meet Laila yet, but perhaps it's best. A lot of changes for her."

"Yes, it is." For us. Was Magnolia tracking the differences in me? My face was fuller, my body rounder in areas. I dressed even more plainly than I used to. I had lived in graphic tees until I'd had to buy scrubs or nondescript clothing for the chemistry lab.

Magnolia hadn't changed much. If anything, she appeared happier. Less stressed than when she'd had kids under the roof. Now they were all responsible adults, and she could be the indulgent grandma.

"Daisy." Weston's voice boomed.

I jumped. Magnolia chuckled and pivoted to my side in time for me to get yanked into another all-encompassing hug.

"Hey, Weston," I said, smushed against his shoulder. Another hugger I didn't mind because he was all-in. My dad wasn't a touchy-feely guy, but Weston was the dad I'd missed all my life. "How are ya?"

"Better now that I get to see the proof." He released me and I nearly went reeling, but a warm hand steadied me on the small of my back.

My heart hammered. I knew that touch. I glanced at the man crowded close. Alder was smiling but his gaze asked if I was doing okay.

My insides were a tangle. I was thrilled to see Magnolia and Weston, but now it was real. For the next several days, I'd have to pretend that I was really married to Alder.

"How was work?" he asked as he dipped his head. Our lips touched briefly but my eyelids fluttered like I'd never been kissed before.

Satisfaction filled his eyes. Did he like the quick kiss? Seeing me with his family again? Or was he relieved his parents seemed to be buying everything so far?

They hadn't really seen us together yet.

"Good," I said.

Magnolia twisted her hands together. "I hope you don't mind. I didn't want you or Alder to feel like you had to make a big meal for us. We put in an order at Rattler's to pick up."

"I was just heading there," Weston said. His gaze lifted to his son. "Care to join me?"

"You afraid you'll get lost?" Alder joked.

His dad rolled his eyes but laughed. "We're city folks now."

They took off, and I was left with Magnolia. Alder probably figured I wouldn't mind. I never had before, and I didn't now. Even though Alder and I were trying to fool them, I had missed Magnolia more than I felt bad about the fib. For one year, I could put off disappointing them again.

"Thank you so much for letting us intrude." She chuckled. "West and I brought our bags upstairs, and it's just so weird. I'm sleeping in Alder's old room, and he's in ours."

Yes. The sleeping arrangements. Another reason I couldn't tie myself up about fibbing to Magnolia and Weston. I was crawling into bed with their son tonight. Something I never thought would happen again. "Did you know this house would go to him?"

She shook her head, a beat of sadness lighting her eyes. "I thought Annie would've sold it. I had no idea she was accruing properties for all the kids or that she'd play games with them."

"The trust?"

Her lips flattened. "It's not right. I mean, Lily and Eliot worked out even if they had to rush the marriage."

I was struck with a moment of confusion before I remembered. Alder's parents wouldn't know that Lily and Eliot had started as an arrangement. As far as my in-laws were concerned, Alder's youngest sister and her husband started as a love match like me and Alder.

"Violet and Evander sort of did too, and now you and

Alder." A line of concern creased her forehead. "I want nothing more than for my kids to be happy, but I'd like for it to be on their own timeline."

I wrung my hands together. She was a mom. She'd worry no matter what, but her concern added to my anxiety. Our rushed nuptials were because of the trust, but they wouldn't have happened without it. "May I ask if Annie was doing okay when she designed the trust?"

"Was she losing her mind?" Magnolia shook her head, her mouth pursed. "No. She got some romantic idea after hearing the guy West replaced. The late wife of Gentry King—the old owner of King Oil—left a trust for their four boys. They had to be married for a year before they were thirty or something before they got it."

"How'd that turn out?"

She released a gusty laugh. "Amazing. I guess the guys are blissfully happy, and Gentry has a ton of grandkids. He also remarried, and his wife is just as amazing."

Envy cut through my heart. Had either of them tried and failed at being married? I shuffled into the kitchen. "What do you all want to drink?"

"Alder had us order lemonade. I'll wait for that, and we went deluxe and requested paper plates and plastic silverware. No dishes or glasses for you to clean up."

I smiled my thanks. Lemonade. I used to always order lemonade to drink, but after having gestational diabetes with Laila, I had cut out all sweetened drinks. I had never regained the habit. Alder didn't know the story, but he'd ordered it last time and I had indulged.

I got my water glass and filled it up. Magnolia was at the table, still grinning at me like I was a dream come to life. From what Lily said, I just might be.

She was going to be heartbroken again. And it'd be

my fault. My stomach cramped as I sank into my chair. They had forgiven me so readily the first time. Everyone had seen how he'd changed once he had his own place and didn't have to listen to his parents. This time, I'd be leaving a suited-up CEO who had fast-tracked his life straight to the top. All I had to show since the divorce was a kid who had to be shuttled between homes, a few exes, and a ton of debt that proved how poor I was at deciding who I should and shouldn't settle down with.

"How are your parents?" she asked.

"Dad's good as far as I know. I think he's in Phoenix. Or Tampa. He moves around." Depending on where his girlfriend at the time wants to go. "Mom's in Grand Forks and happily retired."

"That's good to hear." Her expression filled with sympathy. "I'm really sorry about Lee."

The sudden twist in my heart stole my words for a breath. I blinked back tears. It wasn't often I talked to people who'd known my brother. Lee hadn't lived in a way that made him known and popular, so to get condolences from someone who'd known him brought some of the loss to the front. "It's still hard some days. I'll just randomly cry."

"It'll be like that forever probably."

I nodded. "I've been able to catch up with Violet and Lily. How are the others?"

"I'm afraid I can only tell you how they want me to think they're doing, which is always fine." She chuckled. "Jasper's a little closer now that he's taken over the Knight ranch in Buffalo Gully." She put her elbow on the table and rested her chin in her hand. "Alder's told me all about your job. I'm glad it's going well."

The pleasure that Alder had discussed me with his

parents couldn't be denied, but we were married. Of course he had talked about me. Magnolia had probably interrogated him. "Yes, it's a great environment to work in."

Her smile was knowing. "Alder said he ran into you at Reservoir Barrel and things just took off."

I had taken off much before *things* had. "Yes. It was like no time had passed." The truth of that wrapped around me like a warm blanket. My verbal filter readily switched off around him. He was so easy to talk to. He didn't patronize me. He didn't argue with my perception of events or people. Sometimes, he'd play devil's advocate, but then he'd give me room to change my mind. Alder made life easy. When he wanted. When I'd been worth it. "He's always been easy to talk to."

"Ha! To you maybe. Or when he's talking about you. Otherwise, that kid is like a fortress."

I smiled. *That kid.* Alder was thirty-seven. Eight months older than me.

She got up and moved to a closer seat. "I've seen the pictures of Laila you have in the living room, but can I see more?"

I picked up my phone. "Alder hasn't shown you any?"

"He said he was being respectful. Letting you lead with introducing her."

Yes. Introducing Laila to two people who'd be her grandparents would confuse her when they no longer were. Alder probably didn't have any photos of Laila, or even me, out of respect for our space and privacy. He hadn't said a thing about his mom asking me. He'd kept that pressure off me, just like he had about his conversations with his parents about our marriage.

The cozy sense of being cared for was dangerous.

Alder would lure me in again. Make me fall for him and then figure I was no longer worth the effort. Everyone wanted something out of a relationship. Some guys wanted a housemaid. Some looked for a vulnerable woman with resources to exploit. Others wanted a wife and any wife would do. There were those who wanted a love match.

Alder had needed a wife. Would he ever want a love match? My chest still ached for that young woman who'd had to make the hardest, most embarrassing, utterly isolating decision of her life. Now I had Laila to consider.

I paged through images. "I think it's best to take things slow with her. She's adjusting to bouncing back and forth between houses. And to Alder. But I'm happy to show you some pictures."

"I understand. We'll play it cool."

I pulled up last Halloween's pictures. Laila was a little witch with a green face and a giant smile. Grinning, I showed Magnolia. "She insisted on carrying a broom, but all I had was the one that's taller than her and plastic."

Magnolia chortled, delighted. She oohed and aahed over every picture I showed her, going back to when Laila was born. Jason had taken one of me with Laila snuggled on my chest. I was red-faced and looked half drunk with my sweat-soaked hair plastered against my forehead.

Magnolia sighed, a giant smile on her face. "She looked absolutely angelic. I bet she's just like you."

My appreciation for Magnolia grew. For all of the Dukes. I had missed them. The yearning to be a part of their big, hearty group had stuck with me over the years. I was different from them, but I had been a part of the crew. I'd had my own place.

They had welcomed my small family, accepting my

parents and brother as they were—socially awkward and a little distant. Jason's parents had amplified any awkwardness, and the nicer they tried to be, the worse it had gotten. The more attention they'd tried to give me, the less I knew how to handle it. His folks were sweet, but they didn't get me, just like their son.

Magnolia scanned the room, fondness written into her expression. "Different room or not, it's going to be so weird sleeping under this roof again."

Every muscle in my body tensed. The moment I'd been intentionally not thinking about for days—weeks even—was coming to pass. Tonight would be the first night in fifteen years I'd be in the same bed as Alder.

* * *

Alder

The cloud of tension clinging to Daisy dissipated as the night went on. My parents had always had that effect on her. I thought the lying would be hard for her, and maybe it was, but there was a comfort in slipping back into the familiar. Did she feel it too? She was next to me on the couch. I was in the corner and she was propped on me like she used to do.

All evening, she had laughed with my parents, told stories of Laila when she was a baby—and the real reason she didn't drink much lemonade, and she even swapped stories of when we were younger. She readily answered questions about her school and jobs, although she didn't go into nearly as much detail with them as she had with me.

She still trusted me. At least with her history. Not with her. Because while she wasn't a piece of plywood leaning on me, she was still tense. Hyperaware. Small muscles in her back flinched whenever I moved.

I didn't push the position. I kept my arm wrapped around her, but I didn't run my hands over her. My palm stayed flat on her side, but I inhaled her lemon-vanilla scent. She invaded every corner of my being, no longer a ghost but right here. With me.

Yet still so far away.

Mom yawned and slapped Dad's thigh. "Time for bed, West, my dear. Let's let them have some of the evening to themselves."

Daisy's stiffness returned. As Mom and Dad started to rise, she peeled herself away from me. I let her go, immediately missing her heat.

We exchanged "good nights" with Mom and Dad. Then without looking at me, Daisy walked stiffly toward the hallway.

I gave her space. We had discussed changing beds and that sleeping in the same bedroom tonight was necessary, but beyond that, the topic had been ignored. My only goal was to make her comfortable about the situation.

Each night since my parents had asked to stay with us had ticked by ever so slowly. Mitigated by being under the same roof as Daisy, time had still not gone fast enough until we were in the same bed again.

Ever so slowly, I was getting closer to her.

When I pushed into the bedroom, she crowded around me to get to the bathroom. I used the time it would take for her in the bathroom to change. When I swapped the beds, I had also moved the bulk of my clothing. I kept the rest in boxes. It made it easier to move around while renovating. If Mom and Dad peered into all the boxes in the spare rooms, it'd look like we were still unpacking.

I shucked my pants off and tugged a pair of green plaid flannel sweats on. I'd bake in them, but the long-sleeved shirt I was wearing would push me to sweltering limits. Daisy liked her fluffy blankets.

After I whipped the shirt off my head, I tossed it in the white plastic clothes basket in the corner. I missed, and the material puddled at the base.

Daisy opened the door and her gaze landed on my chest. The same stunned expression as the last time she'd seen my bare chest froze her face, except for the blush creeping along the apples of her cheeks.

I grabbed my lighter T-shirt off the bed. The movement broke her trance, and she blinked away, her gaze landing on my shirt on the floor. Her jaw went tight. "You missed."

I didn't like how she used a small reminder of how I used to be to shut me out, but I was also captivated by the way her loose gingerbread pajamas swallowed her up, leaving only her toes poking out. I'd rather have time to prove myself to her, one piece of dirty laundry at a time. "I know. I'll get it."

Her back ramrod straight, she marched to the other side of the bed.

I hadn't creeped on her during her bedtime routine, but we'd run across each other in the kitchen. I'd have remembered the gingerbread. I tugged my shirt over my head. "New PJs?"

"I got myself a Christmas gift." She tugged the covers back—only on her side.

"They look comfy." I didn't wait to see how she received the quasi-compliment. If she thought I was coming on to her, she might sleep on the floor. I picked up my fallen shirt and dropped it in the basket without even a sleeve hanging over.

When I finished in the bathroom and returned, Daisy was on her side, blankets to her chin, her lamp off and mine on. The overhead light in the room was off. So was the fan. The thick blinds were down all the way, and the walls glowed faintly. Daisy hadn't hung anything up yet. It might take her weeks or months to decide on something she'd hang and then never want to move again. If anything, she might leave them bare. The clean swath of wall probably soothed her.

The block pattern on her comforter matched the earthy brown shades of the blinds. Soft colors. Bold but in a subdued way, like the woman herself. I'd kept it for her, for us, to use. Like a security blanket. I approached my side of the bed, keeping an eye on Daisy. She didn't look at me. My stomach clenched. This was so damn familiar. This was exactly the future I had fucked up. Me crawling into a giant plush bed with her in this house.

I treasured this moment. It proved I wasn't past the point of rescue. That *we* weren't past the point of rescue.

Yet as I crawled in and she didn't move despite the dip of the mattress, the truth was clear. We were still so far away I could lose all progress.

Chapter Eleven

Daisy

My first sense of awareness was the deep, rhythmic breathing against my cheek. The second thing that registered was the darkness. Then that my alarm hadn't gone off yet.

These moments were my favorite. The quiet time before the chaos of the day. When we could just be, and I didn't have to worry about whether he'd listen to me today. I wasn't wondering where he was or who he was with. I could pretend nothing had changed once we'd said I do.

I nuzzled against the hot body and inhaled a shirt. When did Alder sleep in anything more than boxers?

I snuggled closer. More awareness sunk in. My alarm would go off soon. Damn eight o'clock labs. Tucking my hands between Alder's torso and the blankets, I banked as much of his heat as I could until I had to drive to Bismarck in the frigid wee hours of the morning—

Wait. I had a job.

I woke a little more. I had a husband, but not like this. We didn't sleep together. We didn't sleep in the same bed.

Agitation sped my heart rate up. So much for the last few minutes of peaceful slumber. Slowly I rolled away, turning as I went to put my back to the man I should not be cuddling with. Thankfully, he hadn't woken up.

Inhaling and exhaling, I willed my pulse to slow down. That annoying throb between my legs could go away too. I would not remember the lazy weekend mornings having sex. Those long nights when he'd try to break his record of giving me orgasms.

That was not helping the growing desire. My body knew damn well I was in bed with Alder Duke. His pheromones were pouring off him, and I was super susceptible. It'd been fifteen years since I'd had amazing sex.

What torture that had been. Knowing what sex could be like and falling short with each attempt at finding a partner for life.

Drowsiness took over. I had no idea of the time. My alarm could chime in two minutes or two hours. I kept my eyes closed.

The bed shifted. A small groan left Alder as he rolled. My eyelids flew open to stare at the dark wall. He was rolling closer.

Oh shit. Oh shit. Should I jump out of bed? Just sink to the floor? Get up early?

A hard arm banded around me. I held my breath. He'd wake up. He'd realize he was pressed against me, even closer than I had been plastered to him.

Desire built inside me like thunderclouds, one giant

puff stacking on top of another. Even my lungs started to ache.

With a contented grunt, he nuzzled his nose into the nape of my neck and inhaled deeply. His exhale tickled the hair at the back of my neck. I was on fire. Heat swept through my body and the blankets held all the heat in. Add in the burning log that was Alder and I would combust in T-minus five seconds.

But I didn't move.

I could feel every inch of him, including the ones pressed into my backside. God, I had missed him, and I had missed that.

I shifted, trying to use my foot to seek a break in the blankets and get some air, but all it did was make my bottom wiggle against his erection.

"Fuck, Daze," he murmured against my skin. He pushed against me, the hard erection of his grinding against my ass.

His hand started moving, burrowing. My breath stalled once again as his fingers found my waistband, then slipped between that and my skin.

"Alder," I whispered. Electricity zinged through my body, swooping and swirling.

Alder was touching me. Giddiness filled me. *At last!* rang through my head.

"Are you wet, baby?" His deep voice was an aphrodisiac.

My hips rocked, seeking more. No. This couldn't happen. He wasn't awake. "Alder."

"Yeah?" He pushed his hand farther down. My legs widened of their own accord. The disconnect between my mind and body grew even wider.

Hot lips pressed a kiss on the side of my neck. God, yes. More of that.

No!

"Alder, wake up," I snapped, keeping my volume down. If his parents in the bedroom right above us overheard, it'd only sell this thing. Not the logic I needed right now. "Wake up."

He stiffened on a sharp inhale. His arm got tighter and somehow that brought his fingers even closer to where I wanted them. So badly. Need pounded through me.

"I should stop," he finally said.

"Yeah."

One second went by. Another.

"Fuck, Daze. You feel so good. Like warm velvet."

"Alder," I groaned. Having him against me, his hand on me—so damn good.

"Do you need this?"

I couldn't lie when I was trying to figure out how I could get out of bed and accidentally bump my clit against his fingers. "It doesn't matter."

"I think it does."

My leg shifted wider.

"You need to come so hard, don't you?"

It was difficult enough to be strong during the day when I could hide in another room. Under the same covers and entwined together? Impossible. "Yes," I whimpered.

"Let me make you come, Daze. Just this once."

The longing inside of me could weep. Relief was so damn close. I half turned, my shoulder butting into his chest. I snaked my rogue leg over his and bent the one pressed to the bed.

"Nice and open for me." He dipped his fingers down, hitting my clit. Lightning crashed through me, waking up all my nerve endings. "And so fucking wet." He licked the tender spot under my ear, making me shiver. "Just like I knew you'd be."

I fisted the covers. Was he moving or was I? I rode his hand, but he also circled my tight nub just the way I liked it. He didn't ruin his rhythm. He provided the friction and he let me go.

"Alder," I moaned.

He kissed the base of my neck. "Say it again."

"Alder."

"You've had my name on your tongue every time you've gotten off, haven't you?"

There was no room to be ashamed. Pleasure filled every corner, growing stronger. I bowed my back and released the covers to grab the back of his head. I rolled my hips against him, and he continued nibbling that spot under my ear and along my neck that drove me wild. "I'm so close, Alder."

"Take your time. Ride that wave." He said it like neither of us wanted this to end. He couldn't read my mind, but I wanted this to last forever. I could stay on this crest of ecstasy for eternity.

"Oh god." I wouldn't be able to hold back an orgasm that was building this strong, but I had to stay quiet. "Oh my god."

"You're so hot you're going to burn me. Feel how powerful that is."

He wasn't inside me, but I clenched like he was. Like he'd thrust into me and I could hold on to him so tight I'd never let him go.

"Ride the wave." He kept his steady strokes, his voice

right at my ear. This was just between us. "Take it all just like I was in you, thrusting in and out." He ground against my ass.

Another ragged moan left me. I was strung tight and holding on so hard I was shaking, my breath thready. "I'm so close."

I clamped on to my bottom lip as pure unadulterated pleasure washed over me like a tsunami, stronger than it'd been in years.

"Alder." My whisper cracked. "Yes," I hissed. "Yes, yes, yes."

Finally.

I rode the climax as long as I could hold, until the trembling took over and I had to sag against the mattress. Finally.

Alder quit rubbing me, but he cupped my pussy, his hand warm and my wetness coating the both of us.

Nothing but our mingled, uneven breaths filled the room.

Reality pounded at the door of my brain.

Not yet. His hand was splayed on my belly and my leg was still on him. I was cozy and content. For once.

I waited until my heart rate came down. The satisfied thrum between my legs was some sort of code for *Alder Was Here.* Then the lust fog slowly cleared. Our marriage was an arrangement. We were putting a show on for his parents to keep from putting them in a hard spot having to validate our union at the end of the year. Being intimate would only muddy those lines and resurrect old feelings that had taken years to bury.

"We shouldn't have done this." I still didn't move.

"Why not?"

I chewed on the inside of my cheek. I hadn't been

ready to answer a frank question like that. The obviousness in the situation should've been clear. "We're not a couple. It'll be harder to leave at the end-of-the-year timeline."

The fingers of his hand tensed. "What if..."

I couldn't let him finish. I'd tormented myself with various outcomes and possibilities for too long. "There is no 'what if.' There already was, and it didn't work."

"We're different people now."

"I'm not, Alder. I'm not different, and that's why I'm still single."

He pressed a tiny kiss on the shell of my ear. "You're not single. You're married for the next eleven months. What about your pleasure?"

"What about it?"

"You needed that release."

"I've been doing just fine." I thought I had been. Until that orgasm proved how much pent-up energy had been inside me. Before my body whispered insidious things like *Just think how much better that would've been with his magnificent dick inside you?*

I had thought about it. I'd only ever thought about it each time I'd had sex over the years. And I was confident that Alder had not. He'd gone in and done his best with the women he'd dated, and he'd probably realized that he could get so much better than his boring ex-wife. He could land enthusiastic women who had no trouble getting out of their heads. Women who were more adventurous. More flexible. Fuck, I didn't know. Just better.

"I haven't been doing fine," he murmured.

I snorted. "I doubt that."

"You and I fit. Can't we just enjoy that for a while? Can't we be...casual?"

I'd never done casual a day in my life. Horribly awkward? Yes. All-in with hearts in my eyes? Absolutely. Cautious, but never casual. Irritation filled me, but not because Alder had asked. Because I wanted to say yes. "You know that's not me."

"No, you're right." He placed a kiss in my hair above my ear as he slipped his hand out of my pants. I let my eyelids fall shut. "You don't do casual."

I'd turned him down, but he'd only let me know he understood. My alarm chimed, saving me from the answer he knew. I jumped and slapped the screen of the phone to silence it.

"You can use the bathroom first," he said. Distance was between us once again. Like when we'd talked in his pickup. There was intentional space, and once again, it was because I'd asked for it.

I crunched up to a sitting position, swinging my legs down. The lingering arousal didn't dull as I directed my thoughts to work and getting ready for the day.

Damn. It was Friday. Not only did I have to face Alder tonight knowing he'd gotten me off this morning, but we had a full weekend together.

I could be strong. I'd have to be.

I grabbed the clothes I'd laid out last night and shuffled to the door.

"Daisy?"

I didn't answer him, but I stopped and looked over my shoulder. He was stretched out in bed. His erection probably made it too difficult to sit. "Yeah?"

"If you change your mind, I'm here. And I know exactly what you like."

That was exactly why I had to keep what space I could between us.

* * *

Alder

After our orgasmic morning together, I had gone to bed and found a row of pillows lining the middle of the bed, and that was the way it had been each night after. The fondling demarcation zone would still be up tonight.

I'd woken up in heaven only to be kicked back into purgatory. I had pushed too fast. A lonely man, one with a raging erection and the woman he loved in his arms, hadn't been thinking straight. I hadn't put her needs before mine. She'd been willing, and goddamn, I'd hopped on that train and hadn't cared where I got dumped.

Only I had been booted.

At least we still slept in the same bed. I might have woken up with my face buried in a taupe-colored pillow instead of her hair, but she hadn't restricted me to the floor.

There was a chance yet.

I'd take it slow. Daisy was worth it.

I finished cleaning up dinner in the kitchen. Daisy wiped off the table before disappearing into the living room. My parents were at Violet's. She was holding one last get-together before the baby arrived. Daisy and I had been invited.

"You can go to Violet's," Daisy said, settling into the

corner of the couch and tucking her feet under her. "Tell everyone I'm under the weather and wanted to go to bed early."

"I don't want to go." I'd gotten to spend Christmas with Daisy. I wasn't missing New Year's Eve. We'd had a late dinner, and it was only a few hours away. "It might surprise you that I'm not a night owl anymore."

"Alder. You love New Year's Eve."

I used to. Kissing random women at the stroke of midnight had never been my thing. After I'd started dating again, I might've tried for a couple of years before choosing to watch a movie and go to sleep before eleven. Snoozing through midnight was a lot better than forcing fun.

"I enjoyed New Year's Eve when we would play games and drink sparkling juice until midnight."

She cocked a brow and grabbed the remote. "We don't have sparkling juice. Or games that aren't a princess matching one."

"Sure 'bout that?" I grinned at her startled expression and stepped out of the room. I jogged upstairs and ducked into one of the empty rooms. I found the box I had packed Scrabble and checkers in.

On my way back to Daisy, I stopped in the mudroom and opened the door to the garage. I had put a bottle of sparkling grape juice in the garage to cool off. Until I installed a heater, it doubled as a fridge or a deep freeze in the winter, depending on the outside temperature. I hadn't bought a bottle of champagne. Juice was a throwback. A nod to our time together and we both liked it. Champagne might have too many romantic suggestions that would cause her to add another layer of pillows between us tonight.

I grabbed a couple of glasses and carried my armload to the living room. The TV wasn't on when I entered the living room. Daisy had her arms folded under her breasts, a militant but curious expression on her face. She'd changed into pajamas after dinner. I'd kept my jeans and flannel on.

"Up for a game of Scrabble?"

She sat forward. "Is that my game?"

"With the distinctive Q tile? Yes."

Happiness flickered in her eyes, but she suppressed it, like she didn't want me to see. Or she didn't want to get her hopes up about me. "Oh. You kept it."

"Checkers too. Want some juice?" My goal was to keep tonight light. Time with my wife was a precious commodity.

"When did you— You planned this?"

"I planned to have juice and relax. I'm going back to work soon."

The corner of her mouth twitched. "The next time I go to work, you're going to be my boss."

"Do your coworkers know?"

"Yeah, I told them. Not about the trust. Figured that was your business and not the best foot for you to start on."

Touched, I had to clench my fingers to keep from reaching for her hand. "Thank you."

She rolled a shoulder. "I basically told them what you told your parents. We reconnected and waiting seemed pointless."

I poured her a glass.

She gingerly took it from me. "I'm afraid to drink this on your nice couch."

Our couch. "We can always get another."

She sputtered over her first sip. "I can't just go buy new furniture. Not even if I have to assemble it myself."

She wouldn't have to. I set up the Scrabble board. "I have no emotional attachment to cushions."

"I'm getting one. It's like watching TV on a cloud."

I laughed and handed her the bag of tiles. "You go first."

She unfolded her legs and chose her tiles. "I haven't played this in forever."

"So, no seven-letter words right out of the gate?"

Her smile was wicked. "No promises."

That was more like it. We played two games of Scrabble. She won, like usual. Then two games of checkers. I won. Like usual.

"One more?" I asked, stacking the black and red game pieces.

She checked the time. "It's almost midnight. Three minutes."

I picked up the juice bottle and topped off our glasses with the remains. "You've only yawned five times."

Her blink was long. "I didn't plan on staying up."

"I'm glad you did."

She dropped her gaze to her glass. "Yeah."

"Thank you, Daisy. For sticking this out."

"I didn't have many other housing options," she said lightly.

"You would've figured something out."

She lifted her glass. "To having a place to live for the next year."

That toast wasn't good enough, but I wouldn't push it. "Here's to you, for rescuing a poor CEO and giving him a place to stay."

Her laughter chimed through the room. Her phone lit with an alarm. It was midnight.

She lightly tapped her glass against mine. "Happy New Year."

"Happy New Year, Daze."

We each took a drink. Her gaze skated around the room. I'd love a New Year's kiss, but we weren't there yet, and things were going to get uncomfortable if we lingered on the couch.

"You can use the bathroom first," I said. "I'll stay up until Mom and Dad get back."

"You sure?" She slid off the couch, eager to move beyond the awkward stage.

"Of course. Don't worry about the glasses and games. I'll get those cleaned up."

"Starting off the year doing all the work? I like it." She scooted around me. Before she disappeared down the hallway, she stopped. "I had fun tonight."

"So did I. Good night."

"Good night, Alder."

The bathroom door clicked shut a few seconds later. I was alone in the living room. We might not have kissed this New Year's Eve, but if I did everything right, all her kisses for future New Year's Eves would be mine.

· · ·

Mom and Dad were scrolling through their phones on the couch. We'd all slept in this morning after our late night celebrating—or board gaming. Now we were waiting for Jason to drop off Laila. Daisy was busy in Laila's room, arranging and rearranging her furniture as if

I hadn't returned everything last week exactly where it'd been before I had cleared the room. As if she hadn't already checked to make sure the room would pass inspection. She wasn't avoiding me, but her stiffness was ever present, a little less today after our game night.

Just as tires crunched in the snow outside, Daisy appeared and veered straight for the door. Jason had been informed about the visitors, but he'd wanted to drop Laila off himself. The guy was likely being nosy, but since he was also watching out for his kid, I couldn't fault him.

Daisy opened the door and waved. Energy vibrated through her. She was excited to see Laila and probably a lot nervous about how it'd go between our facade and Laila's natural suspicion of strangers.

"Mommy!" Laila plowed through the door and flung herself into Daisy's arms.

Daisy laughed and embraced her tight. I hung back, by where my parents had risen from the couch. Jason stepped inside, his gaze sweeping the room. Instead of the one suitcase Laila had left with, he dropped another duffel bag.

Laila broke away and dove for the new bag. "Look what I got, Mommy." She started pulling out stuffed animals. A red panda. An otter. A tiger.

"We went to the zoo yesterday," Jason explained. "Ma paid for a room at a hotel with a pool over the weekend."

Laila grinned, then her gaze fell on my parents. Her smile froze. She hugged the tiger close to her chest, her gaze guarded. "Who are they?"

Stress knotted up my gut. It was one thing to dislike me. That was understandable, and I could take it. I had to win over Daisy, and I wasn't going to do it by being fake to Laila. Besides, I'd like Daisy's daughter to genuinely like me, but other than being a distant uncle, I had no idea what to do around kids.

Daisy straightened and put her hand on Laila's shoulder. "These are Alder's parents, Weston and Magnolia Duke."

"You can call me West," Dad said and grinned. "Just not North or South."

Laila's little face scrunched up.

Jason chuckled. Dad crossed the living room and shook his hand. "Nice to meet you. Jason, right?"

He nodded. Mom was right behind Dad, taking Jason's hand next.

"So nice to meet you," Mom said. "I hope your week with your parents went well. Looks like it was a blast."

Gratitude wrapped around me like a warm blanket. I could count on them to make sure at least Jason was comfortable about this whole scenario.

"Eh." Jason lifted his ball cap and set it on his head. "It was fun, but I'm ready for a normal schedule now. You know how it is."

Mom laughed. "I don't, but I'm sure a few of my kids do."

Jason joined in with her laughter. The rigid set of Daisy's shoulders eased, and even Laila's expression relaxed.

"They're really grateful they got to spend so much of the holiday with us," Jason said to Daisy. "Thank you." She gave him a small nod, and he squatted. "Until next time, my girl."

Tears filled Laila's eyes, and she flung her arms around him. "Do you have to go, Daddy?"

"Yeah, I do," he said sadly, and goddammit, I hated this as much as them.

A month ago, jealousy would've gnawed away at me over this guy, but now I felt sorry as hell for him. He loved his kid, and whatever things had been like between him and Daisy, he at least loved the idea of a family.

"Your mom has missed you," Jason said to Laila, "and it's lunchtime. I'm sure everyone is waiting to eat."

I caught Daisy's gaze. Her brows knit together with a question. I dipped my head.

"Hey, Jason," she said. "If you don't have to rush off, you can have lunch with us. We're only having sandwiches, but they're, like, gourmet ones."

"I watched how a popular sandwich place in Billings makes them," Mom said. "We add olive oil and salt. Makes anything better."

Jason glanced at all of us, his expression stunned. "I've been spoiled with good food." He straightened his hat but managed to make it crooked. "Hate to go back to making my now plain sandwiches."

Mom squeezed Dad's biceps. "Let's go get it all ready."

"You didn't have to," Jason said, glancing between me and Daisy.

I shrugged like it wasn't a big deal, but it was. If I could carve out a real relationship with Daisy, Jason was part of the Laila equation. I'd rather know him than feel like a stranger. Each time I met him, I understood why he and Daisy had lasted so long. "The more the merrier. My parents wouldn't have had six kids otherwise."

Jason let out a surprised chuckle and shrugged out of his coat. Laila rattled off the names of her stuffed animals.

Daisy smiled and nodded but met my gaze again, gratitude in her eyes.

She'd eventually realize there was nothing I wouldn't do for her. Except quit trying to win her back.

Chapter Twelve

Daisy

I tucked Laila in and gave her a kiss on the cheek.

"Another story?" she asked, her eyelids droopy and her voice groggy.

"We already read four. You need some rest." Her week of adventures had worn her out, and now that she was back in her own bed, she'd been ready to conk out for hours. The new carpet had gotten nothing but an approving grunt from her. Tomorrow, she'd return to daycare, and I'd go back to work. Alder would too.

Right now, he was upstairs tearing out carpet. I could hear the scrapes along the ceiling. He was working in the room above Laila's. His parents had gone, and Laila had actually high-fived them on their way out.

Leave it to Weston and Magnolia to win over my naturally suspicious daughter within minutes. Heck, they'd made fast friends with Jason. He and Weston and Alder had talked all things oil industry for the two hours he'd been over. By the time Jason had left, Laila had come to terms with the transition from Dad-time to Mom-time.

I reshelved the book. Laila's eyes were closed and her mouth was slack. I closed her door and brushed my suddenly sweaty palms down my pants. Thunks of tools hitting the floor resonated through the ceiling. Should I tell him Laila was in bed so he'd keep it quiet?

She'd sleep through everything, and then I'd be left with the reminder I was alone with Alder. His parents weren't here to provide some sort of separation while also throwing us closer together.

Tonight, I would be going to bed alone in his absurdly comfortable king-sized bed.

I wandered into the living room. It was too early for me to go to bed. I'd gotten such better sleep in the last five nights that I wasn't tired.

Five nights of solid slumbering because there was a furnace in bed who breathed so deep and so evenly that I went under with him despite the pillow wall. The only thing that had robbed me of some sleep was when I woke up needy, my body demanding. Alder was right there. Why couldn't I let him make me feel good again?

The stupid thrum was starting between my legs. It didn't take much at all. Thinking of him. Seeing him. Hearing him. I was ready to go. There'd been more than a few long baths and cold showers since that first morning we'd woken up together.

I went to the couch and huddled in the corner. Alder must've figured that Laila was in bed. The tool thumping had ceased.

He didn't come downstairs.

I tucked away my disappointment. How quickly had

I gotten used to sitting snug against him while chatting with his parents? At the table, he hadn't sat on the end. He'd been next to me there, too, with his parents across from us. I'd had his company. Watching an old British series about serial killers was a lot lonelier now.

I yawned. Finally. I was tired enough to go to bed. I shut off the TV and stood. Just as I crossed the kitchen, Alder came down the stairs. His gaze softened when he spotted me.

My feet stopped of their own accord. I had him to myself, if only for a few moments. "Thanks. For today."

"Don't mention it. I'm glad it went as well as it did." His smile was all in his eyes. "It'd be a long year if it hadn't."

"Right." I let out a weak chuckle. "Well...good night."

The humor in his eyes was extinguished. His gaze flicked to look down the hallway. "Sleep tight."

"I will. It's a nice bed." I winced. "You might not have the best night."

"Oh, come on. Dad only said that the bed upstairs made him feel eighty-five instead of sixty-five."

Laughter burst out of me. "Then I should feel sixteen again sleeping in yours?"

"If you were sixteen again, we wouldn't have been trying to have my parents see us go to bed together." Heat lit his eyes. "I would've been cornering you everywhere I could in this place."

"And out in the shop."

He grinned. "And the shed."

Tingles spread over each inch of my skin. I couldn't keep going along this route or I'd remember how we used the excuse of taking the horses for a ride so we could make love in the pasture and get mosquito bites on our asses. "Until Clover busted us when she was refilling the chicken feed."

"The feeder was probably full. Clover was just nosy."

"All your siblings were nosy."

"They still are. Poppy and Clover are constantly asking how this is going. Twice a day before Mom and Dad left."

I laughed. This lightness between us was just like before— No. It was better than before. When we were teens, I was self-conscious for so much of our relationship. I couldn't believe a guy like Alder, the guy all the other girls wanted, was with me. Me! I hadn't had attention like his ever. Then after we'd married, there was the resentment flowing between us, a steady back and forth, each fueling their own.

But this time we were on equal footing. I had my life. He had his. We were working together and then we'd go our separate ways. Living in the same town. Working at the same company.

The refinery was like a small city most days. Employees commuted from the surrounding areas within a fifty-mile radius, sometimes more. But Coal Haven was small. I'd see Alder around. Maybe he'd hang at one of the downtown bars.

Except he hadn't yet. It'd only been a month, but he hadn't gone out unless it was to pick up food from Rattler's. He didn't park himself in front of the TV either. Alder hadn't quit working on the house since we'd moved in.

"I'm done with the TV," I said. "You can watch it."

He checked his watch. "Nah. I'm going to bed too."

He swatted his stomach. "Damn nerves are getting to me."

As if I couldn't be endeared to him more. "Butterflies in your stomach for your first day?"

"Yes, dammit. I was just coming down to get my lunch ready."

"Hmm. You're packing in? I guess I thought the top always just catered in or went out."

"Then it'd be a lunch hour and a half."

"Not if it's catered."

"I don't make that much money."

"Yeah, you do." I snorted. "If I made what you do, I wouldn't have worried about a place to live. I could've paid off all the debt I got stuck with in a few years."

His gaze sharpened. "What debt?"

Shit. I swallowed my rising shame. "Student loans."

I could practically see the calculations running through his head. We'd had to split the two years of loans from when we'd been married, leaving only two years I'd had to get loans in my name only. Those should be almost paid by now.

"Vehicle loan," I added.

"And what else?" His voice was hard. "Did someone get you into trouble?"

"No."

"Daisy."

"Alder." I started for the hallway.

"I know it's not my business, but I care about you."

I turned, my fingers clutching the ends of my sleeves. "I know you do. You're a good man, Alder, but this isn't your problem." It was just another story of how I had messed up my life, and I had to deal with it.

"I might be able to help."

I made a point of looking around the house. "You already are. Have a good day at work."

I scurried to the bedroom just shy of a sprint. I closed myself in and took a deep breath. He might not let the subject go. He'd already walked in on Jason's near meltdown because I hadn't been able to leave him when I should've. Alder didn't need to know about more instances when I should've known better. Especially since he was the prime example of how I'd given up too soon.

Chapter Thirteen

Daisy

It was Alder's first day of work. I couldn't deny it was weird to coast down the driveway and his pickup wasn't parked outside. Nor was it in the garage. I should be relieved. He wasn't around to torment me with his strong body and the way he took care of the house. Of me. And Laila.

We'd left at the same time this morning, but when I shouldered through the door to the house and held it open for Laila to go through, the smell of chicken stew wafted across my nostrils, teasing my stomach and making it growl.

Laila heard the noise and giggled. She flung her arms at her sides to get the sleeves of her coat down. "Alder here?"

"No. He's working." The former CEO used to work long hours. Cameron Barron's expensive pickup would often be one of the last ones in the parking lot though he had advocated for normalized working hours for the rest of us. Alder would do the same. He was at the top now. He could slack off. The refinery practically ran itself. Other than meetings and playing oil industry politics, he could work from home. He could take off whenever he got the urge.

Something told me he wouldn't.

While we ate dinner, Laila chatted about her day and reported what other kids had gotten for Christmas. "They liked Ottery."

"Good." The names for her new stuffed animals were very much on-brand for her naming system. Ottery. Red. Tigger. As we talked, the quiet house screamed loudly in my ears. There was no Alder shuffling through the kitchen, no pounding of nails or whirring drill. He had a job that wasn't caring for this house. Or me.

How would that change things?

I helped Laila get ready for bed and tucked her in.

"Mommy, 'member the zoo trip?" Her little arms clung to Ottery.

We'd gone to the zoo in both Bismarck and Minot before. "The one with your dad or with Grandma?"

"Gramma. We saw an otter, right?"

"Yes, we did." The otters were always the highlight, but Laila loved everything about the zoos she'd been to.

"I took a picture."

She'd taken a ton of pictures and had begged my mom to print them out. We'd gotten a hundred images of various animals. I'd had to buy an album just for the one zoo trip, but Laila still enjoyed looking through it.

"Where is it?" she asked.

"Probably stored away."

"Oh." Disappointment crossed her face and she rolled over, flopping her otter to the other side.

Once she was asleep, I wandered the house. A deep sense of loneliness settled over my shoulders. Alder was still at work. Or maybe out. With someone.

He said he would act as a married man, but the old anxiety settled in. Just because he was married didn't mean women wouldn't try to cross the line. What if he met the one who was worth it? The one who'd be worth losing the house over?

I'd have to find a place to live.

I wanted my year. In the house. It was the house tearing my heart up.

I pushed my hair off my face. I had to distract myself. Tonight was the first of many with just me and Laila. I could watch a show, but the restless energy inside of me needed an outlet. It was dark and cold outside. The upstairs was Alder's domain. So what should I do?

There were some boxes in the hallway closet. Alder had painted the inside at some point in the last few weeks, but the boxes were my stuff. If I was only in the house for a year, I didn't need to unpack. If I stayed to rent the place from Alder, I would have time later.

The zoo album was in one of those boxes. I flipped on the hallway light and pulled one out. I opened the top and flipped it closed right away, but I'd seen all the contents. The fake flowers from our first wedding. The knife with the white opalescent handle that we had cut our cake with. His bow tie and my garter. We had done the auction thing with the garter to raise money and he'd bought it.

Happy wedding memories pounded at my brain, but I shoved the box to the side and grabbed another. It was one of the photo albums my dad had off-loaded on me from his childhood, along with more of his parents' time together. They were stacked on top of the albums my grandma, my mom's mom, had given me before she had died. I had become the repository of photo albums filled with people I couldn't recognize, didn't remember, or had never met.

I pushed that box back into the closet and slid out another. It was mine. I dug through the pile until I found the one Laila had asked about. Good. I set that aside and then picked up an older one. It opened to a page with me and my brother standing by our bikes. We'd been riding around the block, and Mom had popped up to test her new camera.

Tears pricked the backs of my eyes. I folded myself down to the floor and pulled the album to my lap. Me and Lee with the dog we'd had growing up. Me and Lee at the house my parents had bought in Coal Haven. I was short, barely coming to his shoulder. He was gangly, and his smile was filled with crooked teeth. He'd hated the braces he'd worn in high school. Lee on the couch with a cast on his arm when he was nine. He'd been playing at the babysitter's and another kid had jumped on him.

Hot tears poured down my cheeks. The faint vibrations of the garage door opening traveled through the floor, but I didn't move.

I hadn't cried in a while over Lee, and there was no boxing the emotions back up. But I also didn't have to. Alder wouldn't crowd me. He wouldn't tell me everything was okay. It wasn't okay. There would always be a piece of me missing from life, and sometimes I just had to fucking cry about it.

Steady footsteps sounded through the kitchen and

paused. I sniffled and wiped my cheeks. Then clothing rustled as he turned into the hallway.

The warmth of his presence surrounded me as he approached. I couldn't look at him. Just because I was comfortable with him didn't mean I wanted a corporate god towering over a sobbing me.

"Hey," he said quietly as he sat down next to me.

"Hi." More tears fell. I slumped against his shoulder. He put an arm around me and tucked me into his side, like he sensed I didn't mind the connection this time. I was surrounded by his new-leather-and-cedar scent and the buttery-soft fabric of the suit coat he had unbuttoned.

He took the photo album off my lap, set it on his, and turned the page. I wept as quietly as I could while he flipped through.

"Your dad's hair was wild in those days," he said.

A giggle left me, a relief compared to the grief. I traced Dad's image with his bouffant of hair. "It's no wonder I ended up in the oil industry with all that goop he used for it."

"Good thing he didn't smoke."

Another soft laugh gusted out of me. I glanced up at his strong jaw, the dark stubble already dusting it after a long day. My fingers itched to trace along his cheek and over his lips.

"This was always my favorite picture of you as a kid." His rough voice caressed my eardrums and continued further.

My tears were drying up, and the grief was changing to nostalgia. I peeked at the photo he was talking about. I was smiling wide, my two front teeth missing. A giant Christmas gift was open in front of me. A Barbie. The one where she was a doctor, but I had never played with her as that. With the lab coat she'd come in, she'd been a scientist. That was all my imagination had ever made her. "Lee got a GI Joe that year. I used to pretend that it was dating my Barbie."

His chuckle rumbled right through my cheek. "I always liked that picture because I thought that was what our kids would look like. A scrappy little kid with your smile." He looked at me, our faces inches apart. "Your brains and ambition."

Longing and loss mixed together. We'd discussed kids, but mostly that we had wanted to wait until I was at least done with school. I should veer far away from this discussion. We couldn't live in the past, but at the same time, it was a little like the possibility was still there. We were married after all. "What would they have gotten from you?"

"My charm?"

I nudged him. "Your stubbornness."

"I'm not the stubborn one in this relationship."

Relationship. God, I liked the sound of that. "I think your kid will get your dark hair. And your hazel eyes."

The corner of his mouth lifted and his gaze stroked over his face. "Am I that overpowering?" His tone was teasing.

"You're always overpowering, Alder. It's hard to resist you."

"You have resisted me."

"Yet here I am."

Fondness entered his eyes. "Crying on the floor."

"I was lonely and took a trip down memory lane looking for an otter picture from the zoo." I wasn't prepared for my honesty, but sincerity poured out of me. I was lonely, and he listened. "How was work?"

"I have some long days ahead as I learn the ropes," he said quietly.

"I know. It's... You don't have to explain."

"I want to. This isn't like before."

"Neither is this marriage."

"I'm not like before. I'm better."

I wasn't. "I know you are. You'll make some woman a really good real husband."

His expression turned pained. He blinked away and worked his jaw back and forth. "I don't know what I think about my wife telling me that."

"We're not staying married after this, Alder," I said quietly. No matter how much my brain tried to get me to think about it. Alder 2.0 was something to behold. He was driven, considerate, insanely hot, and incredibly sweet. He had a job he'd brushed off as a possibility when we'd been married. After his dad had gotten the CEO position at King Oil and they had moved away, he had stayed behind. People had joked with Alder about whether he was next. He was already working in the oil fields and that was how Weston Duke had started. Alder would laugh and say, "Yeah, right."

His big heart shone, softening the brown in his eyes. "Why?"

The word was a quick stab to my chest. He had to know why. Anger sparked behind my sternum. He knew. He'd been there. "I can't go through that again."

"You don't trust me," he said simply.

"We're different people, Alder."

"I'm still the guy who's in love with you."

My world slowed to a stop. In love with me? It was

too soon. He couldn't. I scooted away from him, but I couldn't go far. My hip bumped into a stack of photo albums. The books toppled, noisy in the quiet hallway. "You aren't. You're in love with what we had." Just like I was.

I pushed a few albums into the closet and haphazardly stacked the others onto them. They slipped and slid until I had to get on my hands and knees to arrange everything.

I peeked at Alder out of the corner of my eye. He had bent his legs and draped his arms over his knees. He wasn't looking at me, but the muscle in his jaw clenched and unclenched. "You can't deny what we have. That morning in bed was only more proof."

My face grew hot, my cheeks burning. "It was a mistake."

"It wasn't, and you know it. Our chemistry is as strong as ever. We're good. We're doing good."

"We're roommates."

He caught my eye, his gaze wounded. "I look forward to the moment you walk through the door. I love watching you with your daughter. You can't imagine how much it soothes me to walk through the kitchen and see you watching those murder shows."

"Serial killer documentaries," I said woodenly, as if that'd distract me from his words.

"I fucked up back then, Daisy. I was scared of growing up, of being an adult, and failing so miserably. I was so damn scared that I let you go, and that was a mistake."

"I wasn't enough to make you change." Had I given him enough time to?

"I would've."

My inhale was sharp. The truth of his statement stabbed me right between the ribs. Would he have changed eventually? Had I gotten too frustrated too soon? I couldn't have. "We weren't soulmates. Or I would've been enough for you."

It was a low blow. I knew that. But it was how I'd felt for so long. Now that I said it, the grown woman in me didn't completely agree. But she couldn't disagree.

A divot formed between his brows like he was in pain. "Fuck, Daisy. You were everything. You still are."

I pushed off the floor. I'd throw my body against the door to get it to shut. I had to get away from a hurting Alder. I shoved the door shut. Albums were in the way. I hip-checked the door. Alder didn't move.

"Do you dread coming home to me? Did you look forward to when I came home from work?"

The door latched. I kept my hand on the cool wood, staring at the swirling grains.

"Tell me you didn't," he insisted. "That you don't wonder how good we could be together. Tell me that you don't wish this was real. Tell me the truth, and I'll drop it."

I needed him to drop it. But he was playing dirty. I struggled to lie. The aggravating man knew how hard it was for me. I could talk my way around stuff, but outright lying was physically painful. All I had to say was that I didn't want him. I was over him.

The words refused to form on my tongue.

I could not go down this road with him. My heart had been shredded. I'd failed two classes. I'd had to take summer school after breaking down in front of my advisor. I'd gotten a job as a phlebotomist just so I had a better chance at getting the internship in the lab after they saw my transcripts. I'd gone from a 4.0 GPA to a 2.5.

I had even more to lose. A kid to take care of. I had a job, and I would not find another without moving—away from Laila's dad and her daycare.

"Tell me, Daze," he said in a hoarse voice.

If I couldn't lie, then what? A future with Alder wasn't unknown. I knew how it ended.

What if it could be different? What if he was the man I had wanted back then? What if...

He'd asked for an explanation, and I couldn't find one, or I might tell him yes, I watched the clock. I had liked seeing him walk through the door. I liked going to work, knowing he was at home.

We were more than in the same zip code. We were at the same company. We lived under the same roof. But I was still that girl who had given up too early and had stayed too long. All it had taught me was that I couldn't be trusted when it came to Alder. Only heartbreak waited for me.

"Mommy!" Laila cried from her room.

I jumped and gasped. Alder put his head down.

"I have to..."

I slipped into Laila's room. "It's okay, hon."

"I had a nightmare," she said in a groggy voice.

"It's all right. I'm here." I sat with her until well after she'd fallen back asleep. I heard Alder's movements on the other side of the door as he got up. The closet door clicked open, I assumed he adjusted the albums. A few minutes later, the door closed and his footsteps sounded above us. Even then I stayed longer.

How could I avoid the man when I didn't want to?

Chapter Fourteen

Alder

I stepped into the empty house. It had been dark when I drove up. It was Friday, and I calculated the days. It was Jason's weekend. The weather was shit, and she should be home by now.

A month had gone by since Daisy couldn't admit that she wanted me as much as I wanted her.

Stubborn woman.

I hung my coat up and shrugged out of my suit jacket. Loosening my tie, I wandered to the counter. No note that she'd taken off for the weekend like last weekend when she took Laila to Grand Forks to see her mom. Cool relief slowed my pulse. She'd be home, and that was good for more than that I wanted to see her. Between my hours and her early bedtime, she was like glimpsing a unicorn these days.

The wind outside howled. A few weeks ago, the weather channel had predicted a mega storm with power outages, dangerous conditions, and maximum snow impact. Three inches and some wind later, I'd heard it had gone farther north than expected. This storm must also be stretching farther north than predicted. The towns along the South Dakota border were being told to watch out. Yet here we were, in the middle of North Dakota, watching out.

I had bashed through a drift that had already formed at the end of the drive. How would her yellow pickup do? I pictured it hung up, like a lemon slice on the side of a glass.

I should go out and shovel before she got stuck. The snowblower was in the garage, and there was a blade for the lawnmower that I had brought from the last house, but it'd be faster to go shovel it.

I jogged upstairs and changed into jeans and a heavy, crewneck sweatshirt. I had overalls downstairs in the mudroom closet I could toss on. It hadn't started snowing yet, but the wind was brutal.

My phone buzzed repeatedly. I hit the bottom of the stairs and dug it out of my pocket.

Daisy. Shit. Was she already out of town and decided to give me a courtesy call? Wouldn't she just text?

"Hey," I answered.

"Alder?" Worry thickened her voice. "I'm stuck."

I stuffed my feet into my work boots. The coveralls could wait. My urgency was too strong. "Where?"

"At the end of the road. My tail end is sticking out where it can be hit by someone who can't see shit in this visibility."

"Stay put. I'll be right there." I rushed into the garage and punched the button on the door opener. Flakes of snow rushed in as the garage door lifted.

As quickly as I could, I loaded my pickup with a tow rope and a shovel. I fired up the pickup and backed out, flipping it into four-wheel drive. More short drifts had built up along the driveway, but my view sucked. The snow had begun, and it was getting heavier by the second.

Daisy's headlights cut through the haze of flakes. The light wavered as the wind blew varying amounts of snow across the beams. Movement around the hood made me shake my head.

Daisy was not staying put. She must've had a shovel in her pickup, and she was working on the worst of the drift around the driver's tire. The pickup was too small to have any power and didn't even have all-wheel drive.

"Get in the car," I called, wading into the storm. Cold cut through the denim of my jeans and snaked through my coat. I tucked my chin into the collar. I should've put more layers on. "I'll hook it up. Once you're free, you should be able to follow me." My pickup would break all the drifts.

She paused, her pale hair getting whipped around her face. She finally nodded and hopped behind the wheel.

I didn't bother with shoveling. The drift was only high enough to hang her up, but I could drag her through without doing much damage. I'd rather hurt her truck and pay to repair it than have both of us freeze our asses off.

The mound had only given us a little resistance. I tugged her ride free, then got out and unhooked everything. Daisy's lights gleamed in my rearview mirror as we drove to the house.

Drifts were already piling up in front, but we both got parked just fine.

Inside, Daisy stomped snow off her boots and brushed her jeans off. "I'm going to have to change."

"Have you eaten yet?"

She popped up, her eyes wide. "Oh, uh. I'm fine."

I gave her a "don't be stubborn" look. "I can throw in a lasagna."

"I'll get a sandwich or something."

"Jesus, Daisy. Can you quit avoiding me?"

She stiffened and planted her hands on her hips. "I am not—" My expression must've called her on her lie. "I'm not that hungry." She was too; I knew it. "And I got groceries yesterday in case it stormed."

Was I stormed in all weekend with Daisy? Alone?

It took an inhuman amount of effort to keep a Cheshire grin from spreading across my face.

I'd make sure she couldn't avoid me.

* * *

Daisy

When Alder had asked if it was butter or olive oil that my mom used to spread across the garlic bread she made, I gave in. My stomach was growling up a storm and the lasagna smelled amazing.

"Dinner's ready," he called from the kitchen.

I shivered as I rolled off my bed and stuck my phone in my pocket. I'd been hiding in my bedroom so much I was tempted to buy another TV to put on my dresser. They were cheap enough, but I could also use that money to put a nick in my mountain of debt. Putting what would've been rent money toward it was slowly chipping away at the total.

Rubbing my arms, I strode down the hallway. I was still chilled from my brief excursion in the snow, and a hot, filling meal was a siren's call.

Alder was too, dammit.

I hadn't seen much of him in weeks, and it'd been hard. Even Laila had been asking about him, like she was worried about his well-being. During our trip to Grand Forks last weekend, she asked if he felt okay or if she should draw him a picture of an otter. I'd told her of course, but if my daughter thawed toward Alder, then what would I do? She'd be sad to leave when the year of marriage was up, and I'd already made her so, so sad when I left Jason.

I tabled the worry for now. It was winter. Alder was fine. When Laila understood that, her sympathy would melt like snow in spring.

Only we were in the middle of winter, and the wind was battering the house. I might be stuck with Alder for the night. Or two nights. A thrill zinged around my belly, but I took a centering inhale. I entered the kitchen, passed my chair at the table, and went to the dining room window.

"It's howling out there." Alder's reflection was visible in the glass, snatching my attention off the drifts piling in the yard light. He set the pan of breadsticks down, then propped his hands on the tabletop, his gaze on me. Warmth swirled through my blood. "I hope Jason and Laila are staying in tonight."

"Yeah. All weekend. He's getting more comfortable having her by himself and not feeling like he has to entertain her all the time."

His gaze dropped to my ass. I stayed where I was for another heartbeat, soaking up his attention on me. I'd called him, and he'd been out in minutes, ready to solve my problem.

I had another problem. An Alder one. I'd had it for years.

I should be in my room, but I sat at my spot. Alder took his at the far end of the table.

A giggle left me. He narrowed his eyes at me.

"How's the weather over there?" Lame joke, but I kept chuckling as I grabbed a fluffy, shiny breadstick. I bit into it and groaned, my eyes rolling back.

"Christ, Daisy. You can't make a dad joke and then make that sound. My dick doesn't know what to do."

My shocked inhale propelled crumbs down my throat and I started coughing. His unrepentant smile only made him look hotter in his crewneck sweater and jeans. The way his hair was mussed could've been used in a salon poster.

I shook my head and downed some water.

"Just kidding," he said. "My dick is never confused around you." I sputtered again, and he held his hands up like he was innocent. He wasn't. Not at all. "I'll stop so you don't choke."

I took a steady breath to make sure I could speak without coughing a lung out. "I'm surprised you didn't make some crack about how you have something for me to choke on."

"That's a given." He pushed his plate close to the lasagna pan and dug a cheesy piece out. "Just tuck that knowledge away."

"You think it might come in handy?"

His wicked smile sent desire ping-ponging through

my body. "Handy is a little different, but you always were a fast learner."

My cheeks flamed, but I chomped on a breadstick before I said something else we could make sound sexual as if we were two middle schoolers.

After a few minutes of eating, I poked my fork into the top noodle. I hated saucy lasagna and this was just right, with extra cheese through each layer, and the meat was actual sausage and not small bits of gravel. "This isn't store-bought, is it?"

"I made some freezer meals when you guys were gone. I kept meaning to tell you that you could throw one in whenever you wanted."

"You made freezer meals?" He'd always been a good cook but never like this.

"Couldn't really do it when it was just me."

"Then what did you do?" Dine out with some sexy woman in a dress that barely covered her ass cheeks? The jealousy turned the cheese sour on my taste buds.

"Grabbed something. I also got to know a lot of the delivery people in Billings. One said they fought for my order."

"You're a good tipper?"

He just shrugged and grabbed another breadstick. Which he'd also made homemade.

"I'm going to be exhaling nothing but garlic all night," I said.

"If you're trying to warn me off, it's not working."

I rolled my eyes. He had always enjoyed giving me a hard time, but after our talk in the hallway, I knew he was serious. Desire ignited inside me.

It didn't matter! I would not test how much garlic breath he could tolerate.

But if we both had it?

I stuffed a big forkful of lasagna in my mouth. I couldn't be turned on when I was chewing.

The thrum between my legs begged to differ.

I shifted. How many nights had I stayed up late wondering if I could give myself as strong of an orgasm as he had given me?

All of them. All of the nights since he'd done it.

"I'll clean up," I said and hopped up once I was done. He still had half a breadstick left.

"There's dessert," he said like he was talking me off a ledge.

"Of course there is," I snapped sarcastically. I blew out a breath. He was caring for me. I could at least not be rude. "Sorry."

"I can take it, Daisy," he said calmly. "Just like you can take the salted caramel cookies out of the cupboard."

"Don't you lose your temper anymore?" The question dropped heavy between us. I set my plate on the island, afraid to look at him. Every time I did, my heart wanted to reach out to him with both hands and never let go.

His amber eyes turned stricken. "No."

"Never?"

"We fought enough for a lifetime."

A sudden sob escaped, made a hiccup sound, and disappeared. We had used up our quota and then we'd been done. "Yeah."

I put my dishes in the dishwasher. He brought his and I added those, keeping my back to him. He dug the cookies out and set them on the counter. I could take one to my room. Then I'd roll around on my bed, trying to get comfortable while watching a show on my phone.

He'd do some project around the house because apparently he never sat down anymore.

Those nights, early in our marriage, when we watched a movie together had been...the best. One of the many things I missed.

Facing a night in my bedroom while getting snowed in would feel as empty as it sounded. "Do you..." My courage faltered.

He tilted his head. Was that a spark of hope in his eyes?

"Do you want to watch a movie or something? I've been bored spitless lately."

"I don't know. That sink upstairs won't unclog itself." His tone was sort of teasing but also like he was giving me an out.

"One night won't hurt you. Just relax for once. You can use the bathroom downstairs." I picked up a cookie and took a small bite, chewing like a rabbit, worried he'd tell me no and I'd have to run away.

He grabbed the whole container of cookies and tucked them under his arm. "No serial killers or I might not be able to sleep alone."

I thought of a hundred titles that would scare us both in bed together, but I kept them to myself. I had some sense of self-preservation. "I'll let you pick."

* * *

Alder

.   .   .

We'd sat on opposite ends of the couch. She had remained burrowed under a blanket. Now she was asleep against the armrest, her feet stretched out and wedged under my butt. I could stay like this forever.

I shut the TV off. We'd started with the original *Twister*, then worked up to *Twisters*. I might've played dirty getting to choose what we watched. *Twister* ended with the couple getting back together, and *Twisters* had a cowboy in a tight, wet T-shirt.

I knew Daisy's kryptonite.

She'd made it through that scene before she'd drifted off.

I rested my head on the back of the couch and soaked it all in. I was with her again. She'd asked me to join her. Weeks of avoiding me and I'd lured her out with garlic breadsticks.

Her breathing was deep and even. I could fall asleep right here and sneak in one more night with her. Only my pride wanted her to know she spent the night with me. I wanted her to want it.

Still, I soaked it all in for longer. We had over nine months left together, but if reconciliation took too long, she'd see the end of the tunnel. She'd tuck her head down and let her stubbornness take over.

I couldn't let that happen. I had given up on us once. I'd made home life hell for her. She'd had to pick up after me, worry about where I was, and then field my attitude when she'd been rightfully upset.

It wasn't happening again. I had worked hard on myself, and she was seeing it. But she was scared.

Remorse coursed around my rib cage. I'd lived in regret for so long, but there was finally room for more. When I looked at her closed eyes and the way her dusty blonde lashes brushed her cheeks, the love burned bright.

I fucking loved this woman.

So I'd make sure she got to bed. Alone. The wind blustered outside, but the power was holding strong. I wouldn't mind getting snowed in with her, but I didn't want us to be worrying about survival. After the storm, I'd get a generator installed so we could run a few lights and the furnace.

Carefully, I rose and leaned over her. "Hey? Sleeping Beauty?"

She wrinkled her nose and nestled farther into her plush, flannel blanket.

"Daze?" I gently shook her shoulder.

A protesting grunt left her. Her eyelids fluttered open, and a dreamy smile curved her red lips. "Hey, you." She extracted a hand from her cocoon and wrapped it behind my neck.

I should stop her, but I didn't. She dragged my head down to hers until our mouths were a breath apart.

"I missed you," she murmured and tugged me the rest of the way down.

I kept the kiss chaste, but that didn't mean I wouldn't try to communicate how goddamn important she was to me. I added pressure, an urgency that told her I was sorry. So goddamn sorry for everything, and that if she could give me half a chance, I'd make sure she never lost trust in me. I'd do anything to let her know I'd never treat her like she didn't matter again.

Her warm tongue licked against my lips. Fuck, I wanted to take this further. She'd be deliciously salty from dinner and sweet from the cookies. I'd get lost in her flavor. But she was half asleep and not thinking clearly.

"Daze," I said against her lips. "I'm gonna carry you to bed."

"No." She whined, and her arms around my neck banded tighter. "I'm nice and warm right here."

"I know." I stuffed my arms under her and picked her up, blanket and all. If I lifted the throw off her, I might stuff myself in right next to her.

She held on to me, burying her face in my chest. I didn't bother with lights as I carried her to her bedroom. Ambient light from the living room gave me enough visibility to get to her bed without tripping.

I set her down on the mattress and pulled the covers back. "Crawl in."

Even in the shadows, I could see her lips form a pout. She tugged a sock off. Then her other one. "The wind is really loud."

"Yeah."

"Sounds like the roof is going to rip off." Her voice was sleepy.

"The house has withstood a lot of storms."

She sighed. "Stay."

My focus narrowed on just the two of us. Only the storm outside made noise. Hope rose like a treacherous promise. Was she still partly asleep? What did they call it? Lucid dreaming?

Did she know what she was asking?

She was watching me from under her lashes, waiting for my answer. She wasn't taking her request back.

I should say no. As much as I wished otherwise, she wasn't ready. I'd been determined to be patient with her. I was ready to give her eternity.

"Where do you want me to stay?" I finally asked, too

fucking weak to walk away. If I made her tell me point-blank, would I feel less guilty?

"Here. We won't— I'm not— I just don't want to be alone right now." She tipped her chin up and her warm fingers sought mine. "Tonight was nice. I don't want it to end," she finished with a whisper.

I didn't ever want it to end. "Let me shut the light off."

My legs were leaden as I left her bedroom. When I was a kid, I'd never wished for telepathic powers, but I did right now. I could've flicked the light switch with a thought instead of risking the time she needed to gain some clarity.

I had to do this right, but there were no guidebooks. No resources about how to win back your stubbornly independent ex-wife.

With the house dark, I made my way back. An especially strong gust rocked against the exterior walls. This storm was supposed to go through tomorrow and part of the next day. Then the town would need time to clear roads and fix any utilities.

I inhaled a deep breath and fortified myself. Entering the bedroom, I waited for the inevitable change of mind. But as my eyes adjusted to the room, all I saw was her curled up on her side of the bed. There was no pillow wall.

The corner of my mouth kicked up. All the knots in my chest loosened. She wanted me close.

As I undressed down to my underwear, I smiled my relief into the darkness. She was trusting me. Slowly but surely, I would win her back.

Chapter Fifteen

Daisy

One of my favorite moments in life was happening again. I loved the quiet time before bed, when Laila was snuggled against me during reading time. Everything was right in the world during these times and we were in sync.

Then there were the early mornings with Alder. I thought I had lost these. Not too long ago, I had gotten to experience one again, and it had ended in fireworks.

Alder's breathing was even, but that didn't mean he was asleep. I peeked my eyes open. Faint light shone through the thick blinds. It wasn't that early.

I strove to get my brain online. I didn't have work. It was Saturday. From the strength of the wind, it was still storming out. I wouldn't be going anywhere today.

This was nice. Hard chest under my cheek. Strong, warm body. I closed my eyes and just breathed. In and out.

I shouldn't be doing this. I shouldn't have asked him

to stay with me last night. I sure as hell shouldn't have wished he'd have dived into bed and devoured me. We'd slept together. That was all.

"Are you awake?" I asked softly.

"Yes." His chest vibrated.

Hesitantly, I slid my hand along his torso. His abs clenched under my touch. I flattened my palm on his hot skin. "I'm sorry I asked you to stay."

"I'm not."

If I slid my hand lower, I'd find out if he was hard or not. I didn't have to check. He would be, but my bravery failed me. I could not go there.

Could I?

Confusion swirled in my brain. I had so many reasons why not. I'd get my heart broken again. I'd have to move, and I had nowhere to go. I'd have to tell Laila. To everyone else, this was what we were supposed to be like. Happily married. Newlyweds.

Could I leave after a year if we were having sex?

Would I have to leave?

Panic welled in my chest, making my blood pressure rise. The hurt. The uncertainty. The anguish. Had I done the right thing back then? Should I have waited longer? Could I ever trust myself again?

I started to roll away, but he twined an arm around me.

"Tell me what's going on in that sharp brain of yours." His deep growl sent shivers caressing over my skin. I felt the loss of his heat, and I didn't want to leave the cozy haven we'd created.

How did I tell him I was terrified? I was scared of him. Of more change. More instability. I was frightened of making the wrong damn decision again.

"I have raging garlic breath," I said, keeping my tone light. "Talking might be a huge turnoff for you."

"I've got the same garlic breath." He tucked me close to him, his chin resting in my hair.

My cheek was back on his fevered skin. How could he be so warm? Being next to him was like finally being free of the cold that had chilled my blood for fifteen years.

"You can talk to me," he said.

I let out a hard laugh. "I can talk to you about how hard it is to stay away from you? I can talk to you about how badly I want to do more than just laze around in bed? I can talk to you about how I'm worried we'll blur the lines and there's no going back and then I'll be left picking up the pieces of me again?"

"Damn, Daze," he said with a groan full of regret. "You're getting me hard and tearing my heart out at the same time."

"Sorry—"

"Don't apologize," he said almost harshly. "Don't ever apologize. None of it was your fault."

The more I thought about those days, the more I wondered. The more I questioned. The more uncertain I was that he was right.

I patted his stomach, barely restraining from petting him like the love-starved woman I was. Then I rolled away out of his grip. "I've gotta brush my teeth and shower."

The blankets slid off me as I sat up and I shivered. "That window is drafty." The chill was taking my mind off the hot guy in bed. The man who would absolutely let me climb on top of him and find as much pleasure as I want.

"They're old," he agreed, staying in bed. "I'll put plastic to cover them on my list."

"Sounds good." When I slipped out of bed, the burn of Alder's gaze on my back stayed with me until I scurried out the door.

In the bathroom, I caught my breath. I was still in the fluffy pajamas that I watched the movie in. The tender way he'd carried me to bed… A tremble whisked over me.

Good thing I hadn't gotten a good look at him shirtless in my bed. Those days his parents had been in town left me with enough images I couldn't forget. Rippled abs. Mussed morning hair. Stubble over a granite chin.

Had his pants been off?

Alder had nice legs, with powerful thighs and a dusting of hair down his limbs. He oozed an addicting masculinity I couldn't get enough of.

I gave myself a full-body shake. My mind kept returning to Alder as I brushed my teeth and showered. Should I hide in my bedroom all day? Should I help him with whatever project he'd work on? Should I talk him into a snow day?

Alder 2.0 probably didn't know what a snow day was.

I finished drying off and looked around. The only clothes I had to wear were the pajamas from last night. I hadn't even brought clean underwear in with me.

Well, shoot. I dug out a bigger towel to wrap around me. All the important bits were covered. I peeked in the mirror and bit back a groan. My damp hair made me look like a drowned cat. My skin was pale except for the bright red spots on my cheeks that never seemed to go away when I was around Alder. At least the towel made my cleavage look good.

Goose bumps spread over my skin as I scurried from the bathroom to the bedroom. It was empty and the bed was made. I shook my head. It'd take a while to get used to that new trait in Alder. He'd been such a slob, even when he'd been a teen. The main argument between him and his parents before he'd moved out had been cleaning his pigsty of a room.

Today's Alder was as neat as a pin. He made Jason's parents look like hoarders.

His voice resonated from the kitchen, confident, authoritative. Work must've called. The refinery had storm procedures in place. Hopefully, nothing had gone wrong.

I dug out a pair of sweats and one of my favorite over-sized, fluffy sweaters. The sweats were navy blue and the top was a soft yellow. Perfect. I got a fresh pair of under-wear and one of my older, more broken-in bras out. I also found a pair of thick, gray socks.

I couldn't be less sexy in this getup.

Dropping the towel, I stepped into the underwear.

"That was work. They—"

I yelped and toppled. Before I hit the floor, strong arms wrapped around me.

"Shit. Sorry." He lifted me completely off the floor, cradling me in his arms like last night.

Cool air wafted under my bare ass. My heart rate spiked through the roof but it wasn't from fear of hitting my head on the dresser. I was naked. My white underwear with yellow smiley faces hung off an ankle.

Alder frantically looked me over, then the jump of his eyes slowed. His attention turned into a perusal. The smell of mint came off him. He must've cleaned up in the bathroom upstairs while I'd been in the shower. He was in a white shirt and gray sweatpants.

"Fuck, Daisy. You're not wearing a goddamn thing."

My arousal was instant. I didn't struggle to get out of his hold. "No. I'm not."

He dragged his gaze up my abdomen, lingering on my breasts. My nipples were hard, begging for attention. Just like me. He finally lifted his gaze to meet mine. "I haven't had breakfast yet, Daisy. I'm a starving man."

All the questions from this morning vanished. The worries didn't. "What if..."

Understanding rippled through his features. He clenched his jaw. "What if it's just physical? What if we just lose ourselves in the pleasure and forget the rest?"

"I don't know if I can do that."

"Do you think nine more months of this is any better?"

"What if—"

He deposited me in the middle of the bed but he didn't move away. He kept advancing until I had to lie back or we'd knock heads. "What if it's real fucking good, Daze?" I opened my mouth to point out that good sex could make things worse, but he silenced me with a firm kiss. "What if it's fucking amazing and we'll be so damn relieved we didn't waste any more time just sleeping?" Another kiss as he spread his comforting weight over me. "What if fucking is the only time that all this feels right?"

All of it already did feel right. Not the part where he slept on a separate floor of the house. Or the fact that my daughter wasn't sure about him. Or how far away he sat at the big dining room table.

The echo of *what if* in my head faded away. I buried my hands in his hair and yanked him all the way down.

A growl resonated from him. He hadn't shaved and his whiskers scraped the sensitive skin around my lips, but I loved it. So familiar. So hot.

Last night, I was the one who had wanted to carry things further before he hauled me to bed and tucked me in. This time, his tongue invaded my mouth, and he took over. The mint on my tongue grew stronger. The idea that he still used the same toothpaste as me soothed me in a weird domestic way. How bad could this be when he hadn't changed his toothpaste from the brand we had bought together?

A whimper left me, and I automatically widened my legs, cradling him right where I wanted him the most. I rocked my hips unapologetically against him.

I'd opened the gate. Now I was barreling through. Everything I had denied myself for so long was at my fingertips.

He ripped his lips off mine. I drank in air, getting loopy on the arousal building inside me, settling between my legs, and begging for more.

"Fuck, Daisy," he said against my chin as he kissed along my jaw and then down my neck. "When that towel dropped, I had no fucking clue how I'd ever get rid of my erection."

My insecurities roared back. "My ass is…"

"Get out of your head. Your ass is goddamn perfection." He shifted farther down, stopping when he reached my breasts. I arched my back into him and attempted to roll my hips against him. Only soft clothing brushed against my pussy.

More friction.

I undulated again. A soft chuckle left him as he swiped his tongue over a hard nipple. He slid his hand between us, and a calloused fingertip landed on my clit. "Is this what you need?" he asked in a sinful tone.

I barked out a cry and rolled my hips faster. He used his big body to pin me in place.

Another whine left me.

"Patience, Daze. I've been thinking about this for too damn long. I'm taking my time." He sucked my other nipple into his mouth while he massaged the wet tip of my other pearled bud between his thumb and forefinger. A shock traveled between us. I couldn't buck against him. He was too strong.

"Can you do that next time?"

He didn't remove his hand, but he went still. My clit throbbed against him, but even I didn't move. My chest constricted. What had I done wrong?

He released my nipple and gently blew across it. A full-body shiver racked me, and he grinned. "We doing this again?" Another blow, another shiver, another sexy grin.

My hips kicked, but he only let out a low chuckle and licked my tight peak. His eyes glimmered when I shivered.

"And what, exactly, are we doing?" His finger twitched, and my eyes nearly rolled back in my head.

"I think you know."

"I want to hear you say it. What do you want us to do?"

This frustrating man. I was naked underneath him and his hand was soaked from me. "Have sex," I gritted out. Embarrassment flooded my cheeks. "I mean, that's only if you want to."

He was giving me an out. It was only fair I gave him one.

He took his hand off me and caressed my lips with the same finger that had been teasing my clit. I opened my lips, and he pushed the tip inside. I tasted myself on him. A mixture of salt and desire.

"Do you think I'm missing out on these sweet juices, Daisy?" He removed his finger and scooted farther down my body, shoving my legs wide with his shoulders. I was open to him, my pussy right in front of his face. "I planned to finally satiate myself on you, to drink up as much as I could in case you hid yourself from me again. But if you want to fuck, Daisy?" He dragged his tongue through my seam until he landed on my swollen nub, then he laved across it. My hips jolted upward, but he put a big hand on my abdomen. "We'll fuck. Because I very much want to fuck you." He circled my clit with his tongue, and I moaned. "What do you want?"

So damn much. I wanted this. I wanted him. I wanted to quit tormenting myself about how losing him again would destroy any chance for happiness. "I want you to fuck me." I could admit that. It'd been true since I first sat in his truck that night. It'd been true for far too long.

"Then I'm going to fuck you. And when you tell yourself it was a mistake, you're going to let me fuck you again. With each orgasm, you'll admit that there's nothing wrong with us having sex. You want to know why?"

My nod was shaky.

"Because you're my goddamn wife, Daisy Duke."

* * *

Alder

. . .

I couldn't take my claim back if I wanted. I might've just torched everything between us. We wouldn't be burning up the sheets—her anxiety would.

I waited as emotions played over her face. Stark shock that I had claimed her. Note to self: Do more of it. Trepidation because she was Daisy. Of course she'd be thinking about the logistics of all this. Then finally, wanton desire because she fucking liked it.

I'd run with that. "You've got me for the rest of our year, and we both want this. It's going to be weird as hell parting ways whether we break apart now and never touch until next December or if we fuck like bunnies until then. I know which scenario I prefer."

Her eyes went wide, and she caught that plump lower lip between her teeth. "I know which one I prefer," she said in a hoarse voice.

"Is it this?" I fit my mouth over the top of her pussy and flattened my tongue on her clit.

"Yes," she cried.

"Good. Then relax and let me make you orgasm." My desire demanded attention, but I ignored it and pushed her knees higher until she was split open, her glistening sex mine for the taking.

And I took. I flicked my tongue across her sensitive bud and then circled her clit. Her moans grew in volume until a shout echoed off the walls. "Yes!"

She was right there. So I eased off the pressure as my own built. She sagged into the mattress with a protest, and I could've chuckled. I slowly ramped up until she was writhing underneath me.

"God." She planted her heels on my shoulders. She was cheating, trying to steal her pleasure.

I'd give her everything she needed, but this would be on my timeline. I backed off again.

"Goddammit, Alder."

My laugh was unexpected, but I kept at it, bringing her within sight of her peak and then whisking her away.

"Please." The pleading in her voice was perfection.

I threaded a finger inside her tight, wet channel and pumped lazily in and out. "I told you I was taking my time."

"I'm going to pass out."

"I'll bring you to with this." I claimed her clit again. Her hips jacked up, but this time I let her go wild.

"Oh my god. *Oh my god.*" She matched my pace. When she went faster, I went faster, until she rolled up and held it. Satisfaction brimmed in my blood. She was at the brink. Then she stuffed her fingers through my hair and cranked my head as close as I could get. "Fuck. Yes!"

Her orgasm was sweeter than I remembered. She was my personal blend of honey pouring into my mouth.

She rode it out like she needed this release to breathe again. I needed her release to keep my heart beating. "Take it all, Daisy."

With a final shout, she collapsed against the mattress and tugged my hair, encouraging me to move up her body. As much as I hated leaving the sweet juncture of her thighs, I did as she wanted.

"I need you now." My voice was guttural.

"Yes." She peppered kisses across my face and the familiarity prodded the scar in my chest wide open. Fear poured out.

My own what-ifs hounded me. What if we never get this again? All the orgasms I'd given her before hadn't been the glue holding our marriage together. There was no guarantee that pleasing her in bed would make her stay.

But that wasn't why I was here, coaxing those greedy moans out of her. I was here because the last fifteen years had left me a fucking empty man. She'd been my other half. She still was.

Right now? I was almost whole again.

Almost.

Maybe once we were connected that emptiness would be vanquished.

I reared up to my knees, her legs still splayed on either side of me. I reached behind my neck and yanked my shirt over my head. Tossing it to the side with one hand, I ripped off my sweats with the other.

My heartbeat was in my dick. No longer strangled by my pants, my erection bobbed out with a mind of its own and only one mission—get inside Daisy.

With the lights off, Daisy was a sultry shadow in front of me. An old dream that came to life but wasn't fully formed. Not completely mine.

Fuck that.

I dropped over her, catching myself with a hand by her head. Her eyelids were heavy, and her face was flushed, the pink spreading down to her chest.

"Spread your legs wide, Daisy. I won't be able to take my time with this."

She nodded and hitched her knees up and out. I notched myself at her entrance and a ragged groan ripped from me.

"So fucking hot and wet." I trembled as I pushed into her clinging, soft heat.

She hissed with pleasure at my entrance, rocking up

to take more. "You feel so perfect," she murmured and twined her fingers back into my hair.

My arm started to vibrate. I wasn't fully inside of her, but once I was I wouldn't be able to stop pumping until I exploded. "So goddamn right."

She made another needy noise.

I pushed all the way in. *Fuck*. I tipped my forehead to hers. She gripped me so damn tight, the little ripples from her orgasms riding over my cock. "Once isn't going to be enough."

"I don't think I can take four orgasms," she said out of breath. Her muscles clenched and released around my dick.

"You can. I'll make sure of it." If each climax stamped me more into her heart, then I'd make it my life's mission to keep going until my brand was permanent. I drew out of her, loving the little whimper of loss right before I punched back in.

"Alder," she breathed.

I did it again, and she moved with me. "Feel this?" The slide of my skin against hers, the way our breathing coordinated and how perfectly aligned we were—this was meant to be. "You were made for me."

Her "yes" came out on a gasp.

I pumped harder. Faster. Her heels dug into my ass and I took her. She was with me the whole way, but she was too far from her peak. I would blow first. I grabbed her hand, licked her fingertips, and guided her arm between us. "I'm close, baby. I need you to come with me."

When her fingertips hit her clit, she arched like she'd been hit with voltage. Her pussy squeezed around me.

"Do it again," I said and punched into her. The

bump of our bodies ground her fingertips into her sex. Her moan said it was the perfect amount of friction. "Rub that needy little clit."

She was squirming under me, and the vise grip she had on me was more than I could control.

"Fuck, Daisy. Make yourself come."

A cry left her and my damn eyes crossed from the pressure she put on my dick. Her legs clamped around me and she bucked against me, against her hand.

"Fuck." I gritted my teeth and squeezed my eyes shut as the detonation hit.

The shock waves of my climax turned my thrusts erratic. The sounds of my grunts and slapping, wet skin filled the room. Then I collapsed on top of her.

For once, I felt like it was all right. That I was all right. Everything was okay. Because I was finally with my wife again.

Chapter Sixteen

Daisy

I held on to Alder like this dream was going to vanish and I'd have no one. I'd be left alone again. I'd open my eyes and find out I was still with the wrong man.

His weight was pleasing. I kissed his hairline and ran my hands over his back. His chest heaved against mine as we caught our breaths.

I'd exploded so many times. In one night, or day in this case. That hadn't happened since... Him. I trailed my fingers over his heated, sweaty skin and along his broad shoulders. The words "I love you" crowded on my tongue. I used to murmur that to him, over and over, in moments just like this. When we were sated and quiet. *I love you, I love you, I love you.* Toward the end, I had said the words as if I willed them to be enough.

He lifted his head and caught my lips in a slow, tender kiss. He tangled a hand in my hair, and inside me, his dick twitched, coming back to life.

His stamina had not decreased with age.

The heat between us kept everything from getting sticky—

I gasped as clarity dawned bright and clear despite the storm outside the window. "We didn't use anything."

He stiffened before jerking his hips back, then he paused before he fully pulled out like he wasn't sure if he was making it better or worse. Alarm beat against my temples. No protection. I might be married, but I was a single woman.

"Are you on anything?" he asked, his tone cautious.

"Yes." I rifled through my brain. Had I been taking my pill every day? I'd been on it for so long that it was rote. Wake up, take the pill with my first glass of water. "I think I've been regular with it. Laila came about because I had the stomach flu for a week."

He was still taut. "I've been checked. I hope you're not worried about... I've always used protection."

"Except for now?" My gentle tease was supposed to hide how pleased I was he'd been out of his mind with me to even think about it.

"It just felt natural. It's us."

We hadn't tried for kids when we'd been married, but we hadn't done everything possible to prevent them. If I had gotten pregnant, we'd just have been parents earlier than expected.

I couldn't fault Alder. I hadn't thought of it either. It had felt natural. "I always used protection too."

He rolled to my side, propping his head on his hand. "And you still had Laila?"

"Yeah. Talk about a perfect storm. Thrown-up doses of pills and faulty condoms."

He traced his fingers over my abdomen. Shivers

cropped up where he touched. I was still warm from him, and he was an oven next to me, but without his heat blanketing me, the chill was back. I didn't believe in signs, but it was like I could only be warm and full with him. "I can grab my condoms from upstairs," he finally said.

I huffed out a laugh. Of course, he'd have condoms. Women probably threw themselves at him. Alder 2.0 was always prepared.

Why the hell was I annoyed? Why the sense of betrayal? I'd been engaged to another man! I'd had a baby with him.

He placed a kiss at the corner of my mouth. "I got them for us. Just in case."

Thoughtful Alder struck again. Worse, an Alder who had hoped to get with me, and I had thought the worst of him. "Sorry." I tilted my face toward him. "It's weird, right? Having this talk? Kind of a sign of how things are different. How we moved on."

"I didn't move on. Not at all." He continued to swirl his fingers across my skin. "I didn't even try."

I barked out a laugh. "I tried." That made me so much worse. "I finally had to admit it was pointless."

"Fuck, Daze. I didn't want you to be unhappy, but I'm sure as hell thrilled to hear that you couldn't bring yourself to marry another guy."

"I did, actually." I held my hand out. The wedding ring caught what little light filtered through the shades. "I married this rich prick who drives a big truck. I think he's compensating."

"They always are."

I brushed my fingers down his cheek. "He doesn't relax though. Like he's trying to atone for the sins of the past."

He didn't respond but his hand went still on my stomach. Only his thumb twitched.

"Sometimes I wonder if he's overcorrected," I said.

A moment went by. Two. "He hasn't," he finally said. "He can't overcorrect when it's impossible to go back and correct what he broke."

"Oh, Alder." I rolled to my side. In the dark, we faced each other. Buck naked and exposed in so many more ways.

"Don't apologize." He skipped his finger down my nose. "I'm the one who should never quit saying sorry." He curled me into his chest. "I haven't yet, have I? Truly apologized."

"I wasn't keeping track."

"That's not the Daisy I know."

A laugh escaped. "Okay, fine. No, you haven't."

I felt his smile from where he rested his face against my head. "There she is." He held me tighter. "I'm so sorry, Daisy. You were right about everything. I was a shit. I invited the guys over and never checked with you, never bothered to think about how it affected you and your studying. Or that, fuck, you felt like your safe space was violated."

I shrank into him. We'd argued about that once, and he'd said he had a right to act like he wanted. He'd lived in a house with seven other people, and he wasn't going to let one person dictate his living space.

"I know," he said quietly. "I did kick Colton's ass when he busted your grandma's vase."

It had been my great-great-aunt's vase. Grandma had passed it down and my mom's mom had not been a sentimental lady. The fact I had anything from her other than the albums was a miracle, and some drunk coworker of

Alder's had knocked it down when he'd gone in our bedroom looking for an extra bathroom.

Then there'd been the dirty dishes all over. The muddy boots and the dirt tracks across the apartment. "Remember when what's his name smoked a cigar and the place stunk for weeks?"

"I was too afraid to admit that I had shared it with him."

"Oh, I could tell you had." I had gone nuclear. It hadn't been about the cigar or that Alder had smoked it with his buddy. I'd come home from a long day of school and working the early morning shift, to come home to a place that made me sneeze and caused my chest to feel tight.

After that fight, he'd taken to going out more and hanging out at bars and crashing at his coworkers' places.

"I'm sorry. I'm sorry for not listening to you. For being a selfish prick. For regressing instead of being the husband you wanted."

The side of my face was pressed against his chest. I flattened my hand on one of his hard pecs. "I understand why you did it, you know. Big family. You finally had freedom. But thank you. For the apology."

"Sometimes, I can't even explain why I morphed into that guy. I take full accountability, but I wish I had some other excuse than that I was an entitled dick."

"Aliens took over."

"There was a body snatcher."

"Oh, that's who gave me four orgasms."

His chuckle was deep against my cheek. "I'm going to keep taking credit for it." He gently rolled me to my stomach and brushed a kiss against the back of my shoulders. "In fact, that means I have to prove I can do it too."

Smiling, I stretched and arched into the light scrapes of his stubble. We'd reached a new understanding between us. The past was over. Done. But we had now. That was all I would concentrate on. If I looked any further ahead, that would only get me into trouble. If Alder 2.0 let me down, I wasn't sure I could bring myself to leave him, and I already had a strong history of staying too long.

* * *

Four orgasms. He'd done it. I could barely move today. It had been like a marathon. Alder must've been tired too because we'd stayed on the couch all morning and watched movies.

This time we weren't on opposite sides of the couch. I spent the day burrowed next to him. His feet were kicked up on the recliner part of the couch and his arm was on me. The movie we'd been watching was done.

Alder flipped through the options. "Have you seen the one about murders in the building?"

"Yes."

He slid his gaze toward me.

I shrugged. "If it's streaming, then I've probably watched it. Unless it's a movie older than five years ago."

"Having a kid kept you homebound?"

"Jason used to work a lot of overtime, and neither of us had family in the area. Our parents love Laila, but they like being grandparents on their schedules, when it's fun for them. Not when I needed the help."

My phone buzzed from the end table. I grabbed it, but I didn't sink back into Alder. I pushed the blanket off me and twisted until I was facing him and my back was to the wall. "It's a video call. From Laila."

His brows drew together, but he nodded. Was he bothered that I was trying to hide how close we were? He knew the deal. We weren't *together* together, and I wouldn't confuse Laila with that concept. She had accepted the whole married-roommate thing.

I hit the answer button. Laila's face came into view. Jason was right behind her like she was sitting on his lap. "Hey, sweet pea."

"Hi, Mommy!" She made a face into the screen. Her gaze was on the little window with her image.

"How's the storm going for you two?"

"Good! We had popcorn."

"Fun. Everything's okay?" I looked at Jason when I asked. He nodded.

"Yup," Laila said. She peered around me. "Where's Alder?"

"Oh, uh..." A moment of panic clutched my heart tight in its fist. I wasn't a kid sneaking around, and I couldn't act like it. Then she'd sense something was wrong. And from the grinding of Alder's teeth, I'd hurt his feelings more than it had. "He's here."

Laila looked around. "Where?"

"We're watching a show."

Jason's expression fell, and he looked away.

Guilt built higher inside me like the snowdrifts outside. I'd told him this was nothing but a marriage of convenience, yet here I was, cozy with Alder not even a quarter of the way through the arrangement.

"You know, with the storm, there's nothing else to do but watch some shows." Geez, I sounded like I was hiding a body I didn't want them to know about.

The muscle in Alder's jaw jumped.

"Lemme see him," Laila said, bobbing and ducking her head like she was going to glimpse him hiding next to the couch.

"You mind?" I asked him.

His features were neutral. "Not at all."

I did. He was in a loose black T-shirt, and while that wasn't out of the ordinary, his hair was ruffled, standing on end from having my fingers through it all night. To anyone who didn't know him, they'd think nothing of it. But they might. Especially since it was past lunchtime, and I was wearing my pajama top with yellow duckies all over it.

We looked like two people who had rolled out of bed together and went straight for the couch. Because we had.

If I delayed any longer, then we really would look like we were hiding something. As much as I hated hurting Jason, I didn't want him to feel like I was hiding something on top of it.

I turned the phone around.

Alder flashed a kind smile. "Howdy, Laila. How's the weekend with your dad?"

"What show are you watching? We're watching *Inside Out*."

"Isn't there more than one?" he asked.

"Yup."

My mouth twitched.

"We're watching a murder mystery series," he said. "They don't scare your mom, but I might have nightmares tonight."

Her giggles carried through the phone. "Hey, Mommy, guess what."

I flashed a smile of appreciation toward Alder, but his face was back to being a blank canvas.

I chatted with Laila about how she planned to help her dad dig out, then I answered her questions about what would happen if she couldn't get home on Monday. Jason planned to take her to daycare that morning, and I'd pick her up after work. That'd change until Tuesday if the roads were still bad.

After the call was disconnected, I held the phone in my lap, trying to gauge Alder's reaction to the call.

Alder stared at the TV as he paged through options for us to watch. "What should we watch next?"

"Were you okay with that?"

He frowned. "Talking to Laila? Of course. I thought maybe she was hoping I froze out in the snow."

"She actually worries about you. She was going to color you a picture last weekend. Hadn't seen you for a while and wondered if you were okay."

He perked up. "Seriously?"

"Seriously." His astonishment touched me. He'd given Laila the distance she needed, and not many people did that with kids. Strangers got frustrated when she didn't want to talk to them. She was another man's kid, but Alder respected her.

At the same time, a tiny pit of anxiety formed. If my kid started to like him, that'd only add another tangle to this web we were creating.

I could leave this distance between us, but that didn't feel right. "I wasn't hiding you exactly. I don't want Laila confused, and I still feel guilty about Jason. I'd rather talk to him first and set the example for when he starts to date."

"It won't bother you when he does?"

"No." I had absolutely no reservations. "The only thing I'm worried about is how who he ends up with will treat Laila." I set my phone on the end table and rose. There was zero jealousy when it came to Jason. All that was reserved for Alder. I tried to stay in the present, but what about the future? What about when Alder moved on? More images of him and beautiful women would devastate me. "I need to take a shower, then I'll make some spaghetti."

I swept into the bathroom, grateful to put some distance between me and the cozy domesticity Alder and I were creating. Being married to him wasn't supposed to be like this. So damn perfect my chest ached.

I started the water and undressed. By the time I was naked, the water had warmed. I stepped under the spray and let it pelt me in the face.

Not even twenty-four hours after having sex and I wanted it all. I could have it all.

But...

The pain of our arguments echoed in my head. The fear of failure.

Warm water worked into my muscles. I turned so it'd hit my tight shoulders. After a few minutes, the door squeaked open.

I froze. I was behind the daisy-covered shower curtain, but I felt like I was behind a pane of glass. Exposed. "I'll be out in a minute."

"I'd like to think I take longer than that." Through the curtain, I could see his shirt was off already, leaving nothing but a swath of sculpted chest. He shucked his sweats down, and my mouth went dry.

I'd seen his chest. It'd been clear in my mind even in the shadows. But his cock was different. I hadn't seen that in years. Last night, I'd felt it. A lot. It'd been in me. In the light of the bathroom, his entire body was on display. Powerful thighs with quads that bulged to his knees. Calves could be sexy, and Alder proved it.

The sex was really good. That was all it was, all it needed to be. I let the rest of my anxiety wash down the drain.

My self-consciousness didn't get whisked away. I kept the curtain as a privacy drape as he prowled to the edge of the tub. "There's not much room. We can sprawl on the bed."

"We can." He propped an arm on the wall, nearly caging me in the tub. He dropped his gaze to where my body was hidden behind daisies on an opaque white background. "You're in your head."

He knew me too well. "Maybe." When he kicked a brow up, I sighed. "I'm not the same." I waved a hand down my body. I'd been scared for the future, for the end of our year together, but I'd share these fears. "You've aged like—geez. Like fine wine is too delicate of a description. You're bigger."

He smirked, and his gaze dipped to his proud erection.

"Yes. I swear even that." My knuckles turned white on the curtain. "I have stretch marks. The perky boobs of my early twenties might be bigger now, but they're just a little tired from fighting gravity. There's more of me, but it didn't turn into muscle like you."

"Ah, Daisy." His lazy chuckle caressed over my wet skin. "You think I find this version of you any less sexy than I did fifteen years ago?"

I feared that he could find better versions. I was scared he'd come to his senses and find out that maybe I wasn't such a big loss. We were in a snow bubble. A snow globe. An idyllic setting that was getting shook, but the excitement would only last until the snow settled.

He gently pried the curtain away. Across from us, I saw myself in the mirror behind his broad back. My stringy hair stuck to my face, but my cheeks were tinged with pink and my eyes were bright. I might fear what he'd think of me in the unflattering light of the bathroom, but it was my overwhelming feelings that were terrifying. A love that had never died.

He set a hot hand on my hip and maneuvered me to the back of the tub. Desire heated his eyes when he studied my body. That beautiful erection of his strained between us. It was millimeters from the water sluicing down my abdomen.

"You want to know what I think when I see you now?" He ran a finger over my collarbone and trailed it farther down, skimming over a breast. "Fucking finally. That's what I think. I get to finally see you without a stitch of clothing again. I get to finally touch you. To be with you." He circled my nipple with his fingertip, then cupped my whole breast in his palm. He did the same with the other one. "I think these tits are more amazing than before, and I thought they were pretty fabulous back then."

Shivers danced over my skin. I wasn't cold, not with him acting like my personal furnace.

"And those stretch marks?" His low groan sounded more like a growl. He traced over silvery squiggles on my hips. "They're a part of you. A badass part. It makes you even more unique. I don't give a shit about your size, Daisy, but trust me when I say I don't mind having more of you to hold on to."

He could be telling me what I wanted to hear to get laid, but he didn't have to do that. I was his regardless. If he didn't want to see me, he could haul me to the bedroom and keep the lights off. But he was standing with me in the shower.

Slowly, the stress inside of me washed out and circled the drain. *Be in the moment. Savor this.*

He gripped each side of my hips before sliding his hands back to palm my ass cheeks. We were pressed together now, and his erection was pinned between us. His cock twitched and pulsed against my stomach.

He placed a kiss at my jawline and nibbled his way to my ear. "Do you mind my bigger size?"

"God, no."

His hot breath gusted across my ear with his soft laugh. "Then, my sweet flower, I don't fucking mind every extra inch you have. It's more for me to get my hands and mouth on."

"You always say the right things."

"I said the wrong ones for too long." He laved kisses down my neck. I tilted my head to the side to give him more room.

He was more than making up for it. When we were in high school, I hadn't thought I could find a better man. He was proving that he got better each day as he strove for perfection. I just wish he knew that I'd be more comfortable around him if he had a few flaws.

But he did what he'd always done best. As he worked his way down my body with his mouth, lowering himself to his knees, I was coaxed out of my head and into this moment. It was only sex between us. So his perfection didn't matter.

Chapter Seventeen

Alder

I didn't get home the Monday after the storm until almost nine. I had fielded calls all through the weekend relating to the weather, shipping delays, production delays, and storm cleanup, but today I'd been meeting with people, getting reports from the damage done, mostly by the snow-removal equipment taking out fences and barriers. No other structures were damaged.

I pulled into the garage. On my way down the driveway, I'd bumped through drifts that had blown in since Daisy had gotten home. The wind was finally dying down from earlier. I'd change and clear snow.

Inside the house, I heard voices coming from the kitchen. The smell of the pot roast I'd put in this morning filled the air. I shrugged out of my heavy wool coat and hung it up. Then I toed out of my shoes, without getting melting snow on my socks, and found Daisy and Laila at the table.

Laila smiled and waved. Brown crumbs stuck to her mouth and smeared across one cheek. "Hi, Alder."

"Hey there." I didn't know when I'd turned the corner with Laila, but I liked her chipper greeting over the suspicious stare. "How are the brownies?"

"Good!"

Daisy and I had made the brownies yesterday. Then after we'd cleaned up, I'd taken her against the counter. I'd pulled down her yellow flannel pajama pants and bent her over the island.

The weekend had been a dream. Today was the first day back to reality, but so far, it was starting off like an extension of my fantasy. I came home to a warm house with my family.

Daisy and Laila were my loaner family. I hadn't earned them for real. Not yet.

The inclination to cross to Daisy, put my arm around her, and greet her with a kiss was strong. The urge was natural. She was as essential to me as breathing. I hadn't been able to take a breath since we'd remarried, but since she'd let me in, I'd been huffing giant lungfuls of air. But Laila was home now.

"Hey. How was work?" I asked.

"Quiet for a Monday." She smiled. "Want some roast? I left the slow cooker on."

"I'm going to push some snow. Hopefully the driveway will stay clear until morning." I refused to push this new reconnection, and eating supper like a family with Laila might've done that.

Disappointment registered in her eyes. "I won't unplug everything, then, so it stays warm for you."

"Thanks." I gave her a regretful smile and jogged upstairs.

After changing into jeans and a sweater, I dove into my coveralls and went outside. It didn't take long to blow all the snow out of the driveway. Between the open garage door, the yard light, and the headlight on the tractor, I could see well enough. The light breeze wouldn't disturb the piles of snow I'd pushed away.

I put the equipment away, closed the garage door, and went inside on a swirl of cold and lingering exhaust fumes. The kitchen was empty. The voices this time came from the bathroom.

I got myself a plate of roast and veggies, unplugged the slow cooker, and sat at the table by myself. With each bite, uncertainty set in. Daisy and I hadn't discussed how we'd act when Laila returned. It hadn't been the elephant in the room, but I hadn't wanted to pressure her for a plan. I couldn't believe I'd gotten as much of her as I did.

Now what?

While I was eating, the bathroom door opened. Laila's chatter and giggles disappeared into her room. Daisy would probably be in there a while, reading her a book or five.

I finished off my food.

I wouldn't pressure Daisy. I wouldn't nag her. I didn't want her to feel like I only came around for sex even though that was what she had wanted to keep our arrangement as. I'd continue what I was doing—make her home a comforting place.

The steady cadence of Daisy's voice came from Laila's bedroom. Smiling to myself, I cleaned up the kitchen, put the food away, and went upstairs to shower. By the time I exited the bathroom, no lights shone from the main level. My disappointment was acute. I just hoped she wasn't hiding from me.

I went into my room and tossed on a pair of under-wear. I found my phone and tapped out a message to Daisy. **Good night.**

If she answered, then I'd know she at least wasn't putting the entire house between us like she had before this weekend.

No reply came.

Had I misread the vibe when I had initially gotten home?

I got my suit ready for the next day. I had a few suits to drop off this week with my dry-cleaning contact. After I was done preparing for work tomorrow, I checked my phone again. No reply.

Well. Damn.

Was I starting at square one again? Had I even advanced to square one or had I been in the negatives?

My heart sunk to my bare feet, I pulled back the covers. There was a knock at the door and I froze. I could not get my hopes up.

I was also only in my underwear. Was our roommate agreement still in effect?

"Yeah?" I searched for a shirt to throw on.

The door creaked open, and Daisy slipped inside. She was dressed in her ducky pajama pants and a loose, long-sleeved top. She clicked the door closed behind her. Another click of the lock followed.

Desire bloomed low in my gut before my brain regis-tered what was going on. "Everything okay?"

"How are we doing this?" she asked, breathless and not from the stairs. Her gaze tracked my chest and down to my boxer briefs.

Finally, the message sunk in. "You didn't change your mind about having sex?"

She shook her head. "Definitely not. You?"

"Fuck no, but I was prepared to crave you all night." All week. For months. But I hadn't planned on giving up.

She dug her teeth into her lower lip. "We'll have to be fast and quiet. I told Laila that if she woke and couldn't find me, I might be up here, talking to you."

My brows lifted. She'd gone as far as to tell Laila that? "Talking?"

Her lips curved. "About the house and stuff."

I crossed to the door and braced my hands on either side of her head. "Just what does the other stuff entail?"

She pretended to think even though her chest was rising and falling faster than usual. "Maybe an orgasm?"

I placed the tip of my index finger at the nook in the base of her neck and traced down between her breasts all the way to her waistband. "I can be fast and quiet, but I can still give you more than one orgasm."

Her lips parted. "What about frequency?"

"You know where to find me. I'm yours."

A pleased expression flashed over her face before giving way to uncertainty. "I don't think we should, um, sleep together."

"I understand."

"I don't want to confuse Laila if she sees us...being affectionate."

"I understand." Frustration built inside my chest, pushing out at my ribs. I wasn't so much as holding Daisy's hand in front of anyone. I wasn't giving her a peck goodbye in the morning or when I came home at night. I didn't tuck her in or slide my hand over her ass each time I passed her, and I didn't push a wispy strand of hair behind her ear. I was doing nothing but holding back.

Still, there was more involved in this arrangement than me. If I didn't play by Daisy's rules, then there would only be me, and I'd been down that road before.

I worked the hem of her shirt up. She lifted her arms so I could slip it over her head. A plain, white, lacy bra cupped her tits. Fucking beautiful. "Any more rules before I make you come so fast and hard you'll need me to carry you down the stairs?"

A startled laugh left her. "Ohmigod. No, now I can't think straight."

"Good." The more Daisy thought about this arrangement, the less chance I had at making it permanent.

Chapter Eighteen

Alder

Now that the snow was melting, I opened the garage doors and let the sunshine in. The cool temps of late April were giving way to warmer weather. I was mostly sure we were out from under the threat of snow.

I took inventory of my tools. Since I'd moved here in the middle of winter, I hadn't unpacked more than what I had needed. Now I was straightening my standing toolbox, opening drawers and lining all the screwdrivers and wrenches up. I had a separate portable toolbox for in the house. For years, I'd had little to spend my nice salary on.

The sound of Daisy's car coasting down the driveway reached me. Daisy had said she'd run to the grocery store after work. This week had been rougher for her, with Laila being sick with a cold and needier. Daisy had only met me in my bedroom once after bedtime.

I meandered into the middle of the garage opening. My pickup was parked outside. I wanted to sweep out all the dirt and grit that had accumulated over the winter, but I'd do that before I went in to clean up. No need to marinate in a dust cloud.

Daisy parked in front of me. In the back seat, Laila waved, her grin wide. I'd never tire of those greetings, not after her dubious frowns when we'd all moved in together.

In the two months since Daisy and I had been sleeping together, Laila hadn't caught us, but she'd made sure to tell me good night and good morning, and if I was home early, she'd give me the daycare report. One little boy picks his nose and it's gross. Another girl wet herself and it got all over the nap pad. And then there was the pregnant teacher who groaned every time she stood up.

As Daisy got out of her car, I went around and opened Laila's door.

"How was school?" I asked.

She giggled. "I don't go to school."

"You're not a senior yet?"

"Preschool, silly." She climbed out, dragging her jacket with her. The purple of the material was grayed out from dirt and mud. She dragged it on the ground behind her.

"You're home early."

I shrugged. "It's Friday. Figured it was time to start working more normal hours." I couldn't finish winning Daisy back if I was gone all the time. That was partly what had cost me her in the first place.

Fatigue lined Daisy's face. Just as she was about to say something, she stiffened, then turned and sneezed into her elbow.

"Uh-oh." I took her purse and her lunch bag, then grabbed the few bags of groceries.

"Yeah," she said, sounding stuffy. "I wouldn't get too close."

I glanced behind me. Laila was just stepping into the house. "That isn't enough to scare me away, but instead of making you come, I can make you hot lemonade and soup."

Her shoulders hung but she smiled. "I haven't had hot lemonade in forever."

"Let me finish out here, and I'll make you some. There are some calzones I'm keeping warm in the oven."

I carried her things inside and set her purse in the mudroom. I took her lunch bag to the island and emptied it out.

She put her hand on my wrist. "I've got it. We'll get the table set."

The weariness in her voice couldn't be missed. "No. Let me sweep and pull the cars in."

I rushed through my tasks, but by the time I returned, the table was set, and steam was coming off the calzones from the center. The girls were just sitting down.

Laila bounced in her chair. "Time to eat, Alder!"

I hadn't started eating with them, but then I'd been working until nearly her bedtime most nights. On the weekend, either she was at her dad's, or I was in the middle of a project—or in the office.

I glanced at Daisy, silently asking if Laila was inviting me to eat with them. Daisy gave me a tired smile and a nod. Triumph swelled in my chest. Another rule crossed off the roommate list.

"Can I shower quick?" I asked Laila. "I don't want to get dust all over."

"Better hurry," she said in a singsong voice.

Daisy coughed into her shoulder. She needed to rest, not wait on me.

"You guys get started," I said. I took the stairs two at a time and ran through the shower as fast as I could. I came down the stairs dressed in my green flannel pajama pants and a hoodie.

The girls were still at the table. Pleased, I took my seat. Pure satisfaction filled me. Sure, there was still most of the table between us, but I was allowed to sit with them. My patience was paying off.

Daisy cut a chunk off her calzone. "Did you make these last weekend and I missed it?"

The only thing I'd been kneading was her ass. It'd been just us last weekend. When Laila was with her dad, Daisy and I lost ourselves in each other. We cuddled on the couch and took showers together. I lived for those days.

But now I was at the table, with them, and that was pretty damn special too. "Store-bought. Sorry."

She snorted. "Don't be sorry. They're amazing."

"I like them," Laila said.

Another win. She was admitting to liking what I cooked. "Then I'll keep getting them." Whatever made my girls happy.

"Can we watch a movie tonight?" Laila asked.

Daisy's blinks were heavy. "Sure."

Laila's smile was triumphant, but she could probably ask for anything tonight, and if it didn't require much energy from Daisy, she'd get what she wanted.

"Want to watch a movie?" Laila asked me.

Delight coursed through me at being included. Eating alone at the table when they were home had been better than getting takeout to eat alone while I answered emails at my old house. This trumped it all. I didn't care if I was two seats down from either of them. "I'd love to. Whatcha watching?"

"*Tangled*!" Laila's answer was instant.

"Haven't seen it," I admitted.

She gasped. "You haven't?" Her eyes were wide. "It's Mom's fav-o-rite," she sang.

Daisy chuckled. "Good thing we're correcting that right now. After bath time." She led Laila to the bathroom.

I wolfed down the rest of my calzone and salad and got the dishwasher going. Then I made a couple of quick mugs of warm lemonade with honey. Daisy was snuggled in her usual corner and Laila played with a couple of dolls in the spot next to her. My insides warmed like I was filled with lemonade and honey.

"This might help your throat." I set the mug for Daisy down on the coffee table and put another with a lid for Laila next to it.

"Ooh." Laila took a dainty drink.

Daisy smiled at me. "Thank you."

"Any time." And I meant it.

To give them space, I sprawled on the love seat.

For much of the movie, Laila would point and say "here" when a funny part was coming. When she giggled, I made sure to laugh too. Before the movie was done, Daisy fell asleep, huddled in a blanket.

I spied on her out of the corner of my eye. Her mouth was open, and I could hear stuffy breaths from here.

"Mommy feels icky," Laila said when the movie was over.

"Yes, she does." I shut the TV off. Daisy didn't rouse. "I hate to wake her. Mind if I read you a book?"

Laila tossed her dolls to the side and scooted off the couch. "Okay. Wait here."

Pleased, I stayed right where I was. Tonight was a milestone. I ate with them, watched a show with them, and now I got the coveted role of bedtime stories.

She returned after several minutes with no less than ten books, and I fought back laughter. I'd been had by a four-year-old.

She scrambled onto the love seat, heedless of my legs. She tucked herself by my knees. Not too close, but not far enough away to be unable to see. I arranged the books into a neat stack. None of them were very long and most were board books. Except one about a Maine coon cat in red Converse. My mom's book. She had sent some books once she had the okay from Daisy.

"Should I start with my mom's book or end with it?"

Laila folded her hands on her lap. "End."

I read through each story. None of them took very long, but by the time we were done, Laila's blinks were as long as Daisy's had been before she'd drifted off.

"How 'bout I walk you to bed?" I lifted the stack and swung my legs down.

Laila pouted and looked at her mom. Soft breaths puffed out of Daisy's mouth. Finally, Laila slid off the love seat. She tucked her little hand in mine.

My heart stopped. This little girl wasn't mine, but the truth was, I wanted to be accepted by her like she was. She was shy but kind like her mom. She was reserved, naturally wary, like Daisy. She was a kid I would've been proud to call my own. Jason got that honor, but...maybe there was a chance I could too.

"Let's get you to bed," I said softly.

When she was cuddled under the covers in almost the

same position as Daisy on the couch, I went to the door. "Good night, Laila."

"Night, Alder," she said in a sleepy voice.

I was smiling when I went to the living room. Daisy was sitting up and rubbing her eyes. She might be sick, but I got to take care of her.

I squatted next to the coffee table on her side of the couch. "Don't wake up all the way. You might as well head straight to bed."

She frowned and blinked around. "Laila?"

"She conned me into ten books, and I just tucked her in." When she recoiled, the pressure was back, pushing against my sternum. "I hope that was okay. I know you're not feeling good."

"No, it's fine. She let you?"

I nodded.

Her lips stayed in a frown. "Jason said she still doesn't let his mom put her to bed."

I wasn't competing, but I needed signs that Laila wouldn't hate me for helping her mom. "Does that woman read her ten books?"

"She probably stops at five."

"There you have it. I aim to please the ladies in my life." I smirked. "Besides, one book was Mom's, so I know she has good taste."

Daisy chuckled softly. "That she does." She pressed a hand against her head. "I feel hot. Am I hot?"

I replaced her hand with mine. "Yup. Get to bed, and I'll bring you some meds."

"I wish you could sleep with me."

"I know." I'd love to crawl in with her, but I would still go to bed a contented man. Tonight, I'd gotten to experience everything I had thought was gone.

* * *

Daisy

I was lying in bed all day. This was the first time I'd been sick as a parent when I'd been able to do nothing but take care of myself. Even if Jason had been off, he'd been overwhelmed with Laila as a baby and toddler. Alder brought me breakfast and lunch, told me not to worry about Laila, delivered hot lemonade with honey and cold meds, and he'd even set up his tablet with shows for me to watch.

I thought he'd plant Laila in front of the TV or toss toys at her, but her laughter drifted in from outside.

Frowning, I got up. I groaned and pressed my fingertips to my forehead. My sinus headache was returning. I grabbed the water Alder left and found another dose of meds next to it.

That man got sexier doing the most mundane things.

I gulped the pills down and stood. At the window, I lifted the blinds back. Laila and Alder were at the edge of the flower beds by the shed. Her red leggings were half covered in dirt, and she held a small trowel in one hand and a tiny hand rake in the other. Her gloves were filthy. I smiled.

Alder pointed at some dried plants and she nodded. Then he retrieved his own rake and spade from where they were propped against the shed and went to the other side.

I watched with the blinds barely pulled back. Every

minute that ticked by, my heart crawled into my throat. This was what I had wanted. Alder as my partner. Alder taking care of me. Alder as an invested parent. This was the life I thought we'd have.

My gaze stayed on him as he worked up the flower bed, his broad shoulders moving under his sweatshirt and his ass flexing in his jeans. If only I could wrap my arms around him and give him a kiss that relayed all my gratitude...and all my love. With none of the germs.

I was sick. He was taking care of me. It couldn't be anything more than that.

And why not?

My illness robbed me of logic. I couldn't think of what a bad thing it would be to nurture and grow whatever was going on here.

Alder had changed.

What if I hadn't? What if I was still incapable of making the right decision with men?

I shook my head. I surely had a fever and this was no time to be making life-changing decisions. I shuffled to the bathroom and then returned to bed. After a nap, I woke to Alder replacing my water.

"Hey. How ya feeling?" His warm smile was more welcome than my cough suppressant.

I closed my eyes to let my hearing get the full effect of his voice. "Like crap." I cracked an eye open. "But also better."

"Mommy, I showered!" Laila called from the doorway. Her light hair was a rat's nest that needed a brush, but she was grinning and dressed in pajamas. "Alder said we can have popcorn."

"Maybe I'll join you," I told her.

Laila disappeared, and Alder smiled. *If I weren't sick, this moment would be damn near perfect.*

"Feel up to eating?" Alder asked. "I got Grandma Annie's potato dumpling soup recipe from Dad."

My stomach growled. "I'm hungry. I can't promise I'll be able to taste it, but the texture sounds amazing."

He grinned. "Less pressure, then." He glanced down the hallway. "But I'll still have the little gardener to impress."

"I saw you out there with her."

"Keeps us busy," he said easily.

Laila flounced around him with an armload of books. She went to the other side of the bed, tossed her stash on the covers, then climbed on. "We can read."

Fondness filled me. Reading was all kinds of medicine for Laila, and she was trying to treat me.

She pulled out a book. "I want a pair of red shoes. Like May-no-la."

I exchanged a smile with Alder. Magnolia had—predictably—left an impression on my daughter. I knew the feeling, and I was grateful Laila could experience Magnolia's zest for life and family.

"She probably heard that from Billings and is already plotting," Alder joked, his eyes soft. He pushed off the doorframe. "I'm gonna grab a quick shower. Have fun, ladies."

He gave me a look that said he would love to kiss me, but he was holding back. He had to.

Did he?

I'd love a kiss from him anytime and anywhere, but our situation was more complicated. Different what-ifs were running through my head. Instead of cruising through all the possible fallouts of this arrangement, I started considering the opposite. What if we tried to be the real thing?

Fear didn't clog my throat like it used to. There was no hopelessness. I started reading Magnolia's book. Laila had two more of hers waiting in the wings.

His footsteps on the stairs sounded, then a couple of minutes later, the water turned on in the second-level bathroom.

I finished the story and set it aside. I had Laila alone, and while that definitely wasn't unusual, I wanted to take advantage of the moment. The hunger in my stomach turned to nerves.

I licked my dry lips. "I'm glad that you don't mind Alder."

She smiled. "I like him."

Me too, kiddo. "I also like him a lot."

She handed me another book. One of Magnolia's.

I flattened my hand on the top. "What if I started liking him as more than a friend? What would you think of that?"

She shrugged and handed me another book.

This was both easier and harder than I thought. "Like, if we started dating or something. Would that be all right?"

She held her hands up. "I dunno. You and Daddy don't date."

"No. Not anymore."

"He dates other girls."

Surprised, I gripped the books she'd handed me. "Really?" I bit the inside of my cheek and inspected my feelings. I was more worried about how he was handling dating with our daughter. "Have you met them?"

She shook her head. "He says they're just friends."

He was probably as friendly with them as I was with Alder. Perhaps just as cautious. As long as he wasn't flaunting them around Laila, I wouldn't worry. He was a more attentive dad as a single guy than when we'd been together.

If Jason was dating again, then maybe he'd take the news that Alder and I had grown close well.

One more what-if popped into my head. What if I asked my husband to start dating?

* * *

Alder

Laila was still with Daisy. I didn't hear the steady cadence of reading. They were talking instead, but I couldn't hear what about. I dished out the soup and let it cool off before calling the girls to the table. I'd burned myself too many times on this damn soup to let it happen to anyone else.

After several minutes, I went to Daisy's bedroom. The warmth in my chest had nothing to do with standing over a stove for the last hour. Laila was cuddled against her mom, her chin resting on Daisy's chest. The stack of books was at the foot of the bed, and they were watching something on the tablet I had set up for Daisy.

As for my wife, her color was less pale and her eyes weren't as glassy as this morning. That nap must've helped.

I stuffed a hand into my pocket. I could stand here for hours, but that'd get creepy. "Soup's on."

"I gotta potty first." Laila rolled off the bed and rushed around me with a grin.

I smiled at Daisy. She stood slowly and stretched, her arms reaching high. Her shirt was too big to show me a glimpse of her abdomen, but my gaze lingered over her hips and breasts as she finished her stretch.

She caught me looking and shyly pushed a lock of hair behind her ear. "Sorry I haven't been to your bedroom much this week."

My feet twitched to go to her. To ease her worries. I didn't like her just for the sex. I wasn't here for the damn house either. It was all her. "There's nothing to apologize for. I'm glad I can be here, helping you."

She hugged her arms around herself. "I, uh...talked to Laila. A little. About us."

The more her words sunk in, the more my shock rose. "Us?" I had to make sure.

Daisy's gaze skated away. "I wanted to find out how she'd feel if we, you know, dated."

"We're not dating, Daisy."

She rolled her eyes and pinned me with her frank gaze. "I can't very well tell her that."

I chuckled, still reeling from her confession. I grew serious. "I want this, Daze. I'm not playing around. Not with you. Not with her. But I'll only move as fast as you're comfortable."

"I'm not comfortable with anything, Alder. You've always pushed me out of my comfort zone. And you do it in a way that makes me want it."

I crossed the bedroom to her and put my hands on her hips. I needed to be close to her for this conversation. "What exactly do you want?"

Her blue eyes shimmered. "You," she whispered.

"Good. Because I want you. It's only you I've ever wanted, and I'm going to prove that I'll never let you down again."

Affection sparkled in her gaze, but a flicker of worry lit the yellow flecks in her irises. "You don't have to be perfect, you know."

I'd been too imperfect before. Too slovenly. Too disrespectful. Too irreverent. Never again. "You deserve perfection."

She snorted. "Neither of us is perfect, though I'm having a hard time finding your flaws."

"I'm trying to make sure there are none."

She placed her hands on my chest. "Whatever we do with us, we do together. We listen and we talk, okay?"

"I'm all ears and all mouth, Daze."

She relaxed and sniffled. "You might get sick if you touch me."

"I'll risk it." I ran my thumb over the back of her hand. "I want to take you out on a real date."

"I can't believe we haven't been on one."

"We're doing things out of order."

She smiled and gripped my hand so our palms were against each other. "Laila's with Jason next weekend."

"Then we'll go out to eat. Get you that steak and sweet potato, nice and fresh."

"That's what I ate on our first date," she said softly.

"I know. And we went to the movies after. So let's hope the horror movie playing right now is replaced by then."

She laughed just as the bathroom door clicked open. Her fingers tensed under mine and she gently pulled away. "I'd like to talk to her more before we do this."

And we were doing this. I was finally going to date my wife.

Chapter Nineteen

Daisy

My bedroom door was closed. I held up one pale pink, long-sleeved shirt, then a loose-knit sweater that was good for cool spring weather.

Alder wasn't home yet. Jason had picked Laila up from daycare, so I'd returned earlier than on a normal weekday. Alder planned to take me out tonight, and I had to decide what to wear.

I had on my best pair of jeans. They made my legs look curvy and would pair well with the brown suede shoes I had.

I held the sweater up. It'd cover my hips and didn't cling to my stomach. I might want to impress Alder, but I would decimate my meal. I didn't get to eat out very much, thanks to an asshole ex and my bad judgement.

My phone buzzed from where I'd tossed it on the bed. I hung the long-sleeved shirt up and shrugged into the sweater. Then I checked my phone.

Alder: Sorry, my meeting is running late.

Disappointment curled through my belly. I fought off flashbacks. The Alder from before never would've texted so promptly. He'd have made me wait for a couple of hours until I reached out and then he'd claim he'd forgotten and tell me I was overreacting.

Daisy: Okay.

I tugged at my sweater and went out to the couch and scrolled through my phone, trying not to watch the minutes rack up.

An hour ticked by. My phone vibrated.

Alder: Should be wrapping up soon.

A tendril of dread swirled through my gut. More like hunger pangs. I'd been dreaming about the meal I'd order. Takeout wasn't the same as fresh. My taste buds could only be placated but not fooled.

I turned the TV on and ordered my stomach to settle down. This wasn't like before. Alder wasn't at the bar with work buddies. He wasn't staying in Williston an extra night because he'd gotten too drunk to drive home after work.

Before long, an engine sounded outside. I popped up off the couch and took a step, then stopped. I had planned to peek around the curtain, but I would not be a desperate woman. I would not be that nagging new wife from before.

Someone knocked on the front door. Confused, I gnawed on the inside of my cheek. I had thought Alder was home, but he would come in through the garage.

I peeked outside only to find Alder waiting on the front stoop.

Opening the door, I frowned. "Is there something wrong with the garage door?"

He grinned, but an apology darkened his eyes. "I wanted to pick you up like a real date. To make up for being late."

I dropped my gaze down, past his charcoal suit coat and tie, over slacks of the same color, to his sharp loafers. He was not dressed for steak and potatoes in a small-town bar and grill. "We'd look like the odd couple."

"I'd look like I was trying to impress you. And I am." He held his elbow out. "Ready?"

I smiled and hooked my arm through his. At the pickup, he opened the door but stopped me before I got in.

He tipped my chin up. "You look sexy as hell. I should've led with that."

I preened inside. "Mm, maybe tell me two more times tonight to make up for it."

Concern creased the corners of his eyes. "I really am sorry."

"I know, but you were working. It's okay."

He studied my expression, his gaze vacillating back and forth between my eyes. Then he lowered his head and pressed a sweet kiss to the corner of my mouth. "If I take it any further, I'm afraid I'll ruin our date night."

"Can't have that."

"Later," he said, his voice full of promise.

My smile didn't disappear all the way to Rattler's. It was crowded for a Friday, but we got a high-top table in the bar. Alder pulled my chair out for me and everything. Self-consciousness rode along my shoulders, but I was too excited to be out. On a date. With Alder Duke. It was like being in high school again.

"Hello, Mr. Duke," an older woman said. She smiled from him to me. She was vaguely familiar.

"Alice," Alder said warmly. "Nice to see you out of the office."

Yes, Alice. She worked in the headquarters office, and her headshot was in her signature block.

"Nice to see you doing more than work," she said. "You as well, Daisy."

"She keeps me out of trouble," Alder joked.

Alice rushed along with a final wave. When we were seated with drinks in front of us, I stared at the handsome businessman across from me, and words vanished from my brain. This was Alder. The boy I'd met when I was a freshman. The guy I'd lost my virginity to. The kid who used to take me on horseback rides and pack picnics. He was also the man who'd gotten through college at lightning speed. The Alder who climbed his way up from the oil fields to the C-suite.

We'd been in the house, living our separate-but-together married life, isolated from the outside world. I went to work married. My coworkers knew, but they weren't the type to get hung up on the emotions of it. I'd remarried my ex, and he happened to be the CEO. But then someone like Alice saw us out and...I was married to the top guy.

"You're my boss," I blurted out.

The couple next to us looked over, and Alder smirked. I didn't recognize them, but Rattler's got customers from all the surrounding small towns and the employees of the big industries nestled among the fields and buttes.

Alder's chuckle was lost in the noise of the bar. "There are a few levels of separation."

"More than a few." I gave my head a shake. He was that high up. And I was that far down. "I know I've seen you coming and going from the house wearing your suits and your shiny shoes, but it just hit me." How far we'd diverged.

He'd probably built up a nice retirement portfolio, while I got only what my job put away for me. I couldn't even put a dime into savings. Forget making an account of any sort for Laila. She'd be in the same boat I'd been in. Years of school loans. I'd have to talk to her about dodgy men who seemed too good to be true.

"You are at the top," I said and I let my pride out. "You remember when you used to shrug off when people would ask if you were following in your dad's footsteps? You didn't think you could do it."

"No." He swallowed hard. "I'd hear that, and I'd know what they didn't. That I was young and immature. That I had almost gotten thrown in jail the night before." When my eyes widened, he gave me an apologetic smile. "I haven't told you about that."

"About what?"

"My antics happened more after the divorce, but the one I'm thinking of is street racing. Lots of straight, desolate highways between here and Williston."

"And now you take a helicopter there? I think you've matured."

"Sometimes it's a private plane."

I laughed. "I'm proud of you. Maybe more than a little impressed."

Instead of shrugging off my words, he sat on them for a few moments, his gaze introspective. Then he gave me one nod, an acknowledgment, as if he'd finally reached the end of a long journey. "Have I told you how sexy you are?"

"You have one more obligatory statement," I joked.

"You're sexy, you're sexy, you're sexy."

When the bartender appeared at our side, Alder didn't take his gaze off me. He ordered for the both of us. The bartender even gave me the side-eye, like he wondered if I was truly okay with that.

Yes. Absolutely. Alder was the only man who'd ever understood me. Being with him was like getting the other half of myself back.

* * *

Alder

We'd been at the restaurant for over an hour, and we'd have to leave soon for the movie. I didn't care where we went or what we did as long as I was with my wife.

I was laughing at a story she was telling of how one of her coworkers performed with an alphorn for them when a shadow fell beside me.

"Holy shit?" a guy boomed. "Crazy A?"

I nearly choked, my eyes bulging out. I remembered a lot from my wild years, but I'd forgotten that godforsaken name.

Tension knotted at my temples. I turned my assessing gaze to the sort of familiar voice. He wore jeans and a hoodie with the name of the coal mine out of Washburn, and his ball cap was embroidered with the green-and-yellow NDSU Bison logo. He had short, dark hair with faint glints of gray. Same with his scruff. He grinned broadly, and the sight tugged at my memory.

"Yes?" I asked politely.

He held his arms out and waited. His smile froze for a moment and he laughed. "Dude, it's me. Matthew." He dropped his arms and nudged me with an elbow. "Matty the Tank."

Awareness dawned on me, and a flood of memories cascaded back that I would rather stayed locked away. Matty the Tank because he could hold as much beer as a thousand-gallon tank, and Crazy A because my ideas had been insane.

"Sorry, Matthew, I didn't recognize you," I said woodenly, sneaking a gaze at Daisy.

Her lightness from tonight was gone, and tension pinched at her flattened lips.

"No kidding." He slapped my back. If I hadn't been concentrating on core workouts for the last ten years, I'd have ended up with my face in my empty sweet potato peel. "You probably don't recognize me when I'm not piss-drunk." He guffawed. "I never would've thought it was you, but I saw the announcement that you're the head at the refinery. No shit? Who'd have thought?"

"Not me," I said honestly.

He shifted his gaze to Daisy, and surprise lit his face. "Daisy? I thought you two—" He sobered, and I admired his recovery. "Nice to see you again."

"Hi, Matty— Matthew."

His smile was congenial. "No 'Matty the Tank' for me." He cocked his head toward me. "The big guy here isn't the only one who cleaned up his act." He waved at someone by the entrance. A woman with ink-black hair in a long braid flashed him a "hurry up" look, then she saw us. She wandered over, more curious than irritated.

"This is my wife, Stella." He put an arm around her. "This is Alder and his..." His gaze landed on Daisy's ring finger and relief crossed his face. "Wife. Hon, remember that guy I told you about when I was working outside of Williston? The one who made us all go ice fishing in nothing but boots and a scarf?"

Ah, hell. I could've done without that reminder. I hadn't been the type to fuck around with other women, but I'd had a ton of other bad ideas. I'd cut loose in ways that should've shortened my life and others'. Thank fuck they hadn't.

Stella chuckled. "The naked ice fishing. Yes, I recall that story, among many."

"Too many," I said, pushing my empty beer farther away. I'd only had one, but it was sitting sour in my stomach.

"I have you to thank," Stella said. She turned her attention to Daisy. "All the wild was out of Matthew by the time we met."

"Had to be or I'd lose my liver." Pride beamed from Matthew's face. "Now, I'm coaching Little League and building sets for the school play our kids are in."

My shoulders unknotted at the mention of kids. He'd grown up and would maybe see our glory days as the wasted time they were. "How many kids do you have?"

"Two," he replied. "They're ten and six. Both boys." He dug out his phone and flashed us his screen. A happy family stared back at us. "How 'bout you two?"

Daisy exchanged a look with me. Did I appear as panicked as I felt? How should I answer?

"I have a girl from a previous relationship," Daisy answered. "Alder and I were divorced for almost fifteen years."

"And now we're married again," I said lightly. I didn't want the past to rain on our night. "Who knew cleaning stuff like naked ice fishing out of my life and getting a good job would help me win her back?"

Stella's eyes softened. "That's so sweet. I'm happy for you two."

"No more pasture polo either," Matthew said.

Daisy lifted her brows at me.

More wild memories, goddammit. "Uh, no. Figured I should give up trying to race bulls."

"Some of them buggers were fast." Matthew slapped me on the back again. "How are we still alive?"

"There were a lot of mornings I wondered that."

"You know what?" Matthew looked around. "I thought I saw— There he is. Hey, Juan. Come here!"

My stomach dropped. Not another blast from the past. What had I expected? I'd grown up in Coal Haven. My worst years were spent here. Witnessed here. Many of those spectators—buddies, bartenders, passersby—still lived in the community.

Shit.

Juan swaggered over. He'd been one of the main crew I'd hung out with. We had worked the same shifts and had carpooled to the job site. Afterward, we had partied.

"No fucking way." Juan grinned and ran a hand through his spiky black hair. Unlike me and Matthew, he wasn't sporting flecks of gray. "Crazy A Duke."

I cringed at the nickname. "Just Alder now. The crazy is over with."

His laugh wasn't as loud as Matthew's. "I heard you were back in town, but I didn't believe it." He let out a wistful sigh. "I guess we all have to grow up sometime. You just fell off the face of the earth, and then when I heard about you again, you're the big guy."

"I decided to work hard instead of play hard," I said.

Matthew's snort echoed in my ear. "I can believe you're the CEO if you worked as hard as you played."

"It was epic." Juan's grin slipped. "For real, I won't be telling my kids about any of the shit I did. How did we not get arrested?"

"By someone's good grace." And I owed that guy who'd told me to never set foot on his land again or he'd call the cops.

Juan stuffed a finger over his shoulder. "I was just at the bar talking to Porter. Remember him? He used to bartend downtown."

I held in my groan. Another person who knew just what an idiot I was. How many of those bartenders and liquor store employees were still in the area? How many more Matthews and Juans? What the hell did Daisy think after hearing all this?

"Wait until I tell Gavin you're back in town. You know he's a loan officer at the bank now? Said his back couldn't take the oil field anymore."

A part of me was happy for Gavin. He'd been less wild, more likely to go home earlier. Now he was an upstanding citizen. But dammit, why'd he have to clean up and stay in town?

I moved here for my career. For Daisy. I didn't expect my past to stop at my table and provide living accounts of what had ruined my marriage.

"Nice to see you again." Juan shook my hand, pumping it hard. "If I see any full moons in the pastures, I'll know it's you."

He and Matthew laughed. Stella joined in. Daisy smiled politely but shot me a concerned look. I didn't realize I was laughing but the congenial businessman in me was finely honed. Charm went a long way.

If I see any full moons in the pastures, I'll know it's you.

Fuck me.

"Well, we'll let you two be." Matthew hugged his wife tighter. I was happy for the man. Mostly grateful my stupid ideas hadn't gotten us killed. They were about to turn away when Matthew pinned me with his brown gaze. "Oh, hey. Do I recall correctly that you used to play baseball? We could always use more coaches."

Me? Coach? "I…"

"We're hoping to field enough teams for everyone interested. T-ball has a ton of kids signed up this year. Daisy, how old's yours?"

"Four," she said.

"Perfect." Matthew grinned. "Bring her out."

"I don't think it's her thing, but I appreciate the offer." Daisy's lips twitched as if she couldn't picture Laila picking up a bat.

Matthew dug out his phone. "Let me get your number, Alder. I'll get you guys the information."

I couldn't see myself having time to coach, but I gave him my number.

When they were gone, I met Daisy's stare, bracing myself for her disappointment.

"Naked ice fishing?" she asked with a wry twist to her lips. "Crazy A?"

"My behavior escalated after the divorce." My ideas had gotten more reckless and dangerous. "Nearly froze my balls off."

She made a tsking noise. "Good thing you didn't. I've found them useful."

I laughed but the humor quickly drained out of me. "Sorry. For all the reminders."

"I'm not sure I recall racing bulls."

"It was after our time too. And also naked." I grimaced. "I sprained my ankle that night and nearly got fired because I was late the next morning for work." I dropped my attention to my empty beer mug. She'd just told me she was proud of me. How'd she feel now?

A server came by to clear our empty plates and glasses. Daisy was looking around the restaurant. Was she trying to guess who else would pop up and recount some ridiculous stunt I'd pulled?

"That whole exchange actually made me feel better." When I looked up, surprised, she nodded. "I pictured you naked, yes, but surrounded by beautiful women, living your best life."

"My best days were in high school and right now."

Her mouth curved up, and those blue gems of hers sparkled. "If you're trying to get laid, keep going."

"We have to finish the date properly, and we have a movie to get to. Then you're all mine."

*　*　*

Daisy

The pickup seat was back as far as it could go, the windows were fogged up, and my pants were in the back seat with my underwear. I was astride my husband and tilted forward so my head didn't hit the top of the cab as I rode him.

Being on a date with Alder, in that suit, had been more than my restraint could take. As soon as he had parked in the garage and hit the button to close the door, I'd been all over him.

"Alder," I whimpered.

"Not yet," he said through gritted teeth. "I've been picturing you like this," he panted, rolling his hips up into me. "Since that first night." Grunt. "You made it impossible for me to get inside this vehicle without getting fucking hard."

His fingers tightened at my hips. He hadn't even touched my clit. He didn't need to. This angle allowed the perfect amount of friction. I ground down on him, my moan ragged.

"Come for me, Daze." He squeezed the globes of my ass. "I want to hear you scream."

My breathing was rough, mingling with his grunts. He didn't have much leverage, and I'd already honked the horn with my butt once.

Pleasure built, from my core to the base of my skull, and mushroomed outward. My nipples were tight peaks and arousal pulsed white hot where Alder and I were connected.

"Alder," I said again, a plea. I was so close.

"I know what you need." He slid his long fingers around my neck and brought my head down for a kiss.

I licked out, meeting his tongue with mine. He broke apart only far enough to slip his fingers in between my lips. I sucked on his rough fingertips. Then he removed them to slide his hand between our bodies.

As soon as the extra pressure hit my clit, energy coursed through my body, hot and chaotic. I bucked, my climax hitting me hard. I bopped my head off the top of the cab. Alder hugged me closer to him as I shook through my climax, keeping me safe from any more head knocks.

I was just coming down when he stiffened under me. His hold tightened as he exploded inside me. My core filled with blistering heat as he pumped in and out.

"God—Alder." I soared back into an orgasm, or a continuation of the first one. I didn't care. Pure pleasure streamed through my veins, holding steady, then I floated back down.

I blinked my eyes open. He gave me a lazy grin, and I started laughing.

"Look at the windows," I said. We'd fogged up every single pane of glass.

He chuckled and ran his hands up and down my back under my sweater. "I don't remember this from our first date."

"Everything's two point oh now, including our dates."

"I love you, Daisy."

We fell quiet. My heartbeat thumped at the base of my throat. He'd said it before, but this time was less urgent. Less desperate. The circumstances made it more sincere.

"It's okay if you're not ready," he said after several moments.

Not ready? I was so ready that it terrified me. I'd been ready for years.

I let my fingertips bump over the faint stubble already dusting his chin. "It's not that. I guess... I'm just afraid I'm going to mess it up. Should I admit that I never stopped loving you? Is that sweet or does it put me in creepy-obsessive territory?"

His easy grin was back. "If it's creepy-obsessive territory, then I'm right there with you."

I stroked my hands over his face. "I love you." The freedom of saying those words would make me float away if we weren't in the pickup. "I really love you."

"Goddamn, Daisy. Do you know how long I have waited to hear that again?" He grabbed both of my hands in his. "Do you know how much I feared I'd never hear it from you again? That you'd never mean it?"

I pressed my mouth against his. I'd had all the same fears, only I had assumed it'd never happen.

He kissed me back, delving in deep with his tongue. His cock twitched inside of me.

I hated to pull away, but I did, easing off him. "I know you can go again, but I can't feel my knees."

"I don't mind. I wanted to crawl into bed with you, wrap you up in my arms, and go to sleep."

I was glowing as I scrambled into my pants for the chilly run through the garage. In the house, I got ready for bed, using the bathroom before changing into loose pajama shorts and a matching pink top. He stripped down to his underwear.

"Remember the roommate rules?" I asked as I crawled into bed.

He got in beside me. "I remember each one, and I'm mostly confident you don't want to enforce them."

I smirked and curled right into him. I snuggled against his chest. His breathing was steady, but a tightness resonated through his body.

I rubbed my hand over his pecs. "Something on your mind, Duke?"

"When can I start going to bed with you again? When Laila's here?"

The real world was impeding on my fantasy time with Alder, but that was a good thing. It should be a good thing.

When should we let my daughter see that I was getting serious with a guy who was sold to her as a roommate? She'd been open to the dating idea, but would that be different than knowing for certain we were dating?

"You can tell me what you're thinking too," he said. "No matter how bad it is, I want you to be open with me. I want to know those critical thoughts swirling around in your head." He trailed his fingers over my shoulder.

My hesitation lingered.

"I know I need to earn your trust again," he said quietly. "I know why you don't want to open up with me."

"No, it's not—" Maybe a part of me was afraid he'd brush me off. That he'd roll his eyes, say *Okay, Mom*, and I'd be standing alone again. Hadn't he shown me how much he was trying? It'd been months. "She's starting to like you. She's getting used to bouncing between houses, and if we date, then we'll start sleeping together like this when she'll know, and I honestly don't know how much a four-year-old can understand. Then we're...married. So you're not a guy I'm dating, you're her stepdad. When we go out in town, people will treat you as her stepdad. And if... What if..."

I hated to say it, but our track record was there in an official document. As much as we wanted to start over, we didn't have a clean slate.

"What if we don't work?" he said, resigned.

"Yes," I whispered as my heart convulsed. If things between us didn't work out a second time, that was it. I'd fall so far there would be no bottom. I'd be single the rest of my life, and Laila would grow up watching me try to pretend to be happy after experiencing what true happiness was like.

"I'm doing everything I can," he said, determination pouring out of him. "I'll even coach T-ball if that'll show you I'm a changed man."

A changed man—or a family man? "I know you, Alder. You've already shown me."

In the dark, I felt the tension ripple through him. "I feel like I should, and not just for you. I can wear the suit. I can run the refinery, but there are a lot of Matthews out there who remember naked me running through their pastures or racing down their streets, and I don't have the excuse that I was a teen. I was plenty old enough."

I draped myself over his chest. I'd been worrying about myself. He was going through his own ordeal from the divorce and how things ended. How he'd acted. I'd noticed how his eyes had filled with dread when Juan had made the comment about finding him running nude through pastures again. Somewhere inside him, he was afraid that no one thought he had changed.

"Seeing your buddies tonight bothered you." I didn't have to ask it as a question.

He didn't answer right away. His chest rose and fell. His heartbeat remained steady. "It bothered me enough to get me to really consider coaching kids, any kids. Hell, I'll direct the summer play if that gets the guys to quit associating me with Crazy A."

"Does it really matter?" I asked. "Look at who you are."

"But to them, I'll always be *that guy*. The one who gave up his wife for all-nighters, mud runs, and hick games in the middle of someone's pasture." He let out a disgusted noise. "All the Barrons are going to be at Violet and Evander's wedding reception next month. I'm sure some of them remember what I was like."

"You're not that guy anymore."

He rolled me over and stretched himself above me. I was in my pajama shorts and top, and he was in his boxer briefs, but that would change soon enough judging from the hard ridge pressing against my stomach. "You're pretty amazing, you know that?"

He used to say that in high school, and I still couldn't figure out what he saw in me. "No."

He lined kisses along my collarbone. "You gonna be there to cheer on my T-ball games?"

"So now I'm going to be the CEO's wife *and* the coach's wife?"

He hooked his fingers around my shorts. "It all means you're my wife."

Chapter Twenty

Alder

It was the middle of June, and my whole family was in town. We were all mingling among the Barrons. Violet and Evander had gotten married last year during the winter but waited until the summer to hold their reception. They held it at their house, with the shop open, grills set up, and tables scattered over the lawn.

The day was relaxed, but I still wore slacks. Maybe I had woken up a little more uptight than usual and dressed like I wasn't the dumbass who hung up my pickup on a mailbox in the middle of town when I had overslept one morning after Daisy had left.

I was no longer oversleeping, but Daisy still wasn't in my bed when I woke. It'd been about a month since our first real date, but she wanted to be cautious with Laila.

I'd put that caution there. So I'd be patient. Daisy and Laila deserved it.

Daisy stayed nestled into my side as we chatted with

my parents. Dad wanted all the dirt about my job. Six months had gone by, but I was still the new guy. Yet I was settling in.

"And you're coaching?" Dad asked. His dark eyes lit up. He'd coached my team one year. He'd been called away during some practices and weekends. That had been the one and only year he'd tried.

"I'm sort of coaching." Organizing a team of ten T-ball players was like herding cats—they went in different directions, made shrill noises, and at a moment's notice, half of them might be off chasing a butterfly.

"Is Laila playing?" Dad asked.

Daisy shook her head. "Not her thing, but she's asked to watch Alder coach."

Dad laughed. "I want to watch Alder coach."

One of Evander's cousins wandered over. Stetson Barron was a big guy, taller than me with shoulders that could block out the light. Dark scruff filled his cheeks, and the gray dotting his temples made it look more like he'd gotten highlights.

"Alder," he said pleasantly. "Been a while."

The fruit punch in my stomach turned sour. Stetson was a nice guy. His dad used to be my dad's boss, and now I was in charge.

Stetson had also not called the police when I'd raced bulls in his pasture.

I shook his hand, meeting his crushing grip with my own. "Nice to see you again," I said. "Are we related now?"

"Any family of Violet's is family of ours." He eyed my slacks and polo. "Keeping out of trouble these days, I hear."

"Trying to."

"And succeeding." He tipped his head toward Daisy. "Since you're an upstanding citizen now, Isla might hit you up to help with the farmer's market."

"Excuse me?"

"She does that. No one is safe." He beckoned his sister over from the long table the food was set up in. Isla smiled and grabbed her husband's arm. They approached us. Isla was a grown version of the girl I remembered. Same long blonde hair. Still taller than many other girls. Her husband was my height, and he kept his hair stylishly shaggy.

"Hi, Alder. Hello again, Daisy." Isla had been in Violet's class, and she and her husband, McCoy, owned and ran Reservoir Barrel.

Daisy smiled. She wasn't tense around the Barrons, but she'd been seeing them around town most of her life. "Hey, Isla."

"You should recruit Alder to help with the farmer's market," Stetson said. "Since he's an upstanding citizen now."

McCoy's brows drew together like he'd caught the "now" and didn't know the story. He wasn't from Coal Haven. Which made him one of the few people who didn't know how I'd blown up my marriage.

"The farmer's market?" I asked to move the conversation along before any stories about me could be shared.

Isla gave a subtle eye roll. "Yes—don't get me wrong. I love the market. I was even fired from managing it before." My brows lifted and she laughed. "It was necessary, and it was my dad who fired me. But then he retired and it's mine again. With two kids, it gets a little overwhelming."

The urge to prove myself to this group rode high on my shoulders. "Sure. I can help."

Isla blinked. "Really? Just like that?"

"I want to give back to the town that made sure I didn't kill myself by being stupid," I said lightly, but the truth landed heavy. Daisy squeezed my hand, the silent reassurance I needed.

Stetson gave me a meaningful look. "Or that you didn't end up in jail."

The image arose in my head of Stetson looming over me, big as a jet plane, telling me to get my ass off his land and that he'd call the cops if I ever returned. Daisy ran her thumb over the back of my hand. She must sense my inner turmoil.

Our dads had worked together for most of our lives until then, yet I was the one in a ditch and he was the responsible rancher. My wife was gone at that point, and my family's pride balanced on a razor's edge. Dad would've been humiliated if this got back to him.

Yet it hadn't been him I'd been concerned about. I had thought that Daisy had been right. I hadn't listened and here I was. Rock bottom.

"But seriously, it's good to see you," Stetson said. "Having you, Violet, and Lily back in the community benefits all of us." He tilted his head toward the newest happy couple. "I thought it'd take a miracle to get Evander back home."

"That's Violet's middle name," I replied.

"I know Dad was glad to see someone competent take his place." Stetson took in my slacks once again, like he was trying to reconcile the immature dick in his ditch with me.

"And I'm grateful you gave me a hand when I needed

it," I said, grateful I could couch my appreciation in vague responses.

A cry rang up, and all the parents in the group craned their necks to see if the kid hollering was theirs. Daisy didn't. Laila was with Jason.

"That's my cue." Stetson jogged off.

"Are you sure?" Isla asked me, her brow creased. "About the farmer's market? I don't want to pressure you."

It was Stetson who'd brought it up, subtly calling in his favor. "You said your dad ran it?"

"For years," she said.

If he had done the same job I was doing and ran the farmer's market, it shouldn't take too much more time. "Send me the details. I'm happy to help."

Relief crossed both her face and her husband's. What was I getting myself into?

"I can't wait to hand off some duties. McCoy and I want to travel a little more this summer."

"Do brewery tours," McCoy said.

"The kids love it, but this one will just be for us." She glanced at the food table. "Oh yeah, I was going to restock the root beer."

She and McCoy went to deal with refreshments, and I was left with Daisy.

She was studying me. "You don't have to, you know?"

I kissed her temple. "I know, but you're not the only one I have to make amends to. Stetson could've pressed charges and he didn't. If I can help his sister and, in turn, help the town, I will."

Sunlight made her blue eyes glitter as she considered what I said. Then she inhaled and her gaze filled with resolve. "Okay. You do what you feel you have to do."

I kissed her again. If we weren't surrounded by family who I hardly got to see, I'd haul her home and keep her in bed all day.

Daisy patted my shoulder. "Poppy told me we're all going out before she and Clover leave town."

"Good. They've missed you."

Her mouth tipped up. "I have been wondering one thing since the night we ran into Matthew."

"I'm afraid to ask." Seriously.

"What exactly was your secret when you were antagonizing the bulls? How are you still here?"

I laughed, but there were plenty of times I had wondered the same. "Stay close to the fence. I don't run *that* fast."

* * *

Daisy

A few days after the reception, Violet and Lily arranged a night I could go out with them before Poppy and Clover left town, just like Poppy had wanted. The bar around us bustled with activity. Instead of sitting at high-top tables, we surrounded a round table, big enough for six. Lily had her feet propped up on the sixth chair. She was due any day now, and it felt like we'd been saying that for weeks.

Lily propped her hands on her rounded stomach. "Your reception was beautiful, Violet, but I'm really glad we can hang like this."

Violet beamed, looking happier than when I'd known

her years ago. "It was really a great day, but sister time is always appreciated."

Poppy lifted her drink. "And finally, all the sisters are together."

Four pairs of eyes fell on me, and all four women smiled.

My brows lifted. "Me too?"

"You were the nice older sister growing up," Clover joked.

Violet playfully slapped her. "She was afraid to get on Mom's bad side. I wasn't."

"I'm still afraid," I said. Magnolia was too sweet.

Poppy propped her arm on the table, and she dangled her beer bottle from her hand. "Dare I say? You and Alder are not pretending to be married?"

My cheeks heated. I'd been prepared to pretend to be close to my husband, but I wasn't ready to talk about actually reconnecting with him. "We're taking it slow."

Clover gasped and pounded the table. "I knew it!" She grabbed my hand. "I knew he looked different. He was actually relaxed, more like 'bossy older brother' Alder and not 'broken-hearted but pretending to be okay' Alder."

I smiled and held still, like a deer frozen in the head-lights. Clover and Poppy had always been more energetic than their sisters, more expressive. They didn't know I didn't like being touched.

It wasn't that I didn't like it, but how was I supposed to act? Hold her hand in return? Giggle? Was my hand sweaty? Should I wash my hands? It felt like I should.

Ugh. This was why I didn't socialize. Alder was my safe zone, and this moment showed me how much I'd isolated myself in the time between then and now. It was also showing me that I'd been seeking the same comfort zone in the wrong men.

Clover released me and relief flooded my body.

I rested my hands on my lap. "I hope it goes well."

"It will," Poppy said with complete confidence. "He'll make sure of it. You're too important to him."

Violet took a drink of her virgin lemon sour. "Unless you don't want it to last."

My gut clenched, and I shook my head. "Of course I do." I wanted forever.

"But you don't trust him." She said it frankly but softened her words like she understood.

"No, I do." I trusted Alder with so much. "He's changed. He's driven and ambitious, and he's really trying to be what I need."

"But?"

"He keeps trying to prove himself. To me. To his employees. To Coal Haven." I supported him, but I saw the reason he was doing everything. It wasn't for his own fulfilment, which I guess was his point. I'd been holding all my concerns in, but his sisters would understand. They cared about him too. And about us. "He's coaching because he wants to show his buddies he's different. He's helping with the farmer's market because he's afraid people will only remember Crazy A."

Lily's brows popped up. "And Crazy A was Alder?"

Violet nodded. "I remember that. I was home from college and came to see him after you two divorced and someone called him that. He only laughed when I asked him."

Poppy worried her lower lip with her teeth. "You're afraid you won't be his priority again?"

My stomach twisted. I was his priority. So what was bothering me?

Clover put her hands on the table, like she would've reached out again if I had made myself accessible. "He's still adjusting. He'll realize that no one thinks he's that guy, and it won't be a worry."

"You're his priority," Poppy said. "Always were." She winced. "I mean..."

I gave her an understanding smile, but my insides were tumbling in different directions. They could see it too. They didn't want to agree with me, but they could see it.

My phone gave a quick buzz. I was going to ignore it, but just in case Laila was having an issue, I checked it. My mom was actually calling. Mom liked her isolation. She rarely texted, and she almost never called.

"I have to answer this. Excuse me." I pushed back from the table, taking my phone with me. "Hello," I answered, weaving my way to the quieter entry.

"Oh, Daisy. Is this a bad time?"

My stomach was still slippery from the topic of Alder, and it got even heavier. "No, it's fine. Is everything all right?"

"Oh, well...I went to the ER this morning, and now I'm just finally getting admitted. Busy place."

Alarm punched through my veins. This was the third time she'd gone to the ER and hadn't told me until after. "What's wrong?"

"I was passing blood in my stool, and I guess my hemoglobin is down pretty significantly."

I ran through what knowledge I would have, but I got stuck on the symptoms she would've been experiencing and how she didn't call me. I pushed the frustration aside.

"I'll come down. Let me talk to Jason and let him know I'll be out of town for a while. I'll call my boss in case I need to take any days off next week."

"You don't have to drive all the way here."

I expected her to say as much, but she didn't have to be alone for everything. It'd be easier to stay informed if I was there. "It's okay, Mom."

"At least wait until tomorrow."

"Okay, I'll be there tomorrow, then." It only took one more time reassuring her that she wasn't putting me out before I hung up. She probably hadn't called earlier because she was afraid nothing was wrong and I'd make the trip for no reason.

I went to the table. The four sisters peered at me. I regretted leaving, but it had to be done. I had a four-hour drive to plan for. "My mom's in the hospital."

"Oh no," Violet said. "Is she okay? I can talk to Raj on Monday if you can't get a hold of him."

"I'm sure Mom'll be fine. Thank you so much for inviting me." I left them on a chorus of byes and, thankfully, before they could all get up and hug me. Nothing was worse than awkward hugs. Except for someone grabbing my hand. Someone who wasn't Alder.

I was home within minutes. The house was dark. Alder was still at work. Or was he coaching? No, it was Friday.

I went inside and called my manager. Raj, of course, said it was fine and to do what I needed to do. Then I talked to Jason. He had no issues keeping Laila, and he was on day shift for the next month if he needed to keep Laila with him.

The house stayed quiet. Alder probably thought I was

still out with the girls. I paced the living room and down the hallway. I held my phone loosely in my hand.

Should I call him?

No. It wasn't an emergency. I wasn't leaving until the early morning. I shot off a text explaining the situation.

I smothered a yawn. I should get to bed. I was leaving early so I'd get to Grand Forks by the early afternoon.

I peered outside in case Alder was pulling in, but the driveway remained dark.

Chapter Twenty-One

Alder

The wind kicked around me and the sand from the baseball diamonds blasted me in the face. I squinted behind my sunglasses, but that didn't stop grit from getting in my eyes. When I clenched my jaw, my teeth crunched over fine grains.

I had only played baseball when I was growing up because it was what kids did and I got out of chores. I had eventually realized that chores had waited for me. But I had stayed on the team because Jasper and our sisters couldn't bug me. Then I'd met Daisy and almost quit to spend more time with her, but she'd come to all my games.

I checked my phone for the millionth time. She should be arriving in Grand Forks anytime.

"I got this one," Matthew said and led a five-year-old boy to the tee. We took turns helping position the kids. The other team's coaches were in the infield, directing players on where they should be throwing the ball. Two kids weren't paying attention and were tying their shoes. I wanted to tell them not to bother, their shoes would never be tied. Never. All the kids tied their shoes. Over and over and over.

I'd find it humorous, but last night was bothering me. And this morning.

Nothing had happened, and that was just it. I'd had a farmer's market meeting after work and it went long. The committee wanted to restructure their hours and their offerings. The debate on what booths to allow in beyond those who were local had raged late into the evening.

I had missed Daisy's text until a half hour after she sent it. Two committee members had been in tears after one had accused the other of ordering goat milk soap off some cheap site and selling it as homemade.

I snuck a peek at the text as if I was checking the time. **Going to Grand Forks tomorrow. Mom's in the hospital. I'm going to bed, so don't call, please. I'll be leaving early.**

To make sure she'd gotten her sleep, I hadn't crawled in with her. Then this morning, I'd been up bright and early, but she'd already gone.

I gritted my teeth. More sand ground between my molars. I took a drink from my mug. God, that tasted like dirt too.

"Hey, Coach?" asked a high-pitched voice.

I looked down. "Yeah, Braxton."

I had a Jaxon—and a Jackson—and a Paxton in addition to Braxton. I was getting better at remembering their names.

"My mom said you used to be called Crazy A."

A spot between my shoulder blades ached. Who was

his mom? It had taken me a while to date again after Daisy, and not until I had moved for school, so I was fairly sure I hadn't slept with this kid's mom. "Yep. I used to make bad choices."

"Oh. Me too." He dug his tiny cleat into the dirt. I still couldn't believe they made them that small.

"We all do, but it's important to try to keep making good ones."

"Mom said you used to buy a lot of beer and chips."

Ah. She had worked at the gas station. Off-sale liquor on one side. Chips on the other. "I don't anymore. I buy lots of kombucha and broccoli now."

He gave me a look that asked why the hell I would do that.

Matthew jogged in, gesturing for me and Braxton to head out. I led Braxton out for his turn at bat. He was the most experienced, and his dad was the loudest in the stands.

The whole time, my mind was on Daisy. I had wanted to call, but Matthew had phoned right away to arrange coolers of water and snacks. Then the texts from parents had started.

Jaxon will be late. His dad hasn't picked him up yet.

Jackson won't be there for the last game. He has swimming lessons.

Does Paxton need his team shirt or will any blue shirt do?

I hadn't been able to call Daisy yet either. We'd had an eight o'clock game.

Who the hell scheduled a tournament for T-ball? And who made the first game at eight in the morning? In between the first and second games, I'd been recruited to help with another team. Their coach had food poisoning.

Braxton made contact with the ball just as another gust of wind blew up, stopping it three feet from home plate. I tucked the brim of my hat down and jogged with him to first base as the other team scrambled to figure out who should field the ball and where to throw it.

Six batters down. Six more to go.

An hour later, the game was done, but Matthew and I had to run down kids and parents with forgotten water bottles, mitts, and hats.

Matthew approached me after one such sprint. "Hey, Alder. Want to go over next week's schedule with me?"

No. Fuck no. "I've gotta give Daisy a call."

"No problem." He brandished some papers. One was a calendar with writing on almost every day. "I'll only be a second."

"Matty, I've gotta call Daisy. Her mom's in the hospital, and I need to check in."

"Oh, shit. Yeah, give her a call. Hope everything's okay."

I didn't acknowledge him as I turned away and pulled up her number.

It rang a few times before she answered with a quiet, "Hello?"

"Hey. Did you get there okay?"

"Yeah, I got here half an hour ago. She's getting an endoscopy right now. I'm in the waiting room."

"How are you?"

"You know. Fine."

I didn't expect her to answer any other way. But it was me. "Daisy."

"What? We're just waiting. She's pale and chilly, but

other than that, she seems good. It's just test and wait, test and wait now."

Daisy had worked in hospitals. The environment wasn't shocking to her, but that didn't mean I wasn't worried. "I'm sorry. About last night."

"It's fine." Her tone was slightly more aloof than before.

"The farmer's market meeting got wild."

Her chuckle was soft. "I didn't expect those words to go together."

"Lots of accusations about what constitutes locally grown. But I'm sorry. I should've been there. I tried to catch you this morning."

"I didn't want to wake you," she said. "I was stopping in Bismarck for breakfast and caffeine, so I left a little earlier than planned."

"I'm just glad you made it. Wish I could've gone with you."

"I don't know how long I'll be here."

"Right." I hadn't thought of that, but I could've gone for the weekend. Instead, I had obligations that included game times and dust. "Do you need any help with Laila?"

"Jason's got it covered."

"Okay." I struggled for a way to lend a hand, but she'd been handling her life without me for a long time. I could at least be her sounding board. "Keep me posted. Love you."

"Love you too."

After we disconnected, I stared at the empty lot. Sand hit my face, and wind whipped my shirt around my torso. Tall clouds gathered on the horizon. The heat and winds would kick up a storm.

I hadn't been there for her when she needed me, but

there was a part of me asking how hard she'd tried to get ahold of me.

* * *

I pulled into the garage after another late goddamn farmer's market meeting. No wonder Isla had needed help. The committee met once a week for no less than three hours at a time, then at least two of us needed to be present for the twice-a-week markets, not to mention the admin work that had to be done, the emails, and the calls.

In no world did I care about heirloom tomatoes enough to argue over the definition of them.

I'd been tempted to take tomorrow off and get a three-day weekend. Maybe I could sneak away and hang out at Daisy's side and help with her mom. No luck. I'd been busy with T-ball all week. Why did they need so many practices?

My phone buzzed. I was still sitting in the car, so I checked it.

Jasper: You bringing the wife and kid out to ride?

My interest reared up. Daisy might love that. Would Laila? If they did, I could fix fences next summer and find a horse or two. I could teach Laila to ride around my coaching...and the tournaments. The farmer's market.

I pinched the bridge of my nose. At least I'd gotten off early today. Daisy would be home soon from Grand Forks. I had fully supported her absence. She'd needed to be with her mom, but I had missed her. I had missed going to bed knowing she was under the same roof. I had missed hearing her and Laila get ready for bed, and I had missed being asked to read a story at least one night a week.

I collected the mail I had grabbed from the box at the end of the driveway and walked into the house, flipping through the various envelopes. Junk mail, car warranty offers, and a credit card bill.

Frowning, I went to the pile of mail I'd collected for Daisy over the week and sifted through it. Another credit card statement. A third credit card statement.

"What the fuck?"

A fourth credit card statement.

I tossed the mail down. Daisy usually checked the mail since she was home first, and I never saw her stuff. We were married, but she'd been keeping things very much separate.

Four credit card statements? I propped my hands on my hips and pondered them. What the hell?

She was on her way home. Would she talk to me?

I only had a minute to ponder before the garage door opened.

I met her at the door to the garage. There were dark circles under her eyes, and she barely lifted her feet off the floor.

"Hey." I pulled her in for a long hug and let the door close behind her. "No Laila?"

She exhaled and melted into me like she'd craved warmth and comfort after getting only hard hospital chairs. "I wanted to come home and decompress first. She'll be excited, and I'm worn out."

"Are you hungry?" I asked without letting up.

She shook her head. "No. I don't have much of an appetite." She eased out of my hold and toed her shoes off.

I took her suitcase from her and followed her to the bedroom.

She sank onto the edge of the bed and closed her eyes. "When I wasn't at the hospital, I was cleaning."

"Was it worse than you thought?" She'd told me her plans to assist her mom by getting groceries and tidying up her place.

She scrunched her face up, like she was keeping tears at bay. "Her house wasn't as bad as Lee's, but..." Color leached from her cheeks. "It wasn't good."

"Yet you stayed there?"

She dipped her head. "Couldn't afford a hotel room, and I didn't want her to leave the hospital and come home to an empty house."

Four credit card bills supported her first statement. Goddammit, were they why she couldn't get herself a decent place and remarried me?

I would be grateful for her debt, but frustration built that she hadn't talked to me about them. I understood she might be embarrassed. She had gone into debt while I had built myself an admirable nest egg.

"She can't live like that. Her house is too big and she's..." Her expression almost crumpled again. "She looked so frail. She hadn't mowed the grass for a month. I did that, and I cleaned out her fridge. And the freezer." She shuddered.

I took a seat next to her. This was one of those moments she didn't want to be smothered. I gripped the edge of the mattress instead of pulling her into me once more. "Does she realize how she's living?"

"Yeah," she said on another sigh. "We talked about that. She wants to move, but she hasn't had the energy to start looking for a new place. I guess an ulcer will do that to a person." She picked at the bottom off her shirt. "I'm going to help her. I'll get Laila after school tomorrow, and we'll head back."

"Another trip?"

"I've gotta get as much cleaned out as I can. Mom's not a saver, but she still has lots of impulse buys stashed around the house." She gave me a tight smile. Stress lined her eyes. "We'll come home Sunday, and next week, I'll make calls. She'd like senior housing. Smaller and no lawn to care for."

Then Daisy would want to return again to help her mom move. "Is she staying in Grand Forks or moving closer to you?"

"She wants the amenities. I can't blame her." Daisy mumbled the last part. "Hopefully we can get it all done before the snow flies."

"I'll be here to help."

"Yeah. Thanks."

Was her default still not to rely on me? I tipped her chin up with two fingers. "I'm here for you. We're in this together." It was on the tip of my tongue to ask her about the credit card bills. To ask why she hadn't talked to me. But she'd had a hard week, and she was emotionally ragged. Now wasn't the time.

"Tell me something that isn't depressing," she said. "Something that doesn't remind me of my brother, or my mom's move, or...everything else."

"Everything else?" I asked. "What other things are stressing you?" This was her opening. She could talk to me. We'd reached that point, hadn't we?

"Just, you know, life."

Disappointment curled through my gut. We'd been together again for six months. What more did I have to do to show her she could rely on me? "Jasper invited all of us out. Said we could ride. Whatever time works for us, he'll make it work for him."

"Oh." Her mouth formed a troubled line. "It's turning out to be a busy summer."

"I can tell him that we'll have to wait and see." I stuffed my disappointment away. She had enough stress, and the trip wouldn't be fun if she felt like she had to cram it in. "It's not horses, but I was asked to join the baseball club board."

She pulled back. "That's quite a promotion from first-time coach."

"That's how it is for me. Straight to the top."

Her laugh gusted out of her.

I grinned. "You know how those things are? They're usually desperate for people, and I'm an easy target. They can sense it."

"You're going to earn yourself another nickname, Duke."

I traced a finger down her soft cheek. "I like being known as Daisy's husband."

She licked her bottom lip. "People know you as that?"

"They're starting to. I'll have to take you out more often. And I want to get my girls to one of my games."

Her mouth curled up. "I get to tell everyone the hot coach is mine."

I put my mouth to her ear. "I have a big whistle."

Her laugh was strong and genuine. My mission was accomplished. She was out of her head, out of the stress cycle, but she could so easily slip back in.

"Still need help decompressing?" I asked.

Her mouth was millimeters from mine. "Think you can help with that?"

I captured her mouth with mine and lifted her onto my lap. She twisted so she was straddling me. My dick got the message and blood immediately rerouted. The desire I'd kept contained all week poured through my veins.

"I need to be in you," I growled out against her mouth.

"I need it too." There was more weight to her words. She wasn't saying it because she was turned on. She needed it. She needed the release. The connection.

Yet as I undressed her, standing her up long enough to get her pants down and to jerk mine off, I couldn't escape the feeling that no matter how much sex we had, how much I reassured her that I would be there for her this time, I only got a part of her.

Arousal blurred my concerns as she sank onto my shaft. I rolled my hips and pumped into her. She dropped her head back and rode me.

I tugged her shirt over her head and let it fall to the floor. Her breasts jiggled in front of my face. I yanked my own sweater off and tossed it.

"Daisy, I fucking love you."

She braced herself on my shoulders and met my gaze. "I love you too, Alder."

When she said my name like that, I was the Alder she had trusted. We were teens again, and it was the two of us against the world. We were partners.

I shoved a hand through her hair and held her close, our mouths millimeters apart. Her breath puffed across my lips as her pleasure rose. She was climbing toward her peak.

"I'm yours," I said roughly. "I've only ever been yours."

"Yes," she said on a pant.

"And you're mine."

She nodded, and her body clenched around me, gripping and rippling over my cock. I was going to explode soon but not before her.

"You're mine," I repeated. "And I'm yours."

That was all I could get out as my vision went fuzzy. Energy zinged down my spine and heat exploded through every cell of my body just as she tensed. My name echoed off the walls.

We came together, pumping against each other, milking every last ounce of pleasure. Our kisses were erratic and messy.

She slumped against me with a whimper. "I really did need that," she murmured.

She had. But did she really need me?

The question haunted me as I rose, holding her to me. I tucked her into her side of the bed, got her a warm washcloth to clean herself up, then climbed in next to her.

The room was dark, and she rolled toward me.

"You have me," I said.

"I know," she replied, her voice drowsy.

"You can trust me."

"I do," she murmured a second before her breathing fell even.

"You can count on me," I said. Asleep or not, would she have heard?

Chapter Twenty-Two

Daisy

I pulled into the parking lot by the baseball diamonds. Alder had been coaching much of the season. Coal Haven only had two fields, but both were in use all summer. Since Alder was now on the board, he'd mentioned that they were trying to build two more.

Also since Alder was now on the board, he'd been approached to substitute coach for another team. For the last two weeks, he'd been helping with a girls' fast-pitch team. The dad who normally coached couldn't finish the season with his work schedule.

"There's Alder!" Laila shouted and pointed.

The game was almost ready to start. Alder stood tall while surrounded by a team of eleven-year-old girls. Their orange shirts looked like flames dancing on the sand.

I took Laila's hand and found a spot on the bleachers. The sun beat down from overhead.

Alder caught my gaze and grinned. Just seeing him

loosened the tangle of tension at the base of my skull. I smiled and waved just as twelve pairs of eyes pinned me and Laila.

My chest squeezed. This was Alder's element, but it wasn't mine. I'd rather be anonymous in the bleachers, but again, he was getting me out of my comfort zone.

Laila had a million questions once the game began. Parents lined the fence and surrounded the dugout in their camp chairs and overhead shades. A few innings went by, and Laila asked to play in the grass by the fence. She ran off, and I squinted at the field.

More like, I gawked at Alder. He wore an orange ball cap tugged down low. He stood at first, helping the players know when to run and when to stay. His voice carried, deep and commanding.

"Are you Alder's wife?" an older woman next to me asked. Her brown hair was in a ponytail, and she had a visor shading her eyes.

I didn't recognize her. "Yes?"

She smiled. "I'm Kayleigh's grandma."

I nodded like I knew who Kayleigh was. I had no idea what any of the team members' names were.

"The girls just love him," she gushed. "They like their other coach too, but..." The woman leaned closer. "You know how it is when it's the dad of one of the players. Their kid and that kid's friends get to play the most."

I didn't know, but I could imagine. My only foray into sports had been for school gym class, so I was familiar with getting picked last and playing the least.

"Alder gives all the girls play time."

Pride cooled the hot breeze blowing against my skin. "He's amazing like that."

The grandma nodded solemnly. "He doesn't know

what a gift it's been to see Kayleigh excited to play again." She swayed closer to me once more. "Some of the girls' parents got upset with him." She snickered. "I was picking up Kayleigh when I saw it, and I heard Alder ask them who the team was for, the players or the parents, and if the kids who got the least game time also paid lower fees. Then he asked for legitimate research referencing how benching the kids was beneficial for them. You should've seen Damien and Mike sputter."

I wasn't familiar with those guys, but if Damien was the lawyer who had ads in the bathroom stalls at the movie theater, so I had to pee with him staring at me, then I would've loved to see Alder knock the smug off his face. "I'm sorry I missed it."

The woman's grin was downright wicked. "You'll get to see it again next weekend at the tournament."

I lifted my brows. "There's another tournament next weekend?"

"In Bismarck. The last one for the season. Kayleigh's really excited."

Cheers rang out, and I turned my attention back to the game. Alder was circling his arm yelling "Go! Go! Go!" as a player rounded the bases. Hoots and hollers rose from the parents, and Kayleigh's grandma joined in. I clapped along with everyone, but my mind was on next weekend.

Laila would be with Jason, but I had to go to Grand Forks again to help Mom direct the movers. Over the last four weekends, I'd been driving to help her pack, donate, and toss to get the house sale ready. Then she'd followed up on the places I had researched and found a nice senior living condo.

When Laila wasn't with Jason, she had come with

me. Alder had offered to watch her, but Laila wanted to see her grandmother, and I hadn't wanted more upheaval in her life. He had also offered to join us and help, but Mom had hired a cleaner for the final clean before the house went on the market, and she'd contacted the movers. No need for Alder to pass on the new duties he was taking on for me.

As I watched the game, letting the heat of the sun soak into my bones, the stress of the last six weeks weighed me down with fatigue. I was tired. I still worried about Mom's health. And... I had no idea what to do about my husband.

Our year wouldn't be up for five more months, but it felt like there was a ticking clock over my head. I hadn't talked to Laila about having Alder sleep with me. Thanks to all the extra travel and his additional obligations, we hadn't been able to act like a couple around her.

Would it mess her up to see us go from friendly to sleeping together? Did we take our time or would the year mark be the end of Alder's patience?

I pushed at my temples. Alder was still an in-demand guy. All for a good, productive reason this time. But he was still stretched thin, and I didn't want to find out that I still wasn't his priority.

* * *

Alder

After the game, I lifted Laila onto my shoulders as Daisy and I walked to the playground on the far side of the ball diamonds. My adrenaline was running high, and the euphoria of the hard-earned win against the Crocus Valley team kept a smile on my face.

Daisy smirked at me. "You like coaching."

We reached the edge of the swing set and Laila patted my head. I helped her down and she ran to the slides.

"I enjoy it," I said and crossed my arms. We stood next to each other and watched Laila go down the slides.

"I got some dirt on you from Kayleigh's grandma."

"She wasn't asking about Crazy A, was she?"

"No, she was admiring what a hard-ass you are. She said some parents got upset with you."

"Oh. That." Irritation itched across the back of my neck. "I had to call on years of professionalism to keep from telling them to fuck off."

"You have another tournament next weekend?"

I nodded. "I don't have the schedule yet, but I'll let you know as soon as they put it out." It was Laila's weekend with Jason, and I had meant to check with Daisy about what she needed from me.

"It's not a problem. That's moving weekend for Mom."

I turned toward her. Sunlight glinted off the strands of her hair. I couldn't gauge her expression behind her sunglasses. "You didn't tell me she was moving already."

Daisy frowned. "I told you she found a place and her house is on the market."

"But not that she's actually moving. I can call in a sub and come with you. I can help you."

"No, it's okay," she said nonchalantly, as if moving wasn't stressful. "She hired people, so we're more just supervising where everything goes. They're going to take the furniture she's not keeping to the thrift store."

All this had been decided and Daisy hadn't thought to bring it up? "Seriously, I can find someone to cover the game. I'm sure one of the other dads—"

"Really, Alder." Her smile was tight. "We have it covered."

This conversation wasn't much different than all the prior weekends. *It's fine. It's okay.* "Daisy, I'm here for you. We're partners."

"I know, but you have responsibilities."

"I get that, but it's not work." And even then, I could take a day off. I got plenty of vacation time. "I can get out of it."

"Kayleigh's grandma said Kayleigh looks forward to playing again because of you. She actually gets to play. It's the last tournament, and if you don't go, some other parent might not have the same stance on playing time."

I worked my jaw back and forth. Yeah, I'd feel bad if the team's morale took a nosedive when they had been more enthusiastic than the first time I had coached. "You're my wife. If you need my help, all you have to do is ask."

A line formed between her brows. "I know."

I cocked my head as frustration built behind my sternum. Her response lacked conviction. "I can at least bring Laila to Jason's when he's done with work."

"He was able to work something out with his supervisor."

Disappointment tightened the spot between my shoulder blades. She'd arranged it with him before checking with me? "He didn't have to. I could've helped. Games don't start until Saturday."

"Oh, well, I wasn't sure, so Jason just asked for a few hours off."

"Daisy, you really can come to me."

Her big eyes blinked behind her dark shades. "I know. I didn't have to this time."

Her voice was just light enough to set off a warning bell. We weren't where we needed to be, and fuck if I could figure out what was wrong. Did she sense it? Was I being paranoid?

No. Because she still hadn't told me about those damn credit cards. Unless she had paid all of them off, another set of statements had to have shown up by now with another four on their way. Yet I hadn't seen them. She'd resumed getting the mail.

Goddammit. I wanted my wife to open up to me in life the way she did about her work history, or in bed, and I had no fucking clue how to do it.

I grabbed her hand and held it between mine. "I wish you'd have talked to me."

Her lower lip pouted out. "I have been, but it's taken care of."

"It's still your life. Your mom is my family too."

She drew back slightly, and my stomach sank. Why was there a clear delineation around where I was allowed in her life?

"You realize I haven't seen her since we've been back together," I pointed out.

"She doesn't like to travel."

"Or talked to your dad."

She scoffed. "I haven't really talked to my dad."

Good point. "Are you afraid of this? Of us?" Was she afraid that we could actually work out?

It didn't make sense, but sometimes figuring out how Daisy's mind worked took some time.

"No." She shook her head almost as if to convince

herself. "No, Alder. It's just been a hard few years for me and I'm cautious. I'm sorry I didn't tell you Mom was moving next weekend. I really didn't think it was that big of a deal."

I studied her features. With her eyes covered, I couldn't interpret the firm set of her mouth. "All right," I finally said. "Just know when I said I love you, that doesn't mean I only love to come inside you. I want to invade every part of you."

This time, she looked away. "You can't say that stuff on a playground." Her tone was light, but my sense of foreboding didn't fade.

I had more ground to cover with her to make sure that at the end of our agreed-upon year, I wasn't left standing with a key and an empty house.

Chapter Twenty-Three

Daisy

Mom was moved. Her house sale was pending, and preschool had started for Laila. She still went to daycare, and twice a week she'd go to a different room for class. Our weeks were a little more normal. I had picked up Laila and was figuring out what to have for dinner from Alder's freezer meal stash. I was at the island with a pack of chicken in front of me.

Alder came through the door, loosening his tie. He grinned. "Put that away. I want to take my girls out for a celebratory dinner."

My stomach did a twirl. I liked chicken, but a meal out sounded way better. "What are we celebrating?"

"Laila's first day of preschool." He came to me and bent for a kiss. I met his mouth with mine, but then he deepened the kiss and I gently pushed him back. "Laila's in the next room."

"She's seen me holding your hand for weeks. Since you two came to the tournament."

And sitting next to each other on the couch. He'd helped tuck her in, and when he wasn't working late, we'd have meals together. Yet I hadn't wanted her to see us making out. I never did with her dad, though she might've been too young to really notice or remember.

"She's had a long day."

He let out a breath. "I know. I don't mean to rush." He dropped a kiss into my hair. "It's getting harder to keep my hands off you. Can I take you both out?"

"Of course."

He stepped into the living room. "Wanna go out to eat so I can hear about your first day of school?"

"Yeah!" Laila ran through the dining room to the mudroom to put her shoes on.

I shared a grin with Alder. Fifteen minutes later, we were seated in a booth at Rattler's. Laila was next to me and Alder was across from us.

Laila tore her little pack of crayons open. "And then my teacher said we have to line up every time the fire alarm rings."

"Is it really loud?" Alder asked.

"I dunno." Laila pushed the kid's menu with the tic-tac-toe board to the middle of the table. She rolled the green crayon toward him. "Green is my favorite color."

My heart spasmed with a little beat of happiness.

"Thank you." Alder wrote an O on the sheet.

Laila scribbled an X.

"You're good at this," Alder said.

She gave him a dubious look. "We're not done yet."

He laughed and added another O. I could sit and watch them forever. The relationship blossoming between them wasn't forced. Alder had let it happen at her own pace, and since Laila could be a lot like me in that regard, my appreciation filled my chest to bursting.

A crack of fear split through it. Alder was doing everything right. He'd proven to me, to himself, that he was a changed man. Crazy A was gone. He was the Alder Duke who had reached his full potential.

But was I doing everything right? He had to see that he was far out of my league. My mouth went dry.

The apprehension grew until my throat got thick. I took a long drink from my ice water.

"I want to play softball," Laila said.

Surprised, I looked at Alder. His expression must mirror mine.

"Yeah?" he asked.

"Looks fun." She started another round of tic-tac-toe. There were three more ready-made game squares. She put an X in the top right corner.

Alder continued playing with no hesitation. "You can do T-ball next year. I'll coach."

"I don't want to do it if you're not coaching." She blinked up at me. "That's okay, right, Mommy?"

An arrow got me right in the chest. How could I say no? Why would I want to? Yet this whole year I'd been feeling like I never knew what came next. Would I be in the house for a year, or would I have to leave partway through? Would Alder get sick of me and move out, or would he ask me to go? Was I doing right by my daughter?

So many unknowns while the whole time had been passing blissfully by. I'd fallen even more in love with my husband. He had become the guy I knew he could be— better in fact. More ambitious, more caring, and more handsome. He did what he had to because he wanted to be a good person and he wanted to care for and love the people in his life.

I was a lucky woman.

Yet I was still terrified. He'd taken on so many outside obligations. The refinery needed him. The community needed him. Little girls like Laila who didn't want to be excluded from a game they loved needed him. I was but one single person who needed him.

The teenage server came to take our order, and then I was roped into a few games of tic-tac-toe.

I pushed everything out of my head. There was no reason I shouldn't enjoy a night out with Alder and Laila. This wasn't our first, and dammit, I looked forward to each one more than ever.

When my food showed up, it tasted like dust. I smiled and chatted, letting Laila lead the conversation.

After the meal was done, we returned home. Laila was yawning and rubbing her eyes. She got out of the car. "Can Alder read me a story?"

"Sure. I'm going to enjoy the beautiful night. I'll be inside in a few minutes. You two read some stories."

Alder shot me a worried look, but I gave him what I hoped was a reassuring smile. I needed some air. Some space. I was happier than ever but also more scared than ever, and I couldn't define why.

I wandered down the driveway. My food sat in my stomach like lead. Why was my anxiety so hard to deal with tonight? Why were things going so well, yet my brain wouldn't shut off the worry?

The late August breeze that brushed my cheeks was warm with a promise of the cold yet to come. In a few days, it'd be September. Then October. Then November.

The year would be up and time would fly by until then. A blink later and I'd have to decide if I stayed married.

Why was it a decision? What made me drag my feet? I loved Alder. I was in love with him.

I reached the edge of the driveway and my heart stuttered. The sun was sinking down in the sky, and the rolling hills around me were no longer the vibrant green of summer. A hint of brown brushed over the grasses.

Just like before.

My breathing came shallow. I'd taken a walk just like this before. I'd come home to an empty apartment with beer bottles falling out of the trash can and dirty dishes piled in the sink. The vacuuming hadn't been done and the fridge was empty. All the groceries I'd gotten so I didn't have to worry during the first week of my third year of college were gone, eaten by a bunch of hungover guys who'd slept on my living room floor.

Why were the past and present colliding?

I was doing it. And I was happy. But there was this anvil poised over my heart, waiting to drop.

I blew out a breath and walked back to the house. Inside, Alder's voice carried through to the mudroom. He was doing the voice of the troll in *The Three Billy Goats Gruff*.

A smile stretched my lips. Why couldn't I just relax and enjoy our reconnection? I worried if I sped it up. I fretted over slowing it down. Alder was getting frustrated. He'd never admit to it, but I could tell.

I leaned on the doorframe and listened to him finish up. Laila giggled when he made the sounds of the goats walking across the bridge. Alder looked over at me as he finished, and the corner of his mouth tipped up.

His hair had fallen out of its strict style. I wanted to

go over there and push it back into place, if only to get my fingers into his soft locks. I could do it now. Laila might not care. She might say something. She likely wouldn't be concerned.

But my feet stayed planted. I'd go upstairs when she fell asleep.

"The end." Alder started to push off the floor, but Laila sat up and wrapped him in a big hug.

"Night, Alder," she said in a sweet little voice.

"Good night." He tucked the blankets in around her. "You've got another big day tomorrow."

When he walked past me to leave, his fingers brushed mine.

I gave him a smile, but my gaze darted away. Today was perfect. So damn perfect. My brain had seen this pattern before, and it kept insisting it'd change. My logical side pointed out that we'd been barely of drinking age, though that hadn't stopped Alder from getting supplied by his older coworkers.

I shook the past off. History wasn't going to repeat itself. I believed that. So what was it?

I sat with Laila for a few minutes. She had questions about her next day of preschool, which wouldn't be until next week. When she was fighting to stay awake, I gave her a hug and a kiss.

The shower upstairs was running. I had a few things to get ready for work the next day. I packed my lunch and then went to my bedroom to get my clothes for the morning laid out. Just as I was about to change into pajamas to head upstairs, I sensed Alder at the door.

Heat flushed my body, and I shot him a smile. "I was just going to head up."

He was wearing gray sweats and a white T-shirt that

was snug against his chest, and his feet were bare. The light glistened off his damp, finger-combed hair. My heart somersaulted.

"I was thinking," he started, shoving his hands in the pockets of his sweats and dragging them farther down his hips, "that I could stay down here with you."

"Oh." Uncertainty cooled off the heat. "Um, I don't know if it's a good idea. I'm sure Laila's asleep—"

"It's not about Laila. Is it?"

I drew back and crossed my arms. His tone hadn't been harsh but more like I'd let him down. Like I'd confirmed his worst fears. "What do you mean?"

He held his hands out, and even though my anxiety was climbing, my gaze dropped to admire his chest. "This." He waved a hand back and forth between us. "The distance you keep here. We're supposed to be reconnecting. I'm your husband, but I'm starting to feel like a friend with benefits."

Acid churned in my stomach. "You said you wouldn't pressure me."

"I'm not," he said calmly. "But I need to know—are you in this with me? I've been doing everything I can think of to win your trust back, and nothing's working. What happens in three months? What happens when this house is ours? Am I still going to be sleeping upstairs? Am I still only good enough to fuck when it's a secret?"

"Alder," I snapped, hating how the discomfort of this conversation slithered under my skin. He was not a friend with benefits. "It's not that easy for me. I have more than me to consider."

"Laila's doing just fine. Hell, even Jason doesn't seem to care. It's you, Daisy. You're the one I'm worried about who'll never come around, who'll never accept me as your husband."

"What do you want? I remarried you knowing damn well I had never gotten over you. I remarried you knowing how easy it was for you to let me leave like it was just another Wednesday."

He flinched. "That was a long time ago. I'm here. I've changed."

"Have your priorities?"

"What's that mean?"

"Your job. The farmer's market." I ticked each point off with a finger. "Coaching. Serving on the board." Those had to be the reasons I had lingering uncertainty. He kept busy, and I was afraid he'd never put me first.

"I would give up any one of those if you asked. Half the time, I don't even know there might be a conflict because you never talk to me."

My defensiveness rose. "I learned to live life on my own."

He threw his hands up. "And you're convinced you still have to. I've given you weeks, Daisy, *weeks* to talk to me about those credit card bills and you continue to squirrel them away and mention not one damn thing."

My lungs spasmed, and shame burned through my face. I hoped he hadn't seen those, and since he hadn't asked, I'd fooled myself into thinking he hadn't. "Those are none of your business."

"I counted four. Four credit card statements."

Tears poked the backs of my eyes, and I looked away. I should've switched to automatic payments long ago, but something about getting those statements in the mail was a painful reminder of how stupid I'd been. Each time I dreaded approaching the mailbox served as a lesson in trusting the wrong person. A tutorial on how I couldn't be trusted when it came to relationships.

And it was five credit cards. "Those are none of your—"

"Don't you dare say it. It was insulting enough the first time." He ground his teeth so hard they should've disintegrated. "Don't fucking tell me that anything that stresses you is none of my business."

"You stress me," I shot back and immediately felt like shit for it.

He stiffened. "So that's it. You're never going to trust me. I'm good enough for a good time, but I can't be let into your life enough to ever help you with the hard times."

"Since those hard times are because of you, no." I gasped and pressed my fingers to my lips. I should apologize, but I was too stunned I had said that.

"Jesus." He raked a hand through his hair. "You're right. I fucked it all up and I can't fix it." He dropped his hand and let out a long exhale. "I'll leave as soon as I can arrange another place to stay. You can keep the house, and we can propose a rental agreement with Aunt Linda."

Panic clawed the inside of my ribs. Leave? Rent? I couldn't afford this house.

His distraught gaze clashed with mine, and he hesitated, like he was waiting for me to say something. I had no words. All my fears were coalescing into this moment. I waited too long. I didn't wait long enough. It didn't matter.

His sigh was long and heavy. "I don't want to be the reason you're scared to live life, Daisy, but I am. And despite what you seem to think, I'm worried about that little girl too. I don't want to hurt her. So I'll start by working long hours. By the time I find a place, she'll be used to never seeing me again."

Would she? Because I had never gotten used to it. "It's fitting, you know," I said, my voice hoarse. "It's the same time of year that I left you."

Sadness filled his eyes. A dark hopelessness. "I guess it was inevitable, just like you assumed it would be."

"I did not," I whispered.

But he only gave me a knowing look and walked out of my room. Forgetting that I could wake Laila, I slammed the door behind him, sank onto the bed, and sobbed.

Chapter Twenty-Four

Alder

Daisy: The house is yours. I'll look for another place so we can move when the year is up.

There were no major holidays between now and when our year was up. Aunt Linda and my dad would likely never know that Daisy and I were done. I rubbed my aching chest and tossed the phone onto the seat of the pickup. I sat outside Rattler's waiting for my order to finish.

The last two weeks had been miserable. I was nothing but a ghost in the house. I'd gotten up at the crack of dawn so I could be out before Daisy and Laila woke. Then I came home after ten. My staff had to know something was up. I was in the office well before any of them, I stayed later, and sometimes, I returned to the office after I grabbed something to eat for dinner.

The farmer's market was winding down now that school had started, but those meetings had kept me busy.

I was half tempted to call Matthew and see if there was any fall coaching to do around town.

I got out of my pickup and walked to the entrance. I had to switch between the Purple Petal restaurant in Crocus Valley and Rattler's. To make it worse, I ordered two meals so it didn't look like I was fucking single and saved the extra in my office fridge for lunch.

I prodded the impending headache at my temples. I'd been sleeping like shit, and there was an ulcer rapidly forming in my stomach lining. I had done the right thing. I had to have. Otherwise I'd torched the only damn chance I had to get my wife back.

My phone pinged. That must be the notice of my meal. If it was Daisy, I didn't want to read it. She was planning to move on without me again. I'd seen it happen once; I didn't need to see it again.

I trudged into the restaurant. My suit coat was left behind in the pickup, and I rolled up my sleeves as I went. Just as I reached the door, Evander pushed out like a battering ram, making way for his wife and kid.

"Alder, hey." He narrowed his eyes at me. No, I hadn't shaved this morning. Or yesterday. Was it the day before?

Violet exited with Willa in her arms. "Alder." Her smile faltered when she took me and the dark circles under my eyes in.

"Hey, guys." I took the door from Evander so the happy family could go on their way.

Violet handed Willa off to Evander. I would've stepped around her, but she blocked my way. "Evander, why don't you head home? I wanna talk to Alder for a few minutes." She peered at me. "You can bring me home, right?"

I wasn't getting out of this. Violet clearly sensed something was wrong, and she had no plans to drop it. "Yeah, that's fine. I'll go in and grab my order."

When I emerged with my bag of food, Violet was by herself.

"I'm parked at the back." I kept walking. I wasn't going to bullshit her, but that didn't mean I looked forward to the conversation.

Once we were in my pickup, I didn't bother to start it. "It's over."

Violet groaned. "I was afraid something was wrong. Daisy's been a zombie for a couple of weeks."

"She's not doing well?" The thought didn't make me feel better.

"It's safe to say no. I suspect she goes to the bathroom and cries."

"Fuck." I pinched the bridge of my nose.

"What happened?" she asked softly.

I gave her the rundown, and unfortunately, it didn't take long. "I tried."

Violet studied me. I itched under her inspection.

"I did everything I could think of," I said, the silence getting to me. "She refused to rely on me in any way."

Violet didn't respond.

"I gave her space," I continued. Why wouldn't Violet say anything? "Her daughter started to accept me, but my own wife? She wouldn't. She couldn't."

Still my sister said nothing.

"Jesus, Violet. What?"

She looked out the windshield. "Do you love her?"

Her question surprised me and fucking depressed me. "I'll never quit loving her."

"Then why are you giving up again?"

The *again* stung real damn hard. "This is different than before."

"Is it? Daisy didn't behave like you wanted, and you're letting her go." She twisted in her seat. "She didn't want to go the first time. She wanted you to try. She wanted you to listen. She wanted you to do better."

"Don't you think I'd give Daisy everything she wanted?"

"Except for time."

My head jerked back. Her words were a real slap in the face.

I had given Daisy time, but I'd put her on my timeline. I'd wanted her to heal faster, to trust me when I demanded it. "Shit."

"Don't get me wrong," Violet said. "Daisy isn't one to open up. She's known me for years—*years*—and she doesn't tell me much. We talk, we go to lunch together, and I barely know why she didn't marry Jason. All she said was that he was a good guy but he didn't get her. I don't know about her exes. She's talked a little about her work experience, and we bitch about our old bosses, but she still keeps things tight to the chest. And the thing is, Alder, I think I'm the best friend she has."

I sighed and let my eyes slide shut. Violet felt like she hardly knew Daisy, but Daisy poured herself out to me. She might reserve some parts, but I got the most. That meant a lot. "What the hell am I supposed to do? She pushed for that damn prenup, probably because of that credit card debt, and she refused to tell me about it."

"She's probably humiliated."

"I'm supposed to be her husband. Her partner."

"Who did *real* well after the divorce. You're the boss

of her boss of her boss…" She mouthed names and counted on her fingers. "Of her boss."

I clenched my jaw and stared out the window at happy couples walking into the restaurant and coming out, greeting each other. My envy chewed through my gut.

How had it looked to Daisy? I'd come swooping in, and I'd had the house, I'd had the funds, and I'd had the history of bouncing back even better. She'd been an almost homeless single mom with an undetermined amount of debt.

My stomach acid flared, searing the lining. She'd been almost homeless because of that damn debt. She'd been in a helluva bind, and I'd taken advantage under the guise of helping. I'd known all along I was going to try to win her back when she'd been trying to survive—for herself and her kid.

I groaned and rested my head against the steering wheel. "Fuck. I ruined it."

"You really are a fan of giving up."

"Damn, Violet." Sisters didn't hold back.

"Look, I don't know what happened way back when. You turned into an Alder none of us recognized for a few years and then you snapped out of it—and right into another Alder none of us recognized. I, for one, have enjoyed seeing you with Daisy. It's like having you back."

I frowned. I'd turned back into myself after Daisy left the first time. "I'm still me, only I argue with Daisy less. Not at all in fact."

"So you two had one argument and then you called it off? Dang, Alder. You're going to have to extend that timeline."

I was going to get a second ulcer. She was right. So

damn correct. The first hiccup and I'd been the one to bail. I had tightened my life so efficiently that I hadn't been prepared for a single delay. I'd finished college over a year ahead of time. I'd climbed the corporate ladder quickly. And I had thought I could win Daisy back earlier than she needed.

"Violet, I need to make sure my wife wants to stay married to me. I need your help."

* * *

Daisy

My real estate agent was barely out of high school, but he was prompt and brutally honest about the properties he showed. I'd taken the Friday afternoon off to find a place to live once Alder got the house.

Mom's house had sold, and she said she'd help me with a down payment. The mortgage on a small house would be the same as renting one. I couldn't pay her back, but she wanted us to have a place that wouldn't get sold out from under us.

I'd reimburse her though. Someday.

That was if I found a house that wouldn't drain the rest of my check from all the repairs. It wasn't looking good.

The first house Hunter had shown me had smelled like moldy carpet and had still been in the seventies. The second had been a giant money pit. We'd gone to Crocus Valley for the next showing.

The house in front of us was also hungry for some

landscaping and general maintenance. I squinted at the roof with the uneven shingles. I hadn't gone inside, but it already looked like it'd need significant repairs.

"Yeah," Hunter said with a lazy drawl. "The roof needs to be replaced. You might even find that it's more than shingles that needs to be fixed." He stuck a hand in the pocket of his slacks and leaned back like he was taking the whole picture in when the sight of the thing just slapped a person in the face. "The original owner built the place."

"So, he was in construction?"

"Nope." Hunter clicked his tongue and started for the front door.

I'd gotten the world's most honest real estate agent. Hunter had saved me lots of heartache with his factual house showings. I'd laugh if I wasn't ready to cry at the drop of a hat.

I followed him into the house. "Oh god," left my mouth before I could stop it. The place smelled like cat pee, and the carpet looked like it'd hosted several ragers. Not even the floor of the apartment Alder and I had lived in had looked this bad when I'd moved out.

"Definitely plan for new carpet and a paint job."

I made the mistake of glancing at the ceiling. The many dark spots told me how bad the leaks were. I walked through the living room to the kitchen on the opposite side of the wall. A hallway stretched to my left. The kitchen linoleum was as stained as the carpet and probably older than me. I looked out the back window at the yard.

Was there any part of this house that would justify me buying it? There were no other places in my price range.

Hunter stopped next to me. "The backyard neighbor

owns a small engine repair shop, and he's known to let his projects creep onto your lawn."

"Oh, okay. Is he a decent guy to talk to about it?"

"Nope." Hunter started for the back door. "He's been in jail a couple of times."

My hopes burst like a stuck balloon. I couldn't afford the renovations on this house, and if I could, I couldn't risk a volatile neighbor with Laila. I blinked rapidly, the tears forming too fast.

The front door opened. Was there another person interested? Hunter would've said if he was entertaining another client. Did it matter? They could have it.

Hunter spun around. "Hey, man. Can I help you?"

The new arrival was a stranger? Alarm pierced my despair, but Hunter was relaxed. I took two steps just as Alder turned the corner, looking like a polished diamond on a dung heap in his suit and tie.

"What are you doing here?" My balloon of hope tried to piece itself back together. Just seeing Alder was a balm, and we'd gotten really good at avoidance.

I'd cried every damn night since he'd left. I'd run our last conversation through my head. I had asked for time, and he had claimed I was never going to trust him.

I did trust him, but I didn't understand why I couldn't let him in all the way. I had no clue why I wanted to vibrate out of my skin to think that we weren't pretending anymore or that we weren't trying. The idea that we were husband and wife in all it entailed smothered me with a fear I couldn't define.

Then Alder had left. Technically, he was still under the same roof. We hadn't come this far to lose the house.

"I heard you were buying." Alder glanced around. His expression flickered with disgust but remained calm. "But you can't. Because I'm purchasing this place."

I sputtered. "What?" Why would he want it? What about his house?

He lifted a shoulder. "I'll buy it and fix it so you and Laila have a decent place."

Shock robbed me of words. What the hell was going on?

"You got, uh, an agent you're already working with?" Hunter asked, grabbing a business card from his wallet.

Alder accepted it from him and stuffed it into the pocket of his shirt. "Thanks. I do need someone. Mind if I have a minute with Daisy?"

"You got it, my man." Hunter left us.

I crossed my arms, stupidly happy that he was here. His presence in this house somehow made it better. "The floor is warped."

"The walls are warped," he said. "This place is a piece of shit."

I bristled, but he was right. "Why are you buying a house I'm interested in?"

He closed the distance between us, so tantalizingly close I could just wrap my arms around him and inhale his new-leather-and-cedar scent. "I don't want you to have to buy a house."

"I can rent." The options were just as dismal.

"Then I'll buy the apartment building so you and Laila can live rent-free."

"You don't have that much money," I scoffed. His gaze remained steady. My stomach fluttered. "You can't purchase every place I look at."

"I can and I will and I won't charge you rent, but let me fix them up first. You and Laila can't live on wavy floors or under questionable roofs." He scanned the room. "Or in a place with both."

I made a strangled noise. He was serious.

"I won't quit taking care of you." He tilted my chin up and ran a thumb over my lower lip. "I walked away, and I shouldn't have. We experienced our first real hurdle, and I retreated. I was wrong. I shouldn't have left you."

"You're still in the house," I whispered.

"I haven't been with you." He stepped back. "But I'm going to be. You asked for time, I'm going to make sure you get it. When you get home tonight, there's dinner in the crockpot. Chicken and biscuits."

My stomach growled. The traitor. "You don't have to — We're not—" A tremble tracked over my skin. We fit a pattern. Bliss, then heartbreak. "This isn't going to work."

"Yes, it will." He took his hand from my chin and all the heat in my body went with it. "I'm going to talk to Hunter. The three houses you looked at today are going to get an offer."

"All three? Alder, you can't."

"I can buy these with the money from the sale of my house in Billings. I won't even have to touch my investments." When I had no response around my shock, the corners of his eyes crinkled. "See you at dinner tonight." And he walked out.

What the hell?

What. The. Hell.

I stared out the window at the various lawn mowers and snow blowers creeping across the property line. If Alder really was buying this house, that neighbor would lose his access within minutes of closing.

I will find a way.

That declaration was not part of the pattern. I believed him. My knees nearly gave out. A boulder rolled off my chest, and I sucked in a deep breath for what felt like the first time in fifteen years.

Fifteen years. We'd found our way back to each other. Two weeks that had felt like an eternity. Yet he was on the front lawn buying this dump. For me.

Only two weeks had gone by. Lightning fast compared to last time.

It all clicked. Time. Deadlines and lengths of relationships. I'd gotten hung up on those.

I charged outside, pushing out the screen door that I hadn't noticed was a screen door because the screen was missing. "Hunter, we're done here for now."

Hunter glanced from me to Alder.

"You have my card," Alder said. "Send me the paperwork."

"On all three?" Hunter squeaked.

Alder didn't flinch. "Yes."

Hunter's mouth dropped open. He snapped it shut. "Of course. I'll lock up and leave you two be."

"You don't have to buy the houses, Alder. I want this. With you." It'd ruin Hunter's day, but I couldn't let Alder buy three damn houses.

Alder didn't take his gaze off me. "Don't worry, Hunter. Send me the paperwork."

Hunter scurried by us. "Will do. You two have a good day."

As soon as his pickup door shut, I sucked in a deep breath. "The first guy I dated after you? He stole my information and opened a bunch of credit cards. I didn't catch it for three years, and he'd run them all the way up.

That's all he was using me for, and I stayed with him *way* too long."

"Daisy—"

I held up a hand. I had to finish this. He needed to understand. "The next guy was a charmer, and I was lonely. So I stayed. I stayed when he came home late five nights in a row with a weak excuse that the office was getting painted and he had to be present to lock up after. I stayed when he went on a work trip with his best friend —*Lilah*. And I stayed when he told me that the fake lashes I found in his passenger seat were mine. I was 'overreacting.'" I threw up air quotes. "I was being *paranoid*." I puffed hair out of my face. "I stayed with him for four years."

"Who the fuck is he?"

"An asshole who's probably cheating on his wife. *Lilah*." I lifted my arms and dropped them to my sides. "Then there's Jason. Poor, sweet Jason. He was safe. I knew I didn't love him. And I knew I had stayed too long as soon as I saw that positive pregnancy sign." I stepped into his space. He blocked the light breeze ruffling my hair. I put my hands on his shoulders. "Before all of them was you. I spent years wondering if I left too early. Should I have stayed longer, given you the time you needed to sow your wild oats? Did I give up too soon?"

Understanding dawned on his face. "You stayed with all those douchebags because of me. I'm including Jason, but he's not a douchebag."

I smoothed my hands over the expensive material of his suit. "I trust you, Alder. I don't trust myself." The tears I tried to keep back rolled freely down my face. "I love you so much. I never thought I'd have a second chance, but I've screwed up every single time before."

He cupped my face, anger emanating from him in waves. "You didn't screw up. Never you. I fucked up. Those assholes fucked up. I mean, Jason—well, damn, I would've stayed with him too long too."

A blubbery laugh left me. "You're the most perfect man. You were then, and I didn't allow you any leeway."

"I was a disrespectful prick. You were the most important person in my life, Daisy. I took you for granted, and when you left, I didn't believe you were gone for good. After we signed the divorce papers, I still didn't buy that we were done. Then you graduated and never came home, and I knew. I knew that I ruined the best thing that had ever happened to me. And I knew I had to do something drastic to get you back." He brushed his thumbs over my cheeks. "Then I took you for granted again. My grandma dropped a miracle in my lap, and as much as I want to find that asshole and throttle him for driving you into debt, I can't help but thank him—just a little—because it created the perfect scenario to get you back with me. I love you, Daisy. I've always loved you. I will always love you, and I'm willing to spend my life showing you, even if it means being the roommate upstairs you fuck."

"Alder...I'm scared. I'm scared I'll mess this up." I already had by not talking to him.

"There's nothing you can do to chase me away from you. One day at a time, Daze. You're mine, and I'm yours. That's all we need to know." He kissed me, capturing my tear-soaked lips.

I gripped his lapel and tugged him closer, then I wrapped my arms around his neck. He hugged me to him, deepening the kiss. For a second time, I thought I had lost this.

Never again. I'd face my fear down a thousand times if I had to.

A low growl came from him. If we weren't in the middle of the street, we'd be stripping each other down. My skin burned for his touch. I wanted him inside me. I wanted him in my bed. I'd talk to Laila—

I pulled back with a gasp. "I have to pick up Laila from daycare."

He checked his watch. "Shit. You need to hurry. I'll go home and get the table set and—"

"Why don't you come with me?" I wet my lips. His taste was on them, right where it should be. "You've never been there, and they should know who you are. I'm sure you'll be picking her up sometimes. Since you're her stepdad."

His whole expression lit up. "I'd be honored to. I'll follow you." He pressed a kiss to my temple. "I'll follow you anywhere, Daisy Duke."

Chapter Twenty-Five

Alder

After Laila had shown me around her small daycare center and introduced me to all the teachers who were still there that late, we went home. Daisy had transferred her car seat. Laila rode with me and chattered the whole way.

"I'm going to change before we eat." I jogged up the stairs and got into jeans and a long-sleeved shirt. When I was back downstairs, I turned into the dining room and stopped.

The table was set. Daisy sat across from Laila and on the end closest to them was a third setting.

Daisy smiled at me. "Figured it was past time you moved closer to us."

Laila patted next to the empty plate.

My heart could've exploded. "I'd love to be closer to my girls."

Tonight turned into the perfect night. Two weeks of

misery—never again. I ate with the girls I wanted to spend the rest of my life with.

After dinner, Laila watched a show with us, then got ready for bed. Daisy joined her to read a book. I waited on the couch.

"Alder?" Daisy called from Laila's room. "Can you come in?"

I wasn't getting out of reading, and that didn't upset me. I smiled at the door. "She can't do the troll's voice, can she?" I asked Laila.

She grinned and shook her head.

"Hon," Daisy said to her daughter, "I wanted to talk to you about me and Alder."

Oh. She was doing this. I perched on the edge of the bed. I wasn't sure exactly what she was discussing with Laila, but I was fine with whatever she wanted to tell her.

Daisy brushed a lock of pale hair off Laila's face. "You remember when I told you that Alder and I would start dating?" Laila nodded, and Daisy smiled. "I'm in love with him."

Laila looked from me to Daisy. "Okay."

"I also want to make sure you know that I was married to him before. He's not just a friend, he's my ex-husband. Now, he's my husband again, and I want it to stay that way."

"You guys were married?" Wonder filled Laila's voice.

Daisy nodded. "I can show you pictures. It wasn't for very long, but Alder's always been important to me."

"Is he going to be my daddy?" Laila asked, clutching the edge of her blanket.

"I'm going to be your stepdaddy," I said, hoping it was okay I was jumping in, but Daisy gave me an encouraging nod. "I'm going to be your mom's partner, and in a way, I'm going to be a partner with your dad too. He'll always be your daddy."

Laila pursed her lips. "Okay. Will I get a stepmommy?"

"Maybe," Daisy said. "And I hope she'll be a good partner for your dad. But you'll be seeing me and Alder act like a husband and wife." She leaned forward. "He might kiss me once in a while."

"Every day," I said, and Laila giggled.

"And he'll be sleeping in the same bed as me," Daisy finished.

It would be inappropriate to cheer, but fuck yes. I didn't want to hide my relationship with Daisy from anyone.

"Okay." Laila yawned. "Make sure he makes the bed."

Daisy giggled. "He's pretty good about that."

We left a sleepy Laila behind. When Daisy shut the door, I pulled her to me. "You didn't have to do that," I murmured.

"I wanted to. We've slept apart for way too long."

Desire shuddered through my body. "I know she's not fully asleep yet, but you need to go into that room and strip down. I'll shut the lights off and be right in."

I made sure the doors were locked and then found Daisy sitting on her bed, still dressed.

I leaned against the doorframe. "Want to just watch a show, and then I'll go upstairs?"

"No." She scooted back and crossed her legs. A stack of envelopes was next to her. "I wanted to show you these. Before we go any further." Her gaze slid away. She chewed on the inside of her cheek and ran her fingers over the hem of her shirt. She'd told me the story, but she was ashamed.

I flopped onto the bed next to her.

"These are the latest statements for each card." She handed me the first envelope.

I took the statement out and opened it. The total amount was substantial. She could've put a nice down payment on any of the houses she'd looked at today.

She slid another over. I opened that one.

My anger flared white hot. "How the hell did he get such high limits?"

"From what I could tell, he lied about our income and then strung it along with regular payments until they kept increasing the line of credit." Her sigh exited heavily. "I had excellent credit, at the time anyway. I'm getting slaughtered by interest, but I can't think of a way out other than to pay them. I've tried to fight him."

I pulled out my phone and pulled up my email. "What's his name?"

"I've tried—"

"My lawyer hasn't."

Her eyes flew wide. "You have a lawyer?"

"One thing all that fucking off did when I was younger was give me the skills to network. I'll pay the legal fees and we'll make this asshole suffer. We might very well lose, but so will he. He'll lose a lot of damn money paying for his own lawyer."

"Alder, we can't..." Her breath hitched and hope filled her face. "I've lost so much of my income to these payments."

I opened the third, fourth, and fifth credit card statements, all with jaw-dropping amounts. That jackass was going to pay. I set all the statements side by side. "I'll deal with those tomorrow."

"You're not—"

I put my finger over her lips. "No more interest. No more debt. It's our money."

"It's not," she said against my finger.

My gaze dropped to her mouth, and I traced her lips with my fingertip. "I had years of bachelorhood to earn an obscene amount of money. Then I got a job making even more money. I did it for us. When I got you back, I wanted to make sure we were set."

"Alder," she whispered, her eyes growing watery.

I rolled her to her back and spread myself over her. The paper crunched underneath us. I pressed kisses along her jaw. "To prove my point, I'm going to fuck you on these statements." I tunneled a hand under her shirt and marked a path down her neck with my lips. "Then tomorrow, while they still smell like us, I'm going to call my lawyer. You don't ever have to worry about these again."

"Tomorrow's Saturday," she said in a needy voice as she arched into me.

"We'll keep having sex on them until then. Once for each card. Deal?"

She stuffed her hands through my hair and spread her legs wider to cradle me. "Deal."

Epilogue

Daisy

I woke to the wind howling outside. The storm had started early last night and was severe enough that Alder had issued the emergency conditions order at the refinery. I got a storm day, and while he'd be working from home, he was still in bed next to me.

He rolled into me and buried his face into my neck. "Happy anniversary."

I grinned. "Happy anniversary."

His arm wound around me, holding me to him. Desire woke and heat spread under my skin. "I told Dad and Linda that it didn't matter when they finished the paperwork for the house."

"You're really trying to sell that this marriage is real?" I couldn't keep a straight face and started giggling.

"I've got to sell it for forty or fifty more years."

I liked the sound of that. Counting by decades

soothed my anxiety. There was no such thing as too long when we were talking about eternity.

"Mommy!" Our bedroom door burst open, and Laila ran in. She jumped up on the bed and wiggled between us.

Alder let out a playful groan. "Oh no, you're late for school."

"There's no school today, silly," Laila said. The schools and daycares had called out yesterday when the storm had moved in. "Can we make cookies?"

"My mom's cookies from the caterpillar book?" Alder asked.

I'd made that recipe with Laila once, and she was hooked.

Laila's hair bounced as she nodded. "Uh-huh."

"Want hot chocolate with it?" he asked.

Laila bolted to her knees and bounced on the bed. "Can we?"

"It's a storm day," Alder said. "That's what we have to do."

Laila squealed. "I can't wait to tell Hannah." Laila was making friends at preschool and Hannah was one of them. Laila went still, a little frown on her face. "She might not be at school next time."

"Why?" I asked. Had I missed preschool drama?

"Her mommy's having a baby soon. Might be today."

I grimaced. "I hope the baby waits until the streets get cleared."

"Are you going to have a baby, Mommy?" Laila asked.

The muscles in Alder's arm rippled over my abdomen.

"I don't know," I admitted. Alder and I hadn't talked about it. We'd been happily drowning ourselves in wedded bliss for the last two and a half months. Sure, I'd thought about it, but I hadn't asked.

When we were teens, I had assumed marriage and kids would be the natural progression. Then my plans had derailed. Now, I didn't want to assume anything, nor did I want to rush it. Yet I couldn't deny that I was aging, and if we wanted more kids, then we should get started.

Alder rolled to his back and propped his arm behind his head. "I'll have as many babies as your mom wants."

Flutters erupted in my belly. I loved Laila, and I didn't regret her, but I had missed the happy pregnancy experience I had envisioned as a young wife. I'd known I wasn't happy with Jason, and I'd been preparing myself to force it. I had written off having more kids because the dad wouldn't have been Alder.

"I do want more kids," I said softly.

Laila bounced again. "Yay!"

"Settle down," I said, laughing. "There are a lot of things that go into having a baby." The first step would be stopping birth control.

Alder's hot gaze burned into me and a flush spread through my body. Yeah, there were some pleasurable activities that went into trying to have a kid.

"Can we make the cookies now?" she asked.

"Give us a few minutes." I laughed. "Go get dressed, and we'll have a decent breakfast before eating cookie dough while baking."

She scrambled off the bed. Before she ran out of the bedroom, she stopped to pick up the carving of Trixie. She did that a lot. Jasper was working on a carving for her for Christmas.

"What would you think of starting to learn to ride next summer?" I asked.

Delight streamed across her face. "A horse?" She jumped up and down. "*Really?*"

"You'll meet Uncle Jasper at Christmas, and he'll show you his horses."

"Eliot raises some too," Alder added.

"Could I get my own?"

Babies and horses. I was back on track with the life I had dreamed of. "We'll have to see how it all goes."

"Yes!" Laila darted out of the room.

Alder rolled to face me. "A baby?"

"We can try." I wrinkled my nose. "I am thirty-seven."

"That means we'll have to try a lot. In all different positions."

A grin spread across my face. "So, say I forget my pill starting today...what sort of positions?"

"Hmm." He pretended to think. Meanwhile, I had to throw the covers off because he was an oven and a fire was sweeping through my blood. "Most definitely a quickie with you bent over the bed." He rolled up. "I'll lock the door."

"Alder?" Laila called. "Can we make pancakes?"

I exchanged a wry grin with Alder.

"Another position is a quickie when the first batch of cookies is in the oven," I whispered.

"Whenever you want me, you've got me, wife. I'm yours."

I held up my hand, the diamonds of my wedding ring glinting in the light. "And I'm yours, Duke."

———————

. . .

When Poppy Duke makes a big move to Coal Haven and then doesn't know what to do, she meets an old classmate, and he has ideas. Jensen Hollis needs help with his business and Poppy needs to be married to get a house that would solve a few of her problems. But it's only a deal between friends. Unless those friends keep growing closer in Poppy Kisses.

Enjoy a special Christmas with Alder and Daisy in a special bonus epilogue, available when you sign up to my newsletter on mariejohnstonwriter.com.

About the Author

Marie Johnston writes paranormal and contemporary romance and has collected several awards in both genres. Before she was a writer, she was a microbiologist. Depending on the situation, she can be oddly unconcerned about germs or weirdly phobic. She's also a licensed medical technician and has worked as a public health microbiologist and as a lab tech in hospital and clinic labs. Marie's been a volunteer EMT, a college instructor, a security guard, a phlebotomist, a hotel clerk, and a coffee pourer in a bingo hall. All fodder for a writer!! She has four kids, cats, lots of cats, and a corgie.

mariejohnstonwriter.com

Follow me:

Also by Marie Johnston

<u>Return to Coal Haven</u>

Violet Promises

Daisy Whispers

Poppy Kisses

<u>Crocus Valley</u>

A Reckless Memory

A Temporary Memory

An Unfinished Memory

A Fearless Memory

An Endless Memory

<u>Coal Haven</u>

Make Me Whole

Make Me Shiver

Make Me Blush

Make Me Dream

Make Me Exhale

<u>King's Creek</u>

King's Crown

King's Ransom

King's Treasure

King's Country

King's Queen